SILVERSTREAM

Jillian
Sullivan

Every reasonable effort has been undertaken to identify the correct copyright holders to the poems quoted in this publication. The publisher welcomes enquiries from copyright holders. The publisher wishes to thank the Estate of Denis Glover for granting permission to quote from "Once the Days".

p.19 "A Farewell" by A.R.D Fairburn
p. 84 "From a Book of Hours" by Charles Spear
p. 85 "Losing the Words" by Glenda Fawkes
p. 108 "The Trapped Hare" by Basil Dowling
p. 120 "Once the Days" by Denis Glover
p. 151 "Victory" by Eileen Duggan

www.pearsoned.co.nz

Pearson
a division of Pearson New Zealand Ltd
67 Apollo Drive, Rosedale, North Shore 0632, New Zealand

Associated companies throughout the world

© Pearson
First published by Pearson 2007
Reprinted 2009

ISBN 10: 1-86970-589-0
ISBN 13: 978-1-86970-589-3

Series Editor: Lucy Armour
Designed by Ruby-Anne Fenning

Text © Jillian Sullivan

Published by Pearson
Printed in China by Bookbuilders

AUTHOR NOTE

Sometimes I dream whole novels. When I wake up I usually don't remember them. *Silverstream* is one I did remember. The sense of being on a mountain in a camp under a repressive regime stayed with me so strongly, I wrote the story down.

When I left home as a teenager I had to sell my pony and I became involved in politics. I knew the freedom I had experienced out on my pony was possible because we lived in a free and peaceful society.

Jillian Sullivan

To know all, to bear all
Quietly, without protest,
To bend never breaking,
To live on, live for another
Day, an equable morning –
Is that what men are born for?
Is that best of all?

from "Cry Mercy"
Charles Brasch

For my daughter Merrin

With grateful thanks to
Joy Cowley and Evie Haverkort

My mother disappeared on Saturday night. She didn't say goodbye and my sister Amanda didn't warn me. They let me go off to bed in a mood, stressed out at both of them because it was show day in the morning and I wasn't ready.

"You should have washed your own jodhpurs," Mum said. "You can't expect me to remember everything."

"Well, some mothers do," I said.

Mum just stood in my doorway looking at me. She was going to say something, I know she was, but I turned away from her. I didn't know when I left Mum standing there that in the morning she'd be gone.

Why didn't they tell me?

Why didn't Mum just stay home that night if she felt something was wrong?

This is what she did. She tiptoed in while I was crossly asleep and put a note on my bed, next to a clean, folded pair of her very own jodhpurs. Then she put on a wig or scarf and a baggy blue uniform and biked a few kilometres through the streets to a dark warehouse.

While I was dreaming of winning at the show, my mum was at a secret political meeting. And, when I woke up to clean jodhpurs on my bed and a note, my mother had been taken away.

"Amanda!" I shook my big sister awake, waving the note in front of her eyes. "What's happening? Where's Mum?"

"What did she say?" asked Amanda, her voice husky.

I gave her the note. "Nothing that makes sense. She said not to worry if she didn't come home from the meeting."

"Well, don't then," said Amanda, passing back the note.

"But she's been to lots of meetings. What was she worried about last night?"

Amanda turned over to face me. Her wild red

hair was sticking out in all directions. "There've been raids lately, that's all. Mum didn't want you to know. She'll be okay. She took another ID. She'll probably be home this afternoon. It's just scare tactics, that's all."

"Are you sure?"

"Course."

"So shall I still go to the show then?"

"Yes. And your bridle's in the laundry."

"Wow. Did Mum get that ready for me, too?"

"No, I did," said Amanda, turning her back on me. I stood there a moment, fingering my note and looking at the large shape of her in bed.

"Well, thank you, Amanda," came her sarky voice.

"Thank you yourself," I said and clomped out. Nothing much had changed about her. Mum would be be okay, I thought.

I went back to my room and got dressed in Mum's jodhpurs. They were too short, but my boots would hide that.

I put my old jeans and jersey on over the top, took two apples and my bridle from the laundry and went out to catch my pony, Lancelot. Mum probably would be home by the time I got back.

Lancelot was grazing on the far side of the paddock. He lifted his brown, shaggy head when I called him. He looked nothing like a show pony — instead he looked like a little Mongolian warrior horse. He came straight over to me, his stubby ears pricked. That was so unusual for him that I got a funny feeling in my stomach as I stood there smoothing his nose.

I'd been looking forward to the show for weeks. I knew I didn't have a chance in the riding classes, but I was sure I'd do well in the jumping. And Mum always came down to watch when I was jumping.

My best friend Rachael was already at the show when I got there. Her mum, in spotless overalls and gumboots, was plaiting up Rachael's horse Mistletoe, while Rachael groomed him. I tugged and plaited Lancelot's black mane and tried not to worry where my own mum could be.

At 8.30 Rachael and I took off our outer layer of clothes and put on our black riding jackets. We rode over to the ring, Rachael taller beside me on her shiny chestnut horse.

When I rode back out of the ring (Rachael first, me unplaced), Rachael's mum was waiting with a big smile for her. I got down and hugged Lancelot.

In the afternoon, when no one from my family was there to watch me, Lancelot got into one of his "I can do it, too" moods. He jumped wide and fast over the hurdles and in the jump-off we beat Mistletoe by seconds to win first prize. I could hardly stop grinning.

If I'd been ten, I would have ridden home with the rosette still clipped to his bridle. Being fourteen, I put it in my top pocket.

"Do you want a ride home in our float?" Rachael asked me. "Mum doesn't mind."

"No, we're going back through the forest."

"Okay. See you tomorrow."

Lancelot wanted to stay where Mistletoe was chomping at his hay.

"Come on, boy." I got him past the line of horse floats and past the brassy horses with silky manes. In the practice ring, horses cantered with their heads and necks arched over. I thought they looked a bit like circus horses, obedient and controlled. I nudged my toey pony and we rode into the freedom of the forest.

Lancelot pricked up his ears and trotted. His

strides got longer. The speed at which I had to rise and sit made me laugh. We cantered around the edge of a small dam, brown and quiet in a clearing. Then the track curved and sloped up a long hill.

"Yeeha!" I yelled. I let the reins go, along with all control over my 400-kilogram galloping beast. The wind buffeted my face and I stretched my arms out wide like a tightrope walker. Then I shut my eyes.

Wild blackness. Lancelot's hooves thrummed on the clay. I felt his legs rising and striking the ground underneath me and I rolled to every thundering motion. I trusted all of him — his eyes, his legs, his sense of the right way to go.

I opened my eyes and held on to a hunk of his mane as the track ahead got steeper. He came to a stop at the top, blowing and happy. We looked out at the views over the valley as our hearts slowed down.

Just as I pictured our house and the paddock with the plum tree, Lancelot turned his head towards the track. The sun had gone down behind Mount Silverstream. We rode home in its shadow.

After I'd seen to Lancelot in the paddock, giving him an extra armful of hay, I ran into the house to see Mum.

The kitchen had been tidied from my dinner cooking the night before. There was a casserole in the oven; the whole kitchen was warm and clean and smelling of good food.

"Mum?" I walked through the house.

I heard something in her bedroom.

"Mum?" I pushed open the door.

There was a man in there, Amanda's new boyfriend, and he was going through Mum's desk.

"What are you doing!" I nearly squealed in my fright. "You're not allowed to touch Mum's things."

He stood up. He had a box with him and it was full of Mum's things — her computer discs, her precious books of writing.

"You're Lorna, aren't you? I'm Michael Hadlow. I'm actually . . ."

He didn't get a chance to finish because I leapt across the floor and grabbed at the box.

"Lorna!" Now Amanda was at the door.

"Amanda, what's happening?" I'd tipped the box and Mum's notebooks had spilt to the floor.

Michael knelt down to get them and handed me my red rosette, which I'd dropped.

"Congratulations," he said.

I grabbed the rosette from him and stuffed it in my pocket. "Amanda, what is he doing here?"

"I'm taking your mother's latest manuscript, Lorna." Michael stood up. "I'm her editor."

"You're not. You're Amanda's new boyfriend, Michael, from the chemical laboratory. You wash bottles there. Amanda told me that. I know."

"He washes bottles because the Authorities closed down his publishing house and make him do that work," Amanda said. She strode across the room, taking the box from Michael and putting it on Mum's bed. "Mum left me a note telling me to get this stuff to Michael."

"I'm publishing underground now," Michael said. "We'll still get this in print."

"What note?" I said to Amanda. "You didn't tell me there was another note."

"You don't need to know everything. It's better that you don't."

"I'm not going to blab, Amanda. I'm not eight any more. And, anyway, you said Mum would be back by tonight."

Amanda looked at Michael.

"You *said*!"

"Lorna . . ." Amanda sat on Mum's bed and pulled me down beside her. "Everyone else was released from the raid this afternoon. They were held overnight, but no one was hurt."

"Everyone else is back?"

"Except Mum. She didn't come back."

"Well, where is she then?" I swung round to look at Michael, too. "Where is she?" They didn't say anything.

"She's at the camp, I'll bet. They've taken her to the camp. I'm going to go down to the Central Office and I'm going to ask."

Amanda grabbed hold of my wrist. "Lorna," she said, quietly and fiercely. "Calm down. You are absolutely not to go there. You are not to do anything, not say anything, not tell anyone."

"Especially not Rachael," said Michael.

"Oh, and who are you to bring up my friends?"

"Do you promise, Lorna, for Mum's sake?"

I looked at Amanda's face. She looked more worried than I'd ever seen her.

"It's just like what happened to Dad, isn't it?"

"No, hon, it's not at all," said Amanda.

Did I believe Amanda? I looked from her to Michael and back again.

"She's gone to camp, though, hasn't she?"

"Yes," said Amanda.

"Probably," said Michael.

"Well, what for? You can't go to camp for being at a meeting, can you?"

Michael spread his hands out.

"But Mum's famous. You can't lock up somebody famous."

"Lorna, don't get hysterical. Mum's gone and we have to carry on as if she's still here. That's safest for her. The Anti-camp Committee know about it and one day soon, I'll bet, she'll just be back."

"Oh, the anti-campers . . ." I said. "Since when have they got anyone out of the camps? They didn't help Dad, did they?"

"There was nothing they could do for Dad," said Amanda.

"Because he was dead. And Mum could end up dead too. But you wouldn't want to do anything so radical as ask questions, would you?" I stormed out of the room.

"Lorna!" Amanda called after me.

"Leave her. She's just upset," I heard Michael say before I slammed the door into my own bedroom.

I opened my wardrobe door and pinned up my red rosette in there, starting off a whole new row under the photo of me and Lancelot that Mum took the first winter I had him.

Shaggy, hairy Lancelot. Like a mountain pony, Mum said. She loved him almost as much as I did, before she got so busy with her meetings.

We used to go everywhere together — Mum on her horse Mongo, and me on Lancelot. I wasn't 1.7 metres in those days, and my legs didn't hang down Lancelot's sides as they did now.

I closed the wardrobe. I used to hang my ribbons on my bedroom wall, until I went round to Rachael's. She had three sides of her bedroom completely covered in ribbons and rosettes, even fat, purple championship ones.

Rachael never said anything about winning. She was my best friend, and that Michael Hadlow had no right at all even to mention her.

I changed out of my jodhpurs and jacket and tossed them, hairy and horse-sweaty, into the corner of my room. Then I remembered that they were Mum's jodhpurs. She'd thought about me, even as she worried about going out. I picked up her jodhpurs again, folded them and put them on the end of my bed.

Her note said, "Lorna love, there may be trouble at the meeting tonight. If I don't come home, DON'T WORRY. Most important, don't say anything to anyone. Listen to Amanda. She's in charge. I love you. Mum."

There may be trouble . . . but what did she mean? It was supposed to be a secret meeting. A man had come back from Silverstream Camp and was giving a talk. He even had photos. Why were the Authorities doing raids? Did they want to find out who was joining the anti-camp movement so they could fire them from their jobs?

The elections were next year and Mum said the Government was getting nervous. There'd already been a protest march, which was dispersed right away by Authority police. Pamphlets and speeches had been produced on Mum's computer when she was supposed to be in her room writing. She'd told me that's what she was doing, working on Chapter 16, or something, and to be quiet and get myself some dinner.

Mum is a children's writer. She's won awards and everyone knows her. That's why she always thought the Authorities would leave her alone.

She wasn't some activist trying to undermine the country's morals. She wrote books that helped the Authorities' children learn to read. She was sweet, with a kind face, and she looked after me the best way I could imagine.

That was when she was working on a book. She would wander around in a vague way and smile at me, but she didn't tell me anything. So I made up my own instructions. Amanda got to hate it when I said, "Mum said I could," because Mum could never remember if she had or not.

I got to cook and eat odd meals at strange times, go riding in the dark, watch DVDs when I should have been doing my homework, and slouch around in my dirtiest, horse-hairiest jeans. As long as I did well at school, Mum didn't mind.

And now she was gone and Michael was in her room like a vulture, when the trail wasn't even cold, taking Mum's work as if that was all that was important.

Amanda, she'd been a goody-goody for far too long. She had a highly paid job and a clean reputation. She didn't want to ask questions about Mum. She was scared she'd end up next Monday working as a rubbish collector or whatever else Central Office decided was a suitable job for you when your own job mysteriously disappeared.

Like Michael's publishing job.

Like my dad's job as an English teacher.

Dad spoke to his pupils too much about individual rights after the Government came in. One day, he was called before the newly set up Central Office and told he was redundant to their teaching programme. It mostly went over my head — I was eight at the time — but this was how my mother talked about it.

Dad was offered a job back at his high school as a gardener's assistant. He refused. They sent him to a work camp. They had just set those up. Silverstream wasn't built then, so they sent Dad 160 kilometres away to a factory.

Dad organised the first work camp protest meeting. Three hundred people came, and in front of all of them Dad was hit by a car. The driver was a man in his seventies, almost too old to be blamed — that's what the Authorities said. Dad was killed straight away and the Anti-camp Committee went underground.

I remember I told everyone at school that the Authorities had killed my dad. I told my friends. I told the teachers. I was eight so I didn't understand.

I'm not eight any more. I'm fourteen, and I wouldn't tell Rachael or the school or even my teacher, Mr Jacobs. If Mum said don't say anything, then I wouldn't.

But I wasn't like Amanda. I wasn't going to sit back and say it'll be all right. My mum was in trouble. I knew she was, and I was going to do something about it.

THREE

It was Rachael who told me about Dana Dixon.

Dana was pregnant to Rachael's cousin Davey. Dana was seventeen. You're not allowed a baby at seventeen. You have to put them up for adoption or go back home to live with your parents until you're twenty years old. Otherwise you have to get married.

Rachael said Dana didn't want to adopt out her baby. And her mother was dead and her father hit her till she left home a year ago. She wanted to marry Davey and Davey wanted to marry her, but there was a complication.

Dana had been too nervous and embarrassed to buy a pregnancy test kit from the chemist shop she worked at, so she stole one, and got caught. Now she was going to a work camp for a month. This was whispered on the way to English class.

"So?" I said. "She can get married after that, can't she?"

"No. My uncle and aunt won't approve of her if she's been to camp, and because he's under twenty Davey can't get married unless they say he can."

"Oh." Then my brain started racing with an idea. "When's, um, Dana going to camp?"

"Next week," said Rachael. "Davey's frantic. He doesn't know what to do."

I walked into English with my mind spinning. Dana had to go to camp. My mum was probably at the camp. Dana was desperate not to go, but someone had to go, someone called Dana Dixon — and that someone could be me!

My teacher, Mr Jacobs, wasn't himself in English. I sat close to Rachael and, just because I kept whispering questions about Dana to her, he really lost his cool. He banged his hand down on my desk.

"Lorna Bennett, I've had enough. You go and stand in the corridor for the next twenty minutes."

"But Mr Jacobs . . ."

"I said I've had enough. All of you. What does it take?"

He was really agitated and walking up and down in front of the blackboard, waving his arms like a wind-up toy.

He usually only did that when he was excited about a poem, and he was definitely not excited about a poem, this time. I'd never been kicked out of English before. I pushed my chair back loudly so it scraped, then sauntered across the classroom.

I stood in the corridor looking out the window while Mr Jacobs droned on inside, and I thought about Dana Dixon and going to camp.

I'd miss two weeks of school. I could handle that. And then there'd be the holidays. A month I'd be away. I'd have time to find my mum and help her, and Dana would have time to suck up to Davey's family and get a ring on her finger before her stomach started showing.

Then, through the door, I heard Mr Jacobs say, "The poem on page ten, Sarah please. 'A Farewell' by A.R.D. Fairburn," and all of a sudden it wasn't just Mum I was thinking about, but Dad as well.

"*What is there left to be said?*" read Sarah, and

I was back at the river where we scattered Dad's ashes and where we went every year and took him a rose. We had turns each year to choose a poem, and last year on Dad's anniversary, it was Amanda's turn. This was the poem she read.

"*There is nothing we can say,*
nothing at all to be done
to undo the time of day;
no words to make the sun
roll east, or raise the dead."

At that point, where the river rushed into the sea (confronting its greater power, Mum said), Mum and I held hands while Amanda held the rose and read on.

"*I loved you as I love life,*" read Sarah, in her flat, careful voice and without Amanda's passion,

"*the hand I stretched out to you*
returning like Noah's dove
brought a new earth to view,
till I was quick with love;
but Time sharpens his knife,
Time smiles and whets his knife,
and something has got to come out
quickly, and be buried deep,
not spoken or thought about

or remembered even in sleep.

You must live, get on with your life."

With the last words, Amanda had thrown the rose into the water and it swirled in some eddy near the bank and lodged itself there. Mum bent down and picked it up again. She pulled her hand back to throw it into the river again, then changed her mind. We took it home instead and laid it under the rose bush it had come from.

Mr Jacobs left me outside till nearly the end of class. By then I had tears wet on my face and was sitting slumped on the floor with my back to the wall.

"Lorna, I'd like a word after class," said Mr Jacobs, standing in the doorway. I rubbed at my cheeks with the back of my hand and went and sat back in my chair. Rachael peered at me, so I pulled a face at her.

The bell rang for lunch. I hoped he wasn't going to keep me in for a boring lecture on my behaviour. "Not like you at all, Lorna," or, "What would your dad have said?"

I waited at my desk while the class emptied, my

legs stretched out and my fingers playing with my pen. Mr Jacobs came over and settled his weight on the edge of my desk.

"Did your mum get home okay?" he asked me quietly.

My eyes snapped up to look at his face.

"Of course," I said. Then I thought, what if he knows something, what if he could help?

"I was at the meeting, Lorna," he said, and then, keeping on in the same tone but a bit louder, "And I'm not happy with the last assignment or your behaviour in class this morning."

I stayed still, but out of the corner of my eye I saw that someone was standing in the doorway.

"I'm sorry, sir."

"It's not like you at all, Lorna," said Mr Jacobs, then he stood up and turned. "Ah, Donald, come in. That will be all, Lorna."

The deputy principal, Donald Meads, walked into the room. His eyes stared into me, black and secretive. No one liked Meads at school; he was always appearing silently and watching.

"Lorna, is it?" he said. "Bennett. You're that writer's daughter."

"Uh-huh." I pulled my legs back under my

chair and pressed my toes hard into the floor. Mum had said to me that some people in our city held a lot of power. One man Mum told me about was Rachael's father, but I never believed that. The other was Mr Meads.

"Tell me," he said. "Is your mum working on a new book at present? It's hard to believe she finds the time, with all the things she's involved in."

"Mum never discusses her work with me," I told him.

Mr Jacobs looked at me and nodded his head imperceptibly at the door.

I picked up my bag and got up and walked across the room, not looking at either of them.

Thank God I never said anything about Mum to Mr Jacobs. Suddenly, school seemed a dangerous place to me. Dana just had to agree to my plan.

Dana lived in a small house on Greenwood Street, a long way from our house. I biked there straight after school.

"I'm a friend of Rachael's," I blurted out when she opened the door. "My name's Lorna Bennett."

Dana just looked at me.

"I think I could help you."

"I don't need any help," said Dana, and went to shut the door.

"About the work camp," I said in a rush. "I thought we could swap."

Dana opened the door again and looked over my shoulder to the house next door, then down the road.

"You'd better come in."

I followed her through the door. Iron Maiden was thumping out of the stereo and a kettle was sending billows of steam up the wall behind the kitchen bench.

Dana went over and turned the kettle off. The music she left on. "Do you want a hot chocolate? I'd make coffee, but I can't stand the smell of it at the moment."

"I know. Rachael told me you were pregnant."

"Yeah. I hope she isn't blabbing it everywhere. If her dad finds out . . ."

"She wouldn't tell her dad. Davey swore her to secrecy. She only told me."

Dana pushed her hand through her ragged, spiky hair. I looked at her face. Could I look like her? She was tall like me, that was one thing.

"Sugar?"

"Two please."

She clunked the teaspoon into my mug and passed it to me.

"Swap? What kind of mad idea is that?" she said as she sat down at the table.

So I told her about my mum — how she was gone without even a work camp notification, and how everyone else at the meeting was back home and we hadn't heard a thing.

"Your mum. Yeah I know her, she's a writer."

And I told her about my dad, but Dana said no, she didn't remember him. She was having too much trouble with her own dad at ten to think about anyone else's.

"School will be okay. I'll only miss two weeks and then it's the holidays."

"And I would have to meet Davey's family and be safely engaged before you make any noise at Silverstream."

"I know that."

"It could work. Yeah. But it's a hard camp. It'll all backfire in a major way if you get there and decide you can't handle it."

"I'll handle it."

"You're only, what?"

"Fourteen."

"Fourteen. How do you know what you can handle?"

"I'll handle it okay. Mum's all I've got. They killed my dad, remember."

Dana leaned back in her chair and stared out the window. Her fingers made drum rhthyms on her mug. Behind her, the music stopped and the house was suddenly silent. I couldn't take my eyes off her face.

"Okay," she said. Just like that. And everything about my life was changed.

"Oh wow, Dana. Thanks." I grinned at her.

"But you can't take my ID card. I'll need it."

I hadn't thought of that.

"I'll get a forgery. I'll look in Mum's drawers. She might have a contact somewhere."

"You've only got till next week."

"I know."

"Mmmm." Dana looked at me. "And another thing. Your hair." She picked up a long length of it. "I wouldn't look like that."

She took me down to the bathroom and sat me in front of her mirror. We both stared at my face. Then Dana picked up the scissors and cut off a huge hunk of my hair, right next to my skin.

She left a long piece hanging over my forehead and at the back, and clipped the rest close to the side of my head.

"That's better," said Dana. I just stared in shock. "Are your ears pierced?"

I nodded.

"Try these."

I pushed some black chain earrings into my ears. We studied my face in the mirror again.

"I look . . ."

"You look seventeen, at least," said Dana.

"My God," said Amanda.

"What?" I kept stirring the chilli beans.

"Mum's not out of the house three days and you're . . ."

"*You've* got short hair."

"And it doesn't look like that."

"Oh, I don't know, it kind of suits her," said Michael.

I turned around, the pot of chilli heavy in my hand.

"No one said you were coming for tea." I hadn't forgiven Michael for poking round in Mum's bedroom.

"I'm not."

"Yes you are. There's enough," Amanda said. "And she's not a bad cook when she puts her mind to it. Even if she does look like . . . like . . ."

I raised my eyebrows at Amanda. "You are becoming culturally biased, Amanda. You should be careful. You might just end up a bottle washer yourself one day and not a high and mighty chemist. Then see how you feel." I banged the sour cream down next to the plates.

"You've become extremely political in a very short time," said Amanda.

"Oh, and I wonder why."

"And what do you think I've been doing the last five years while you've been mucking around at the pony club? I've been typing pamphlets and helping Mum and you've never once even offered."

"This chilli's good, Lorna," said Michael.

I picked up my plate and fork. "I think I'll have mine in my bedroom."

"Good," said Amanda.

For the second time that week, I slammed the door at her.

Everything had just gone too fast. I went and sat on my bed and shovelled in mouthfuls of chilli to calm me down.

One day I had had nothing else to think about except jumping Lancelot and riding with Rachael. And the next Mum didn't come home. I was planning stories in my head about how I'd go and rescue her. I'd take on the Authority police, Central Office, the whole Government. I, Lorna

Bennett, was invincible.

And the next thing you know, everything was settled. There was this person Dana Dixon. It wasn't a story any more. It was real. She had a baby growing inside her, bigger every day, and I went and got myself involved.

I would have to stand there at the desk at Central Office with a false ID (which somehow I still had to get) and lie to them. Not even Amanda would lie to Central Office.

I was only fourteen. I shouldn't be worried about anything bigger than next week's maths test. And, on top of that, it wasn't just my life I had to worry about. There was also Lancelot. I put my empty plate down by my bed.

I'd be away for a whole month, right when he needed to be covered and fed, and exercised to keep him happy. Amanda got home too late most nights to care for him. And I couldn't ask Rachael to look after him. Her father would ask questions.

Who else then?

I had no time to put an ad in the paper or on the board at the saddle shop. I didn't have time to ask at the pony club. I had to lend him to someone, and straight away so they wouldn't ask questions.

I went up to Mum's room and rang Riding for the Disabled. They knew Lancelot from before I bought him.

"A rather stocky pony, isn't he, and a bit of a grump?" said the woman.

"If you'd rather not have him . . ." I said.

"No, he's a good sensible fellow, and we're busy at the moment. Bring him over tomorrow night."

I hung up and went into the kitchen. The dishes were done. Amanda was making some tea. I looked around. "Where's Michael?"

"Gone home. Do you want some tea?"

I nodded. The half-dead pot plant on the bench looked even deader. I poked a finger into the dry soil.

"We're not very good at keeping plants, are we?" Amanda said. She moved the plant to the end of the bench and put a steaming mug in front of me.

"Are you okay?" She peered at my face. "Not still mad at me are you?"

I shook my head and she opened the cake tin of chocolate fudge biscuits and held it out to me. "Better take two. Sugar always helps."

I managed a smile.

"And, hey, about the hair. Once I get used to it, I might even like it."

I dunked my biscuit in the tea. I didn't even want to think about my hair.

"I've heard some news about Mum," said Amanda.

"News? What do you mean?" I nearly choked.

"Ernest rang."

"Ernest Jacobs? My teacher? Why didn't you say before?"

"Shut up and listen, Lorna. All he said was that he heard this afternoon that someone of Mum's description definitely checked in at Silverstream. She was there the next day, but nothing after that."

"What do you mean nothing?"

"Just gone," said Amanda. "From her duties, her bunk room, everything."

Silverstream was one of the tough camps, as Dana had said. It was way up in the mountains. Most of the workers had to work in the gold mine or forest. Even the women were put on hard labour.

I thought of Mum, who just lived in her head all day and only ever held a pen. Maybe she was strong enough to work up there, but now no one knew where she was.

"What are we going to do, Amanda?"

"Do? I don't know. What *can* we do? Just wait for now. That's what Mum said."

But Mum had never said anything about disappearing.

At school I got harassed about my hair. Rachael didn't say much. Just, "I don't understand."

I suppose we had always planned and done things together, and now I'd just come to school with most of my hair shorn off.

At lunchtime Kim Bloomfield came over to talk to Rachael about the pony club trials. She and Rachael were both taking a float to it but, as we had no horse float, and Mum had said we couldn't even tow one with our car, my name wasn't down to compete.

It was bad enough missing out, but it was worse having Kim and Rachael go on and on about it in front of me when they knew I wasn't going, and I knew I wouldn't even have a pony by night-time.

Kim had long hair like Rachael. It was pulled back, thick and tidy in a golden ponytail. I sat and listened to them going on about jump heights and judges until I couldn't bear it any longer.

"I'll see you later," I said to Rachael. We had separate classes that afternoon.

Rachael looked up. "What about tonight? Are we going riding?"

I shook my head. "Can't."

"Hey, I could ride over," said Kim. "We could practise our dressage test."

"Okay." Rachael turned and smiled at Kim. I put my hands in my pockets and walked away from them.

On the way to Riding for the Disabled, I had to pass the turn-off to Parkers Road, where Rachael lived. I reined in Lancelot and sat there for a moment, looking up the road. I could just ride up there and forget about everything — Mum, Dana Dixon, Silverstream . . . Lancelot sensed my mood and swung his head around.

What if one day I came home and Amanda said, "There was an accident at the camp. Mum . . ."

"Come on, boy." I turned Lancelot's head and urged him past the turn-off.

A girl was waiting for us at the RDA grounds. "He's beautiful," she said. "Look at his fluffy ears. Oh, he's adorable."

I slid down from Lancelot's back. He pushed his nose into the girl's chest, demanding more attention.

I handed the reins to her. "I'll pick up my saddle later."

My arms almost trembled. I wanted to throw them around Lancelot and cling to his neck. I wanted to say goodbye, but not in front of someone.

I reached up and touched his neck, up under the warmth of his mane where his coat was the softest. Then I turned away and started walking.

All of a sudden he let out a long ringing neigh. I turned and saw the girl struggle with him as he swung his body around. To watch me? Or was it the other horses in the paddock? I started running and the sound of his call followed me to the end of the driveway.

It was an eight-kilometre walk home from the paddocks. I scuffed my boots through the grass that Lancelot had just trotted through. Halfway home, a car slowed and pulled up behind me.

"Lorna?"

I turned around.

"Couldn't mistake that hair. Need a ride?" It was Michael. He leaned over and opened the door for me.

"I've given Lancelot away for a while, but I don't want to talk about it."

"Okay," said Michael. "Get in anyway."

I got in. "I'm lending him to Riding for the Disabled. I even left my saddle behind, the one that used to be Mum's. But what was I supposed to do, walk home eight kilometres carrying it?"

"Would you like me to go back for your saddle?"

I shook my head. "I don't want to see him. I've just said goodbye. But next week, could you?"

"I'll take you then if you like."

I looked down at my hands. "I won't be here."

"Lorna?"

"What?"

"What are you up to?"

"You're in Mum's group, aren't you?"

"Her writing group?"

"You know what I mean. The anti-camp group. You must be. Mum trusted you with her stuff.

And don't say it's just her manuscript, because I've been in and checked and all her DVDs have gone, the speeches, booklets, everything."

"Mmmmm," said Michael.

"So can you get ID cards as well?" I looked up at his face and met his brown eyes.

"What makes you think I know anything?" he said carefully.

"I need help, that's all. I've got to ask someone. And Amanda wouldn't let me, I know it."

"Wouldn't let you what?"

"Swap. I'm going to Silverstream Camp next week," I said.

Michael's face didn't change at all. He just kept watching me.

"So I need a forged ID card. I can't take hers — the person I'm swapping with."

"Swap," said Michael. "You're going to miss school and possibly end up doing hard labour at camp, so you can single-handedly find your mum and get her out?"

"I'll find her and make sure she gets out. I don't know how exactly. I've got to get there yet. So can you get me one?"

"Yes, I can. But I can't let you do this."

"It's not up to you, is it? It's up to me."

"I can refuse to get you the ID card then."

"Okay." I put my hand on the door handle. "I'll just find someone else. I might end up asking the wrong person, though. Or I might just turn up to the work camp bus without it and bluff my way through. Either way it could cause trouble."

"Lorna. You're fourteen. Leave it to the anti-camp group. They'll track your mum down and get her out."

"No. No way." I opened the door of the car. "I couldn't help Dad but I'm going to help Mum." I got out and went to shut the door.

"Lorna, get back in. Just let me think," said Michael.

I looked up and down the road, then back at Michael. I got back in the car and waited.

"For your mum's sake. And Amanda's," said Michael. "I will. But only because I believe you are strong-willed enough to go off anyway and do something risky."

"That's right. I will."

A logging truck rumbled past at high speed and the car rocked in its wake. Michael waited for the noise to fade. "There have been rumours about a second camp at Silverstream," he said. "If it's true, your mum could be there."

"A second camp?"

"There's something going on. Something that's beyond our normal sentencing system. A man who'd just come back from camp, supposedly holding photos, never turned up at the meeting he was meant to come to. There's no reason why your mum should be in danger, but we're worried."

"I knew something was wrong."

"I'll help you Lorna, on two conditions. One — you do nothing to put yourself at risk. You do your job, keep quiet and listen. Thousands of people go to camp, do their term and come safely home. There's no reason for it to be any different for you. How long is this girl's term?"

"A month."

"Lucky it's almost the holidays. Condition two — if there is any trouble, any hint of trouble, you get word to me and we'll try to get you out. That girl will just have to go instead. Does she understand that?"

I thought of Dana's growing baby and my promise not to make a noise until she was safely engaged. "Yep. It's fine," I said.

"Okay." Michael smiled at me. "I'll get your ID. You go to camp and keep your eyes and ears open. And Amanda . . ."

"Amanda's going to be wild."

"I'll have to deal with Amanda. Now where do we find this girl and her card?"

I took a deep breath and looked at Michael. I hoped I really could trust him with Dana's name. Michael looked back at me, his eyes as steady as those of a horse resting in the sun.

"She lives in Greenwood Street," I said. "Her name is Dana Dixon."

"Here, you might as well have this, too." Dana passed me a photo in a frame. It was of her and Davey. They had their arms around each other and they were laughing. Dana had on a brown felt hat and Davey had a grin a bit like Rachael's.

"Put it by your bed there or something," said Dana. "They probably expect that."

"That's a good idea," said Michael.

"Davey and I are going to talk to his parents on Wednesday," said Dana. "And remember, till then . . . "

"Yes, I know," I said quickly, and looked across at Michael.

In the car on the way home I peered in the bag of clothes Dana had given me. At the bottom there were more earrings, and the brown felt hat. I put it on and looked in the mirror. It felt good on my head. I turned and grinned at Michael and he smiled back at me.

I had ideas of locking myself in my room when I got home, to try on some of Dana's clothes, but Amanda was in one of her major tidy-up moods.

"The thing I really cannot stand," she said, appearing at my door with hands on hips. "Is how you manage to get horse hair everywhere in this house."

"I don't."

"In the bathroom, in the hand basin. On the couch. And in the kitchen they must just sort of hang out in the air, because I was making a cake and guess what got in it?"

"Lancelot can't help it. He's moulting."

"He's moulting! You're the one moulting. Just look at your jeans. They're covered in horse hair. They look as if they haven't been washed for weeks."

I looked down at them and it was true.

"Just because Mum's not here doesn't mean you're getting away with everything."

"Oh, Amanda."

I looked at her standing there, her red hair illuminating her face and her cheeks pink from scrubbing or whatever she'd been doing. Amanda was a chemist. She liked everything to match up to some formula and be precise. She was so unlike Mum and me that I wondered at times where she came from.

I knew that Dad had been tall, 1.88 metres, which was where I got my height and big shoulders from. But, though Amanda was tall, Mum said she took after Dad's sister, who had milky white skin, a fine neck and "alluring" eyes.

I think I just took completely after Dad: his height, his shoulders, his mousy-coloured brown hair, his freckles. The only real hereditary advantage I got from my family was a big, wide smile (my best asset, Rachael had agreed in front of her mirror) and that probably came from some obscure uncle.

But I was like Mum, too. I was messy and disorganised and I liked it. And now that he was gone I especially liked the thought of Lancelot's hair all over the house.

"I'll wash the bath then," I said "and clean my bedroom, I suppose."

"For a start," said Amanda. "Your dinner's in the oven, by the way. I'm going out for a while."

"With Michael?"

"Yes." She had turned to walk back up the hall when I called her back.

"What?"

"Do you think, well, do you know more about Mum than you're letting on? Do you, honest?"

She came and sat down on my bed. "Lorna, you're cared for, aren't you? You've got a home and a pony and friends."

I shrugged my shoulders at her.

"Don't you worry, okay? Mum would want everything to go on the same for you. And she'll be all right, Lorna."

"But look what happened to Dad. They killed him."

"That was an accident — an unrelated bizarre accident. They proved that at the coroner's court."

"The Authorities' court," I said.

"Come on now. Don't go thinking everything's a major plot against you. Mum said for us to carry on. And we can't go asking questions, because they don't know it's Mum who disappeared."

"Because she was using another ID?"

"Yes. *Now* do you understand?"

"So who is she?"

"She's . . . It doesn't matter. Mum didn't want you to know any details. Hey, I've been thinking. I could borrow a car and horse float so you can go to those pony trials in Greyfield."

Now she said it, when it was too late and Lancelot was gone and the trials belonged to another future that wasn't mine.

"I don't want to go."

"Why not? You made enough fuss about it a few weeks ago."

"Because. I'm not good enough. And I'm too big on Lancelot — you know I am. Only people whose parents spent thousands on their ponies are going."

"That's not true."

"Yes it is."

"Well." Amanda stood up. "The offer's there if you want it." Then she was off down the hall, calling back, "The bathroom, remember."

The bathroom, as far as I was concerned, could wait. I took the bag of Dana's clothes out from where I'd hidden it in my wardrobe.

First I tried on a blue jacket. It looked good. I turned sideways in the mirror and checked out the profile.

45

I took off my hairy jeans and took them to the laundry, where I dropped them in the basket on top of Amanda's sheets. Then I came back and pulled on shiny black tights and a black ripped skirt.

With the chain earrings through my ears, I pulled on the felt hat and looked up.

Someone else looked out at me from my bedroom mirror. I could have been Dana Dixon.

In the morning, I put on my school uniform for Amanda's sake. There was no way I was going to school, though. What for?

I pushed the lever down on the toaster and stood there, knife in hand, waiting for it to pop. Just to have teachers try to stuff facts in my head. Specially in social studies, and that unit we were doing on "our society today" — how wonderful it was, how clean our streets, our cities, our schools. Everyone was working; the houses were full of model families.

Single parents didn't exist, of course — they

were called extended families. Unemployment didn't exist, either. There were work schemes and camps everywhere. Think of a job? Somewhere someone was being forced to do it. And, if you didn't like your option or you failed at all, there was always a place at a camp for you.

What about the people who didn't agree? They biked around in the dark with borrowed IDs and went to late-night meetings. They organised protests that never made it on to the news. They wrote pamphlets to push into letterboxes and kept their eyes and ears open everywhere they went.

They also disappeared.

I slapped peanut butter on my toast and listened to the radio as I ate. Amanda whisked around smelling of perfume, had her coffee and muesli, then rinsed her dishes in the sink before calling out the usual, "Don't be late now, Lorna."

Silence.

I went up to my bedroom. There was a plastic bag on the bed containing my jeans and a note from Amanda. "Scrub these before they infect the entire household."

For God's sake, the world could be coming to an end and Amanda would still be vacuuming.

The phone jangled. I let it ring, then suddenly thought it could be Michael and raced through the house.

"Lorna?" It *was* Michael. "Thought you'd be home. I can take a photo for your ID at half past ten. Okay?"

I was wearing a black singlet of Dana's and the black skirt when I met Michael at the door. Just for a moment, when he first saw me, I knew he didn't see scruffy, horsey Lorna, but someone else.

I hadn't liked Amanda's last boyfriend. He wore suits all the time and worked in a bank and spoke very correctly. Sometimes he looked at me as if I was something that needed to be cleaned up and put away. I hope horse hairs landed in his coffee, I thought. I hope they're still surfacing in his suit pockets.

Michael wore a brown leather jacket and jeans and he treated me like an equal. We were partners in this, and Amanda didn't know a thing about it. After coffee he took head and shoulder pictures of me against the white sitting room wall. Then he talked to me about what to pack.

"Nothing personal of your own, like photos or journals. Except the photo of Dana and Davey.

That's good."

"What about my poetry book?"

June the eighth was the anniversary of Dad's death. This year it was my turn to choose the poem. I liked reading them and thinking about my dad.

"A poetry book would be fine," said Michael.

I didn't ask about Lancelot's photo. I'd taken my favourite one of him and me off the wardrobe door and put it in the frame on top of Dana's photo. I knew what Michael would say about that, but there was no way I would leave it behind. Lancelot was coming with me wherever I went.

"Michael," I said. "Amanda keeps telling me everything's all right, to keep quiet and not worry, and you're helping me get out of here."

"Have you said something to Amanda?"

"No, but you wouldn't like me to, would you?"

"You need me, Lorna, and I'm helping you, that's all. My guess is, if Amanda knew what you were up to, she'd have you packed off quick to live with some eagle-eyed auntie."

How true that was. Aunt Isobel would be able to spot a stray horse hair at twenty metres.

"But why does Amanda think everything will be all right?"

"I suppose because, up till now, apart from helping your mum sometimes, she really does have faith in the system."

"She's scared she'll lose her job."

"She has worked hard and played by the rules to get where she is. Why shouldn't she think the rules will be fair in the end? She thinks they've made a mistake with Harriet and one day there will be an apology and she'll be back."

"She doesn't want to think about the truth," I said. "She likes all the streets being clean and no unemployed people hanging around."

"Be fair. For the first three or four years, most people liked it that way, too," said Michael. "In a way, the camps were a good idea. They gave people a place to live and work to do. But what's happened is they've become a way to control people. You do what Central Office says or they'll send you away to a camp. We're only just starting to wake up to what's happening. But people like your mum and dad — they saw that coming from the start."

"I think Dad would be pleased I'm doing something," I said.

Michael smiled at me. "I'd have liked to have met Jethro. But, Lorna . . ." He suddenly had a fatherly look on his face. "If you've got any doubts, it's still not too late to pull out. It won't be your fault if Dana has to go to camp."

"No." I shook my head slowly. "I've decided. And that's that."

On Sunday morning, I packed. All Dana's clothes and some things of mine fitted into my canvas sports bag. I'd left out a pair of jeans, black boots and the blue jacket for the bus trip.

I was sitting on the bed, thinking hard about what else I'd need, when there was a knock on the door and Michael called out. I went up the hallway.

"Amanda's not home. I've been waiting all weekend to hear from you."

"There was a hold-up with the card."

He followed me into the kitchen and shook his head when I offered him a cold drink.

"Here, have a look." He handed me the new ID card. All the details of Dana Dixon were there, but it was my photo in the space above her name.

"It will pass, won't it? They won't look twice at me after seeing this?"

"You'll be fine. Have you got everything else ready? What about school books?"

I pulled a face.

"Amanda said you wanted to be a vet. That's a lot of hard study."

"I'm doing all right. I'm going to have to work up there though, aren't I?" I pulled another face and Michael laughed.

"That's another thing. They'll pay you for it. Here." He produced a bank slip. "That's your account number in Dana's name, but it's your money. Look on the bright side. You could end up with a new pony after this."

"What do you mean?" I said slowly. "Do you think I'm just doing this for money? I didn't even know about the money."

"Be practical, Lorna. You'll be working for a month. Why shouldn't you get money towards a new pony."

"A new pony!" He looked so reasonable, I nearly flew at him.

"Why not a new pony? You're too big for Lancelot anyway, Lorna. I've heard you moan about how small and bad-tempered he is."

"To you? Have I? I have not!"

At that moment, I hated Michael more than anything. He was so far off understanding about horses. I didn't know how I had even thought I could like him.

"It's good you're mad, Lorna," said Michael. "You need to be taking this seriously."

"Oh, as if I wasn't."

"You need to be," continued Michael evenly, "because there are important issues at stake. Dana, for one."

"Oh, shut up. I know all about Dana."

"You can't just go up there, get sick of it and come home."

"Shut up," I said.

"It's four whole weeks."

"Shut up, shut up, shut up."

"You're repeating yourself, Lorna."

"And you — don't you know when to leave it? I know what I'm doing. I started all this myself. I don't need you bossing me around. And I don't want the money, either. Here!" I threw the slip of paper back at him. "Give it to Dana. She can have the money. Does that show I'm serious?"

Michael picked up the piece of paper and put it in his pocket and I picked up the ID card from the bench and put it in my pocket. We looked hard at each other, then he turned away.

At the door he said, "I'll pick you up at 9.30 tomorrow for the bus." Then he walked out.

I didn't want to stay in the house, either. I put the ID card away in my sports bag. Maybe I'd bike around and see Dana myself, even though on Friday he'd told me to keep away from her house — just in case. Just in case what? I slammed the back door after me and went out to the shed for my bike.

When I came out into the drive again, wheeling my bike, Mistletoe was standing there and Rachael was sitting on his back smiling at me.

"Hi, Lorna," she said.

I nearly dropped the bike in shock.

"Are you okay?" she asked. "I thought you must be really sick or something."

"I know. I'm sorry I haven't rung." I leaned my bike against the shed. Mistletoe dropped his head and started eating the weeds on the driveway.

"Mr Jacobs asked about you in class. You want to come riding? I mean, you don't look sick."

I looked back at Lancelot's empty paddock, then at Rachael. I decided to tell her.

About Aunt Isobel, that is. About how Mum had to go away for a while to do some research, and she was making me go and live with my aunt, who was really strict. That's why I had got my hair cut, to make some sort of stand before I went. And Aunt Isobel was bossy and tidy like Amanda. They even looked alike. In fact, I didn't know why Mum bothered sending me there. She could have left me with Amanda and it would have been just the same.

"Yes, but what about Lancelot?" asked Rachael. She tugged on Mistletoe's reins to stop him getting too close to Mum's rose bush by the garage. "Are you taking him?"

I nearly kept lying. And then I thought — she only has to ride past him and see him one day. So I told her how I'd taken Lancelot to RDA, and how Mum was going to get me a bigger pony next year. I nearly choked on those words.

Rachael had known Lancelot as long as she had known me, right from when we first went riding together when we were ten. She had been on her smaller pony, Abacus, then, and looked up to me on towering Lancelot.

"It's all right," I said. "I'm getting used to the

idea. It's just . . ." And all the feelings of sadness and worry that I'd been holding back for days threatened to burst out in one big torrent. Right then, I just wanted to tell Rachael everything.

"I know," said Rachael. "It was horrible when Abacus had to go. I even hated Mistletoe when he first arrived. But I love him now, the big, fat greedy guts." She rubbed Mistletoe's neck. "Hey, would your aunt let me come and stay with you for a week?"

I looked at Rachael on her shiny pony.

"I hope so. I'll ask. But I have to go now and run an errand for Amanda."

Rachael pulled Mistletoe's head up and turned him around. "Ring me up, okay?" she called.

"Goodbye," I called after her.

I didn't feel like going to Dana's after that. I didn't like how Rachael seemed to be part of a life that didn't exist any more.

So I rang Dana instead and said what I wanted to say, that I wished her luck for her engagement. She wished me luck, too.

The house was full of sunlight — even the wooden floors beamed. I turned the radio on loud, though the music was interspersed with stupid ads. It was amazing how empty a whole house could seem with just Mum gone from it. I suppose that's how Mum felt after Dad died. I remember the radio was on loud all the time then, too, filling up the spaces where people would be have been talking.

Amanda had left me a note telling me to cook some dinner. I looked in the fridge. There was no juice and I'd drunk all the milk. I scrubbed potatoes and put them on to bake, then poured a glass of water and went into the dining room. I sat with my feet up at the table, looking out at the fig tree.

Amanda's sheets were flapping on the line. I thought I should probably go and get them in, but I didn't. It was better just to sit there, while the potatoes gave off warm smells in the kitchen and the light in the house dimmed around me: thinking of Lancelot and of Mum and the whole new life that would start for me in the morning.

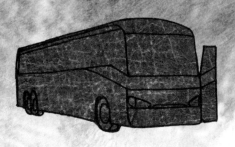

SEVEN

Michael was early to take me to the bus, but I was ready even earlier.

"How are you feeling, Lorna?" he asked as I got into the car.

"Okay, I suppose."

"You look great."

But nothing could shift the cold feeling in the pit of my stomach.

When I'd got up that morning and put my T-shirt under my pillow, it was as if I'd put myself away. I wore my school uniform until Amanda went to work, then I put that away as well. Everything of Lorna's got put away, and I dressed in Dana's clothes, gelled my hair and put on heaps of eye make-up and the earrings.

I didn't go to Mum's room to sort of say goodbye, as I thought I'd do. I just picked up my bags and walked straight through the house, and it was like I was a stranger already. When Michael's car pulled up in the driveway, it was Dana Dixon who walked out to meet him.

"Got your ID?" Michael asked.

I gave him a withering look, but he only laughed and passed me a wage card in Dana's name.

I looked from the card to Michael's face. He was watching for my reaction — to see if I was going to throw it at him again, I suppose. But I'd made my point and I didn't have the energy just then to keep arguing.

"Thanks." I pushed the card into my pocket. Michael looked relieved.

We drove down Arrow Street towards town. There was a work group working on the drains along the edge of the footpath. One man, portly in his uniform, pushed his cap back and wiped his red face with a hanky as we drove past.

"Oh no!" I turned round on my seat to stare out the back window. "That was Mr Jacobs. My English teacher. Michael, what's he doing in a work gang?"

"Sit down, Lorna," said Michael.

"But Mr Jacobs . . ."

"It was only a matter of time," said Michael. "Harriet had been worried about him for a while."

"But he was my best teacher."

The car swung into Courtney Street and the work gang was left behind.

"Don't worry about Ernest Jacobs now. You've got to concentrate on being Dana Dixon." Michael pulled the car into a parking space. "Now, about your mum. She was arrested with the ID of Sheila Wilcox."

"Sheila Wilcox," I repeated. "But, if Mum's using her name, where is the real Sheila Wilcox?"

"Where indeed. She's disappeared from her home. Amanda's going to visit her family again this week. Don't worry about that. Now, one last thing, Lorna. There's a farmer who lives in the last farmhouse going up towards Mount Silverstream. His name is Douglas. He's a friend of mine and he can be trusted, if you need help."

I swallowed. "Okay, thanks" I managed to say. "Otherwise, at the end of my month, they'll just send me home on the bus again, won't they?"

"I'll be there to pick you up," Michael said, and he smiled at me. "Good luck, Lorna."

I smiled back at him, a sort of sick excuse of a smile. Then I got out of the car with my bags and crossed the road to Central Office, where the bus was waiting.

I had a seat by the window. It was like carsickness — the feeling in my stomach. If only I could see Michael, I thought. Someone familiar after all those security policemen in Central Office. I stared out the window while the bus idled. There! Michael was just down the footpath a bit. How normal and safe he looked in his jacket and jeans. He didn't look up at the bus or acknowledge me at all. He just crossed the road and walked away.

Michael! I wanted to yell after him.

Someone sat down next to me, a dark-haired girl. I looked at her, but she didn't look at me. Her face was lonely and quiet, like a seagull on an empty beach.

The bus lurched, then glided forward. I held my bag so tight that my knuckles whitened.

Streets flashed past, then long country roads — roads I'd galloped along on Lancelot. Then we turned up a road without a verge, and wound past farms I'd never ridden by.

I tried to see the last farmhouse, the one belonging to Douglas, and just caught a flash of a square letterbox with no name and a driveway hidden by trees before we entered a forest. The bus juddered and swayed through dark, green corridors. I watched the trees and the edge of gravel slip by, searching — for what? Secret paths out of there? But the forest went on and on and the bus began to slow, still climbing.

EIGHT

I hadn't thought about the wind or the cold. Back in town, I'd only thought how to look like Dana and what to pack to remind me of my own life. Down there, the name Mount Silverstream meant a mountain lit up by the sun against a bright blue sky.

When I got down from the bus, my legs felt the first blast of frozen air. I climbed down on to the gravel and into a mountain climate.

A woman led us through an entrance foyer to a courtyard and into a hall, where at least the wind had stopped, even if the cold hadn't. Her arms were covered in blue angora — she was knee to neck in the stuff and looked like a policeman pretending to be a woman pretending to be a friend of ours. But she wasn't.

"I'm Andrea, your camp superintendent," she

said. "I like to greet each one of you so you know I have seen you and I am watching you." She looked at us. "How your future goes from this moment on is up to you — you and the choices you make."

I felt the bolt of her blue, staring eyes at mine, then she moved them on to the girl with long black hair beside me, and the man beside her, and the old man beside him, and on and on for a long minute of waiting until she had stared at the whole busload of us.

I looked out the window to where another mountain range loomed. There were yellow-bellied snow clouds already above it. You couldn't see that range, the Devil's River Peaks, from town. All you could see from town was Mount Silverstream, Mount Crusader and High Peak Hills. From here, we couldn't see Arapiko or any other houses or buildings or roads. The camp was in a clearing on a mountain, ringed by yet more mountains, and somewhere in this wilderness I hoped I would find my mother.

"You there, the gangly one. Your name and number?"

Had I missed something?

"Number 557."

Andrea waited. I looked at her puffy face and tried to clear my mind. My mother had been here, now I was here. I was Lorna. No — I had another name.

"Dana Dixon," I said. The name surfaced from the darkness that was growing round the edge of my thoughts. I wanted to be Lorna, but I couldn't. I had to let that name and the memories go. I had to be Dana. Dana. Dana.

"Is there anything else you need to remember, Dana, apart from your name?" Andrea held out her arm. I looked at her hand. She kept holding it out and realised what she wanted and handed her my ID card. She flipped it open, looked at my face and then back at the photo. Even in this cold room I felt sweat begin to slide from under my arms and run down my ribs.

She passed it back.

"Dana is a thief," she told everyone. "I know what she stole and why she's here. I know why every one of you is here. I know where you live. I know what you last went to the doctor for. I know who died in your lives."

The old guy just down from me slumped to the ground. I heard his head hit the wooden floorboards. His glasses slewed sideways on his face, which was so white it was almost translucent.

"I know how little education each of you has," Andrea continued, "and how much you think you know."

"Excuse me," I said. I pointed to the man on the ground, then looked around at the other faces. The girl with the dark hair, the one I'd sat next to on the bus, held my eyes for a moment, then turned away. On the floor, the old man's knitted cardigan was rumpled up on one side, showing a patch of clean white shirt. He took a sharp, deep breath and opened his eyes.

"Leave him alone," said Andrea. "I know what jobs will be best to teach you what you need,' she carried on. "And if everyone does what they're asked . . ."

This was stupid. I looked at the people across from me — a young dark-skinned guy, a girl in flowery pants, an older woman whose eyes slid from mine back to Andrea. I looked down at the old man and he was looking up at me. I knelt down beside him.

"Are you okay?"

"I said leave him alone," said Andrea.

"He's an old man," I protested, looking up at her. Then the man grasped my hand and squeezed it hard and I helped him stand up. His head only came up to my cheeks.

"Name and number," barked Andrea.

"Number 337. Mr Edward Avison."

"Mr is it?"

Somebody laughed.

At school once, in assembly, I fainted. Before I fell, I felt my stomach convulse with nausea and my throat close up like squashed spaghetti. When I'd looked up from the floor, there were uniforms and faces crowded over me. Miss Thompson had cleared a path. "Stand back and give her room," she'd ordered. She sat me up slowly and got me to tip my head forward. That's what teachers did when they needed to — they took care of you.

Nobody normal would let an old man fall and just leave him. Andrea carried on telling us the conditions of our stay.

No cellphones, no Internet, no phone calls, no TV. Work as directed. Stay in your own accommodation block . . .

"The mining area is completely out of bounds. So is the native bush past the signs in the forest.

Anyone caught trespassing will be dealt with. Escaping is pointless. Several have tried — they don't do it again."

I stood perfectly still. What if Mum had tried and they'd caught her?

When Andrea started giving out the jobs, I wanted an outdoor one. Mine workers got to go on the bus each day. They got to work outdoors and not be anywhere near Andrea. And they got to check out the mining area. It would double my chances of finding Mum, I thought.

Andrea had her own method of delegating jobs. Males went to mining jobs. The older women were given chainsaw duties. Old Mr Avison was given laundry duty. I was young and fit and strong, and Andrea put me on dishes. Did she have a hotline to my sister?

"What Dana doesn't know, because I haven't had a chance to explain it yet, is that we have a system of discipline here," said Andrea. "Major issues are dealt with using isolation and, for men, physical punishment. Rudeness and disobedience are sorted out immediately with twelve-hour shifts. Yours starts now, Dana."

"Pardon?"

"Your twelve-hour shift. Report to the kitchen now. Leave your bag with me. I'll take it to Blue Block."

"I don't even know where the kitchen is."

"This isn't a city, Dana. It's a camp." She pointed to the door.

NINE

The thing I learned about twelve-hourers is that they do all the lunch and dinner shifts, because they are there to serve. And, when the meal is over, there's no food left worth eating, only a million dishes still to do.

By dinner time, my stomach was graunching like a learner driver changing gears. The smell of rubber gloves on my hands, hot from the sink, made that squishy feeling rise up in my throat again.

I wouldn't have thought that one kitchen could have enough cleaning in it to last till eleven at night. But Flossie, my boss, pointed out the light and power switches, the lamp shades and the cupboards. I had a fair idea of the sorts of meals we were going to get after heaving crates of cabbages, troughs of lentils, sacks and sacks of rolled oats and the cheapest brand of instant coffee on the market.

Finished at last, I found Blue Block easily enough in the courtyard on the other side of the hall. A sign said "BLUE BLOCK" in big blue letters. Lights from the courtyard shone through the high windows, so I could see down the row of flat beds humped with bodies till I came to one with my bag beside it. I pulled out the photo of Lancelot and put it on the cupboard by my bed. Then I just took my shoes off, lay down and pulled the blankets over my clothes.

My legs were so surprised at being horizontal, they almost floated upwards.

"Dana?"

I turned my head to my neighbour. It was the girl with the black hair.

"I'm Rebekkah."

I strained to hear her whisper.

"Andrea went through your bag. You need to be more careful."

"But why wouldn't anyone help that old man?" I whispered back.

"The thing is not to be noticed. One person isn't worth risking the bigger picture for."

My cheeks flushed hot, despite the frigid air. Finding Mum was *my* big picture and here I was, on the first day, already known as a troublemaker.

"I have to find Sheila Wilcox," I whispered.

"Do you know me?" Rebekkah whispered back. "Don't ask things of people you don't know. This is not the place for questions." She turned her back on me and lay still. I heard her take a deep breath and, when my heart stopped thudding with shame, I heard the snoring and breathing of women all around me. Had anyone else heard me name Sheila?

My jeans weren't functioning like an electric blanket. Instead of getting warmer, I felt colder. It was as if my bed had been aired outside in a frost. I thought of my socks and jersey in the bag by my bed, but I didn't want to make a noise. I didn't want anyone to think about me. I hunched up my knees and thought about Lancelot instead — how soft and warm his neck was under the heavy fall of his mane.

The clock in the dining hall said 5.30 am. The sun hadn't risen. The sky hadn't even lightened. It was the black of night still, and we were all up and having breakfast. Porridge. And a cup of pale tea.

I lined up for a second cup. It gave me a chance to look around each trestle and at the workers. They wore blue kitchen smocks, orange mine overalls or yellow chainsaw trousers. None of them was my mum. One guy turned and stared right back at me. He had freckles blasted all over his face. I'd never seen him before.

Flossie shook her head at me from the kitchen doorway. What? No one else was starting work. But she aimed her thumb behind her, and I put my cup down and followed her into the kitchen.

She took me through to the sinks. "Did you leave that pile there?"

I looked at the stained and damp tea towels and cloths I'd put on the end of the bench. "I didn't know where else to put them."

"Get your act together, girl. It's not clean until the job's finished. Take them to the laundry."

Rebekkah was just putting her white cap on to start work in the laundry. She smiled at me. "Everything okay?"

"Sure," I said. "A-okay." I dumped the tea towels in the chute and looked at the black window. "If it's dark when we start and nearly dark when we finish, how do we get to look around the place? If it's okay to ask you a question, that is?"

"They don't want us looking around the place. That's the point."

Mum had already been gone ten days. I had to look around. "I might have to be sick this afternoon."

Rebekkah opened the first machine and started loading overalls.

"If Andrea asks . . ." I began. But Rebekkah didn't look up again.

TEN

The guy with the freckles was on lunch duty. A twelve-hourer then. He stood by the pot, ladling out cabbage soup, just as I had yesterday. Rebekkah went up for seconds, but I didn't like the way he looked over at me, as if he knew something.

I could just go up and hold out my bowl and ask, "Have you got a problem?" or "Did you want something?" But what did Rebekkah say last night? — "Don't ask questions of people you don't know."

What if he said, "You're not Dana Dixon. I know her." What then?

One thing I felt sure of. If he did know Dana, he certainly didn't like her.

I looked out the window. Wisps of grey cloud drifted past the bus shed. Down in the town, it might be hot and sunny, for all I knew. Up here, we were inside a cumulus the colour of rain.

What if Mum was injured somewhere? Yet she'd been seen right in this room. What job had she had? One like mine? Then Flossie would have known her.

After the lunch dishes were done, I folded tea towels and I watched Flossie's face for something I could trust. Violet, our chef, leaned over and said something to her and Flossie lifted up her head and laughed out loud. Even when she saw me watching, her eyes stayed smiling.

I made my decision. "My aunt was here last week," I said. "Sheila Wilcox."

"Hey, she thinks that's something to be proud of," said Violet and they laughed again.

"I'm proud of her cooking," I said. "Was she working in here?"

Violet merely shuffled over to the pantry and heaved out a bag of soya beans. Flossie went on stirring the curry.

Time to get sick, then.

The beech forest came right up to the grassy space behind the buildings and leaned over it. One moment I was alone in the bare camp ground, the next I was in the shelter of trees, walking up and past the sign that said KEEP OUT. I kept going.

Beech leaves wafted and fell from the trees as I walked. The forest floor was bright with their golden colour. Far off a "whoomph" sounded from the mine, and then the forest was silent again; even the birds were mute. I had no hat or gloves, and the air was icy on my cheeks and ears. I pushed my hands into my jeans. I didn't even have a jacket. I'd gone straight from the toilet, where I was supposedly suffering from diarrhoea, and out the back door.

If there was another hidden camp, could it be up here somewhere?

The sun broke through the forest canopy in a circle and lit up one beech leaf on a rotten log, as if for its own starring role. I climbed upwards and the sky came down to meet me. Whiteness crept and hazed through the trees until all I could see were the damp trunks rising up around me.

Then I heard the buzz and crash of machinery and the whine of chainsaws. From behind a boulder, I looked down into a wide, open area that stretched out of my vision. A row of square houses lined the road into the factory and mine. Three buses and a single van waited in the greyness of gravel and air.

I waited, too, crouched on the sodden beech leaves with my arms holding my knees warm against my chest, watching.

At knock-off time, the workers in their orange overalls walked to buses. The windows steamed up and the buses drove off. Now lights were coming on in the houses. If there had been a sun in the sky, it would be almost setting. Somehow I had to find my way back through the dark trees — unless I scrambled down the bank and ran along the road.

Still I waited to see what the van was for — staying or going? And then, out of the first house, walked a line of people in pale overalls. They all had short hair. One woman staggered and a man in jeans and a black jacket held her elbow and guided her into the van. I peered at the shape of the woman, at the shape of her head. She could have been my mother.

If you live with someone all your life, you get to know their outline. It's like a word where you keep the first and last letters and scramble the rest, but your brain will still understand it.

Pale, shapeless clothes, short ragged hair. I would have known if she was my mum. But she wasn't. None of them were.

The man slammed the van door shut and his headlights swung my way. I jerked back behind the boulder. When I heard the van accelerate away, I looked again. The mine yard was empty, the house lights yellow in the twilight mist. I slid down the bank, braking with numb hands, and when I hit the road I started to run.

Blue Block was lit up and the high squares of light shining through the windows patterned the courtyard. I stepped through the light and up to the door. The women sitting on their beds in groups stopped talking and turned to look at me. I pulled at the twigs stuck in my hair and took off my damp, dirty boots to carry them to my bed.

Rebekkah watched me changing my damp sweatshirt for a clean one and putting on my big, blue woolly jersey — one Mum knitted for Dad.

"Did you see anything worth seeing?" she asked in a quiet voice.

"I went up to the mine. And, after the workers left, I saw these people come out and get put in a van."

"Anyone like this? Did you see him?" She took a photo off her bedside counter and showed me — a young guy, dark hair, dark eyes and his lips curving up about to smile.

"My brother Anthony. He should be here."

"No one like that," I said. "I looked really hard."

She sat back on her bed and blew out a long breath through her lips.

"Did they all have short hair?"

"It was weird. They all sort of looked the same. One of them tripped."

"They're the drugged ones. They're the ones we won't see again. Do you see what I mean now? That's what could happen to any of us."

I looked around the room.

"Oh, not *them*. They'll just do what they're told and go back. Ones like us, I mean, who won't put up with it."

"If someone is supposed to be here but they're not, where are they likely to be held?"

"Andrea puts people in isolation. That's where I think Anthony is."

"Did Andrea see that I was missing?"

"She wasn't there. You can bet she knows, though."

My stomach gripped, but that could have been hunger. Hours of clambering and running, fuelled by watery soup. And that was only one bowl.

"Did you learn aboout Aktion T4 at school?"

I shook my head.

"It was the Nazi programme that killed off unwanted people in the Second World War. It started with children who had something wrong with them. Then it was for killing anyone who was 'unproductive'. There were lists, and if three doctors put a red cross next to a name, without knowing that person or what they were like, that was it — that person was killed. They called those people 'Life unworthy of life'.

"And, when that plan got sprung by some priest, the Nazis did it another way — they got rid of people by starving them and drugging them."

"Do you think they're starting here with our food rations?"

"Huh. It's still nutrition," Rebekkah said. "Enough to keep us working. But those ones in the van — who's going to see what happens to them? If we can't prove anything, how can we stop it?"

"I saw them, though," I said. "And now *I* know about it."

The babble of voices around us stopped. I looked up at the sudden quiet. Andrea stood in the doorway.

"Evening, ladies," she said with a grim smile. She advanced towards me. "Diarrhoea today, Dana?"

I nodded.

"I can't let you infect a whole room. Get your things."

"I'm all right now, Andrea."

"I don't think so. I think it lasts, oh, forty-eight hours at least."

She stood there. Rebekkah turned away from us and picked up her book. I pulled my bag out of my cupboard.

She took me to a white room. A white bed, white walls, a white light hanging from the ceiling. I thought the tray with Flossie's curry on it and a white paper napkin was a nice touch.

I woke up in my own bed in Blue Block. I remembered someone walking me back through the courtyard — it must have been work time. The dining hall was quiet and Blue Block, when I got there, was empty. I remembered that one foot went in front of the other — that's all I knew how to do. Turn when the woman next to me said "Turn". Stop when she said "Stop". Go through the door. Lie down on my bed. Then not so much sleep, I think, as faint from being upright.

I know I wasn't making up the diarrhoea or the vomiting. The ends of my hair stank and were stiff with sick. My stomach felt like a hollowed-out skull, scraped free of any sense.

I thought of those people shuffling to the van in the twilight. Was it just last night? Or days ago? Their feet taking them up the step into the van.

The van driving them beyond the reach of this camp or my memory.

I reached under my pillow and pulled out my poetry book. I thought of Dad's hands opening it. How he would read the old words of dead poets by my bed. He called it his roll-call of heroes, his welcoming answer to the dark.

At his funeral, when each friend stood up to read the words he loved, nothing made sense to me, nothing gave me comfort. It was all words, just sounds out of open mouths. Mum sat in the front row with her face lifted up, as if the words were flowing over her, like a potion that could make you forget everything.

For that day and awful night, I hated poetry. There was nothing that could make "*the sun roll east, or raise the dead*".

A year later, when the rock from the river was put on Dad's grave, we got these lines put on it. Mum said them out to the river, to the sunshine and the cold, clear day:

"*And all is peace. Slowly the daylight fails
and voice and lute bring back the stars again.*"

Then Amanda stepped forward with her rose and I saw how words could make you feel again.

And what you felt, you could bear, because you had to, and that was how you carried on.

I opened my book in my bed in Blue Block and silently read "Losing the Words".

There are
rumours
of words that were,
words that
have gone
from dictionaries.
The names
of strange
slow birds
no one living has
seen
are gone.
The word
for water to
catch in
the hand and drink
and
that for rich
earth nourishing
families
no one

remembers.
Forest *is slipping*
away.

I think
of the word
green
and I am afraid.

I shut the book and lay back on my bed with the pages resting on my chest. The cold in the room was starting to seep into my empty body.

What would Dad do? He would stay clever. He would know the cost of standing out too much. But wouldn't he want me to keep on trying?

What would Amanda do? I almost heard her voice in my head: "Look at the state of you, lying on those sheets."

I thought about the shower block, with no queues and maybe even hot water.

Afterwards, I put on Dana's brown felt hat and walked over to the laundry block, newly clean and still unsteady on my feet.

"You're here! Are you okay?" Rebekkah put down her iron and looked into my eyes. "We thought you might end up disappearing."

"It'll take more than food to do that."

"Was it horrible?"

"Pretty gross. Where's Mr Avison?"

"Doing your kitchen duty."

"Oh." I looked around for somewhere to sit and ended up on the overalls hamper. I was warm there, next to the driers.

"So why are you here?" asked Rebekkah.

"At camp? Same reason as you."

"That doesn't really answer my question."

I looked across and met her brown eyes, considering me. I considered her back. "Do you like spaghetti or baked beans?" I asked.

"What?"

"Which one?"

"Spaghetti."

"Same."

She shook her head and went back to ironing.

"Now ask me."

She set her iron upright and turned over the overalls. "Do you like loading or unloading the dishwasher? Washing the dishes or drying them?"

"I hate it all."

"Someone has to do what no one wants to do," Rebekkah said.

"Well. You know that woman I asked you about, Sheila Wilcox? That's why I'm here."

"Okay then," Rebekkah said.

At lunch I sat at the end of a table with Rebekkah and old Mr Avison. He reached over and squeezed my hand. "We're blessed to have you back."

"And so is my brother Anthony. Look, Dana, he came out of isolation." She was beckoning a young guy holding a plate full of food to come and join us. He sat beside Rebekkah and I looked from one set of dark-lashed eyes to another. Her hair was pulled back in a ponytail and his fell forward on to his eyes. He had a smile as wide as mine.

"So you're Rebekkah's workmate."

I looked to Rebekkah.

"Dana's one of us now," she said and I gave her a quick smile.

"Try to eat," she added, pointing to the heap of soya beans on my plate. I pushed at them with my fork and looked around for bread, but there wasn't any.

"Dana saw a group taken away."

"Five people," I said, remembering the grey

sleeves lined up in the window of the van before the van drove away.

"Do we know if anyone is missing?"

"Simon Singh," said Anthony. "A law student. He went into isolation last Wednesday with us, but he didn't come out yesterday."

"There were two guys in the group," I said.

"What do you think?" Rebekkah asked her brother. "Dana said they looked drugged."

"If they're kept drugged, they haven't got a chance." Anthony looked around the room of trestles and back to us. For a moment, our eyes met.

"We have to make enough disruptions here to force people to look at the camp," Rebekkah said.

"Like with machinery and vehicles," Anthony said. He nodded at Mr Avison.

"Yes, like that. And we have to be able to get back and tell people what is happening here. Only those two actions aren't necessarily compatible." She scraped the rest of her soya beans up and ate them.

I looked down at my plateful. It was as if food was another country now, and one I wasn't so sure about visiting.

"A cup of weak tea and sugar will see you right,"

said Mr Avison, looking at my face. "It does the trick for most things."

"I reckon bananas," said Anthony. "After a big night, it holds everything together. There were some on Andrea's desk when she was having her little interview with me about 'right behaviour'."

"Yes, Anthony," said Rebekkah with a frown. "Putting your artwork on the sides of buses doesn't really count as a major disruption. Not worth getting on her radar for."

"Ahh — but that is exactly the role of art, sister. Art is the provocation, it gives people motivation. Anyway," he smiled at me. "If I'd known what she had done to you, I would have stolen you a banana."

"Don't even joke about it," Rebekkah said. "He's all I've got now," she told us. "And speaking of radars, Dana. You've been making blips on their screen."

"Once on my account. I won't forget that," said Mr Avison.

"Are you guys all anti-campers?"

"They wish," said Rebekkah. She pushed her chair back. "I'll get some tea for us."

"Well, I am," said Mr Avison. He reached across

the table for the sugar bowl, looked around, then tipped half its contents into his pocket.

Camp life must be really getting to him. He looked up and saw the look on my face.

"Sugar in the petrol tank, Dana. It can ruin engines. True, it takes days to do the job, but it takes even longer for them to find the problem. All contributions for Bus No. 2's engine gratefully received."

"She's got you doing destruction for the cause now, eh?" Anthony passed down a sugar bowl from further up the trestle. "She's been a one-woman band ever since our parents . . . You know, our dad was here. Last year. I've painted him on every bus now."

"That's right, lad. You keep painting the buses. Everyone's got to protest in their own way. I'll take care of their engines. And," he patted his top shirt pocket, "I found a key in the van driver's overalls when I put them in the wash." He winked at me. "No doubt she'll have a job for you, too."

"When did you join the anti-campers?" I asked Mr Avison. He might have known Mum.

"Essie and I joined right from the start. The first day. That was my Essie. It didn't matter that she had cancer, she was delivering pamphlets, doing what she could, right to the end."

Rebekkah was back, plonking four steaming mugs in front of us. "I know the anti-campers did a lot to educate people and to protest," she said, "but things are getting worse. Like Simon — if he's one who has disappeared. The time for talk has passed."

Rebekkah might be past talking, but for now I needed to keep my mind on Mum. I turned to Anthony. "I have a friend named Sheila. An older woman. Was there someone like that who went into isolation when you did, Anthony?"

"No-o-o." He moved his head from side to side.

"So," Rebekkah said, "the plan is we take out the power supply for the camp and the mine."

TWELVE

Over by the kitchen door, a man was watching us. I sucked in my breath.

"What is it?" Rebekkah turned her head.

"That man. I know him."

"He was up at the mine last week," Anthony said. "I saw him watching Simon."

It was Donald Meads, deputy principal of my own high school. He knew me. He knew Dana from school, too. He especially knew my mother. My heart was suddenly so loud in my chest it was a wonder Mr Avison didn't feel it vibrating through his cardigan.

"Please, Anthony, don't stare at him," Rebekkah said. "Save your keen eye for your painting."

"Do you ever draw horses?" I tried to make my voice sound normal, but it had an odd squeak in it. If I just talked normally, looked normal, then

Donald Meads wouldn't feel the fear surging out from me across the room towards him. I sniffed air deep into my stomach to try to keep it calm, instead of sluicing around, empty of everything except adrenalin.

Anthony plucked a pen out of his overall pocket. "Pass your hand," he said.

I held out my hand to him and he turned it over and laid it palm down on the table. Then, on the back of my hand, he drew a horse's head so fresh and so wild it could have been Lancelot looking up at me.

"How did you know what to draw?" I asked him.

"Art knows what the heart comprehends," said Anthony.

A shadow fell across my arm. I barely had the courage to turn and look but, when I did, it wasn't Mr Meads, but the freckle-faced man, his overall sleeves rolled up to show tattoos of twisted trees.

"Hey man," he said to Anthony.

"What's up?"

"Do you know her?" the man asked, pointing at me.

I put my hand under the table.

"Dana Dixon." He turned and looked at me. "Authorities' little friend. It was her lies at court that got me sent here. I wouldn't trust her, if I were you."

I looked down at my thumbs intertwining in my lap. Lancelot stared back at me.

"Just thought you should know," he added. There was a silence at the table. Mr Avison, with his pocket full of sugar, and Rebekkah, with her latest plan just out of her mouth, looked at me. Anthony put his pen away.

"I wouldn't betray anyone," I said.

In bed that night, I lay and looked up at the windows. Outside in the courtyard the night lights glared coldly, but, inside, the frames of glass held the sky and a spattering of stars. In the next bed, Rebekkah lay still with her back to me. My stomach churned with unanswered questions. Who was that guy and why did he say that stuff?

Stress had flushed my cheeks, despite the frigid air. I remembered the way Anthony and Rebekkah had looked at me — as if I would betray them. And I had so liked how Anthony had held my hand and drawn on it. I took my hand out from under the sheets and stared at Lancelot by starlight.

The day I rode him to RDA, he had stepped through the long grass so confidently, his ears up, trusting the way I wanted to go. Had I betrayed *him*? He was my own pony. And now he was someone else's.

But maybe he liked being in a paddock with six other horses. Maybe he liked the grass better there, too.

I turned over, away from Rebekkah's silent outline, and pulled my feet up, searching for warmth.

In the morning, the horse drawing was paler and smudged. I kept my hands inside rubber gloves and out of Flossie's sight. There were elements of my sister in her, particularly the way she could spot a stray hair at ten metres. I had my own hair slicked down, my earrings out, my smock clean and I stood there slicing carrots finer than toothpicks, my hand steady on the knife. Flossie stopped to watch.

"Not bad," she said. "They'll think it's gourmet food tonight." I smiled back at her.

"Did you get food poisoning from my curry?"

I nodded.

"I hate the idea that the food I make might be used to poison people. Are you okay?"

"Pretty much."

Flossie considered me. "You look pale. You know that aunt you were asking about?"

"Sheila Wilcox?"

"Yeah. Well, she was here for one day. Made a fair salad, too. I don't like to hear what's happening to her."

I put down my knife.

"She's over at the mine houses. There's always a group of them over there, doing some sort of research. Sheila got sent to isolation first — for stealing paper."

Oh, that would be right. My mum, with a book bursting to be written, stuck without pen or paper.

"The mine super there knew of her. She babysat his kids when they were little, so he grabbed her to help with their correspondence school lessons."

"Well, that's good, isn't it?"

"She wasn't too good yesterday. My son-in-law, he's one of the drivers here. He said she was too quiet. All her hair was cut short. He liked her because she always had a story for him. Not yesterday."

"Maybe they gave her curry, too," I said.

"Listen, I'm only telling you this because I don't like what happened to you. You lot here, I think it does you good to have some discipline, clean up your lives a bit. I mean, look at you — you've got promise, you're shaping up in the kitchen. But good food is good food, and it's for nourishing people. It's not to make them sick."

"Do you think you could pass a note from me on to her?"

"I can't do that, but I can pass on a message."

"Can you say . . . can you tell her that Jethro's daughter is here."

THIRTEEN

I sure hoped that Dana had got engaged to her Davey back in town last night. It was Thursday, and I had to make a move to save my mum. I was thinking a lot about that key Mr Avison had.

As soon as the wet tea towels had piled up, I took them to the laundry. Rebekkah was at the ironing board, but she kept her back to me. I went over to Mr Avison and put them by his machine.

"I'm still the same Dana," I told him.

He wrinkled up his eyes to peer at me. "I know that," he said.

"I don't know what that guy was talking about. But now I really need your help." I glanced back at Rebekkah, who was standing still and listening, no doubt, as much as she could over the thud of the driers.

"That woman I've been trying to find, you may

as well know — and Rebekkah, you, too — she is my mother. And now I know where she is. She's like the others. She's had her hair cut short and she's not herself — she must be drugged as well. But what if they're coming to get her soon? What if she just disappears as well?" Outside, the sun, which had been trying to make up its mind all morning if it was around or not, suddenly blazed through the clouds and lit up Mr Avison's face.

"We can't have people's mothers disappearing," he said. "That's taking it too far."

"People shouldn't be disappearing," Rebekkah said. "It doesn't matter who they are. And it doesn't give you first priority for action, Dana."

"So, I'll give myself priority. I'll just go there. She's at the mine houses. I'll go by myself. I'll try to get her out — and anyone else who's there. And I could try to walk her all the way down the mountain. But I don't know how drugged or sick she is. That's why I need help. I need a vehicle. Mr A?"

"Dana, that would be my pleasure."

"Oh, thank you!" He got my best smile.

"No," said Rebekkah. "It doesn't work like that. What if, now that you know what we're planning here, you go and take that vehicle straight to the Central Authority? Or maybe you're leading Edward here into some other kind of trap? All of us."

"I can't help it if you believe that, Rebekkah."

"I *have* to think like that, don't you see?"

"What . . . you would trust that guy's . . ."

"Barry Drew. His name's Barry Drew."

"Trust his word, over mine. Why? He could be the one setting a trap."

"Barry is . . . he's okay. He says you stopped him at the shop you work at and made out he was stealing something. He thinks you lied to make yourself popular with the Authorities."

"Great."

"*Thinks* you did. That doesn't mean you did. But whatever — I have to be careful of everything."

"I wouldn't do that. I'm against the Authorities as much as you are. And I can't risk my mother disappearing because of your carefulness. We have to get her. Tonight. Mr A, is that possible?"

"Of course. I have the key to the van."

"All right. But you come with me on my job first," said Rebekkah. "You help me, and then you go and get your mother."

"Why not Mum and the others first?"

"I have to know I can trust you, that's why. And I can't leave you out of this in case — just in case — you decide to report us. Besides, if they discover your mum has gone, there'll be guards everywhere. This way, we can take the power out quietly and then it's done. And the darkness will help you."

"It looks like it's her way or the highway," said Mr A. His ears stuck out energetically from the side of his head.

"I don't want to do something that could be dangerous," I said. "I just want to get my mum." Then I took a chance. "You must know her. She's not really Sheila Wilcox. That's a false name. She's Harriet Bennett, the writer. You know her?"

"*Harriet* is here?"

"Please, Mr A, can we just get the van and go and get her?"

"Don't you think I would have wanted to save my mother, too?" said Rebekkah. "That is, if that *is* your mother over there and she *is* Harriet and you *are* her daughter. I mean, if her name is Bennett, how come you're called Dixon?"

The iron on the ironing board suddenly hissed

steam. Rebekkah glanced at it and I took a breath. I knew who she was — Rebekkah de Havalon. And she was right. It was time to trust each other.

"My name's Lorna Bennett. Not Dana Dixon. I swapped places with Dana so I could come here and look for my mum."

There was a moment's silence as Rebekkah and Mr Avison took this in.

"Okay. So, whatever happened between Barry and Dana, that's got nothing to do with you anyway. That's good," said Rebekkah. "But Dana ..."

"Lorna," corrected Mr Avison.

"Lorna, this isn't just about you and me and you finding your mother. Your mother is just one person. And the only way to stop this whole craziness, to change what's happened to our society, is to work on a big scale, to do what can be done for as many people as we can. For a start, we have to shut this camp down. We have to expose what is happening here."

I looked out the window behind her head. "Andrea is coming this way."

Rebekkah looked at me a moment longer, then she half-turned and flicked her eyes towards Andrea's blue shape walking past the window.

Rebekkah went back to ironing the overalls. Mr Avison opened a washing machine. I went to the first drier and took out an armload of hot, wrinkled tea towels and went back to the kitchen with them.

A new busload of workers came to the camp at lunch time. I saw Mr Jacobs, my English teacher, as he walked through the door. He was wearing the yellow trousers of the chainsaw gang. He saw me, too, and his face flushed with pleasure.

When lunch was served, I took my bowl of broccoli soup and went over towards him. He was looking so pleased to see me I hoped he wouldn't call out "Lorna". Someone who knew me from the kitchen or Blue Block might hear him. I couldn't risk any more questions about who I was. Had Michael told him I was called Dana now?

I lifted up my bowl and squeezed past the trestle where Barry sat. Suddenly, he leaned back and knocked my arm, so that soup splashed out and burned my wrist.

"Hey!"

"You should watch your step," he hissed.

I went and sat beside Mr Jacobs.

"Dana! By jingoes, it's good to see you're safe and well and healthy."

Oh. I breathed out. He knew my name. "Yes, I am. Safe and well," I said. I put my bowl down and rubbed at my splashed wrist. "How's home?"

"Good. Michael filled me in on what you are up to. He's worried, though."

"I'm fine. See." And I gave him my big, cheesy smile, mostly out of relief at seeing someone familiar, someone from home.

"Have you had some of this soup? It's actually not bad."

"It should be good. I peeled about a million onions for it." I looked over at Barry, then listened a moment to the guys next to me, talking about a truck. "How did Amanda take my going?" I asked in a quieter voice.

"You mean you didn't hear her from here? I thought you would have." He smiled at me.

I let myself smile back. "Oh, she'll be missing someone to boss. I just hope Michael can cope with her."

"Any news on your mum? Because, thanks to our wonderful system, I'm here now."

"I know. It's stupid they took you away from teaching."

"At least now I'm here I can take the load off you."

"Well . . ." I looked up and around the room. I saw Barry, only too ready to report me. And Rebekkah, who didn't know whether to trust me. And Mr A, who would help me if I did my part. There was Flossie, who had risked her position to give me information. And Andrea, who wasn't in the room, but was always watching us. Mr Jacobs had no idea what he was walking in to. "I heard Mum was at the mine. She was looking after the mine manager's children."

"So she's all right for now? Oh great. Good. That's good. I can take over from here. The main thing now, Dana, is that you stay safe." He reached down by the seat and took my hand.

Nothing was as simple as he thought, but I held on to his hand anyway, as if to gather strength from him for the night that lay ahead.

FOURTEEN

"It's just a poetry book. I'm not reading the Central Authority manifesto."

"I didn't say you *were* one of them," said Rebekkah. She lifted her pack on to her bed and looked quickly around the room. A girl was playing her guitar down on the far bed. Another was filing her fingernails next to her. They weren't taking any notice of us. The rest were still back at the dining room.

"Anyway, what *is* that you're reading?"

"I was trying to find something that would give me inspiration."

"Well, read it out then."

"It's about a rabbit. I don't want to."

Rebekkah unscrewed one end of the aluminium pipe frame of her pack and tipped out three rusted rods. They clunked with a dull thud on her bed.

She looked up as two more women came into the room.

"Just read it," she urged. "It will cover up what I'm doing here."

"*This morning I found a hare gaoled alive in a gin,*" I started. "*One red forepaw held bitten in clenched iron. / With ears laid back and large eyes full of woe.*"

Rebekkah looked sideways at me.

"*He crouched on the scoured floor of his open prison. / Resting, poor creature, and gathering strength for his struggle . . .* Shall I go on?"

"You've started now," said Rebekkah. "Finish the story." She pulled up cargo pants over her tights and put the first three rods and a slim torch into one long pocket.

"Um . . . *Set him free, urged my heart, but my mind made excuse*

As it will often at sight of familiar wrong.

My hollow sophistry said, End his pain — Better to enter life maimed, pleaded those eyes.

So I dallied too long between thinking and doing

Until the practical farmer came without scruple.

Then the hoarse feminine scream and spinal blow . . ."

"Oh," said Rebekkah.

"*And the limp body dangling . . .* Poetry evening," I said to Jess, who had come over to her bed on the other side of mine.

"Whatever turns you on," she said. She wrapped a scarf round her neck and went back to the guitar corner.

I put the book down next to Lancelot's photo. "You asked for it," I said.

"Yes, thank you for your wise, inspiring choice," Rebekkah said. She pulled a wry face at me.

"What about jackets? Listen to that wind."

"I know," said Rebekkah. "But we don't want to look like we're going somewhere."

"They've got jackets on but they're inside."

"True," she said.

I zipped up my jacket, and then took the photo of Lancelot out of the frame, putting it in my pocket. Lancelot would come with me.

I was glad of Dana's staunch boots out in the cold air. If my heart was pulsing in my throat and my stomach was twisty with nerves, at least my feet felt strong. I glanced up at the sky. No moon yet, but luckily the clouds had gone.

We crossed the courtyard towards the dining

hall. A group of men stood around the entrance to Red Block. They had their hands shoved in their pockets and looked like Russian sailors taking a break on deck, their faces chilled and watchful. I didn't see Barry. I didn't like the thought of him turning up somewhere in the dark.

"So where are we going?" I asked.

"Across the sports ground."

Sports ground. That was a joke. Working seven days a week left no time for sports.

"We cut through the bush. Then round the hills to the surge tower. Sshh."

Two security guards with flicking torches came around the edge of the bus shed. We walked in a circle back towards the laundry, and waited there in the shadows as their footsteps passed.

Someone else was waiting there. There was a movement on the edge of the bush and a figure walked out and stood looking at the backs of the guards as they walked away.

"What the hell is that guy up to?" whispered Rebekkah.

I watched Barry watching the guards. "Looking for me, I'll bet."

"I told him you were sweet, and that you were

coming with me tonight," Rebekkah said. "He should just leave us to do our job. Or volunteer to do it for us."

"I wonder what actually happened with Dana and him."

"Maybe she really did report him to Central."

"Well, whatever happened, I'll bet he's said lots of stuff about me to Anthony."

"You think Anthony's cute."

"No." I shifted my weight from one foot to the other.

"He's not cute. He's a smart-arse."

"I thought all brothers were smart-arses."

"Have you got some?"

"Just my sister. Queen Amanda."

We watched Barry move off towards Red Block. When the tussocky grass in front of us had stayed starlit and empty for a couple of minutes, we ran out across it and into the blackness of trees.

FIFTEEN

One step into the bush and the darkness stopped us like a wall. Talk about going into the unknown. There was nothing even hinted at. Only when I looked up at the sky, visible in patches high above the canopy, was any shape revealed. Up there, the trees sorted themselves out into separate trunks.

Back on earth, our legs were lost in blackness. Any step we took could be over a sudden drop or into a hole. The only way forward was centimetre by centimetre, not by strides. My hands reached out to protect my face from branches, tree trunks and thorny creepers.

As my knee nudged a fallen trunk, I put one hand down to touch it and felt the softness of moss. For a short way at least, I kept my hand on it, as if it were a trusty dog that walked beside me in safety.

There were no voices calling out, no shouts

from guards. The forest was calm and eerie and, up above, the wind surged in the treetops like a wild surf foaming on the rocks. Our light remained off to keep us safe, and yet we could be blundering towards a hole blacker than extinction.

Rebekkah stopped and I walked into the back of her. Then we waited. My eyes might as well have been shut. My ears searched the darkness for any form of life. She flicked the torch on.

"I think we're okay now," she said. We went on with the thin beam of light like a leash leading us forward, around the tree roots, the blunt-faced rocks and the wide, black trunks of forest giants looming up before us.

"Do you really know where we're going, to this surge thing?"

"We just keep going downhill. I've seen it on the Internet," said Rebekkah. "It's halfway between the dam and the power station."

"But what's it for?"

"It's for letting off pressure from the force of water falling. Mum and I studied it. I'll throw the rods down the vent and they'll get washed straight down into the generator and hopefully wreck it."

"Where's your mum now?"

Rebekkah kept following the torch through the shapes of trees.

"Is she dead?"

After a while, Rebekkah answered. "Yes."

"How did she die?"

Rebekkah stopped and turned around. I could only see the shape of her with the torch pointed on the ground.

"She died raging against her death to the last minute. And raging against this government that destroyed my father."

"And mine, too," I said.

I heard a snapping sound off to my left, like branches breaking. Then a grunt. Rebekkah kept walking. She hadn't mentioned wild pigs, so I thought I wouldn't either. I followed so close, I was almost on the back of her heels.

"They'll be more scared of us, you know," she said.

"What will?"

"Pigs. I heard it, too."

We started walking faster, but the crashing, snapping and grunting kept pace with us. Every few steps, Rebekkah played the torch around the banks of fern and fallen branches. Suddenly, the black shape of a pig burst out of the undergrowth and ran through our torchlight before blundering away into the darkness again.

"See?" said Rebekkah. "We're safe."

My heart was still crashing and snapping like bracken being trampled and, whatever she said, I'll bet hers was, too.

We came out of the pig territory on to a slope of tangled grass. After the denseness of the trees, I stood and tipped my head back and stared up at the sky. It was so clear and so full of stars, it was like a forgotten landscape, both startling and familiar. Rebekkah turned the torch off and stood beside me looking up.

"Do you ever think about your future?" she said. "About the point of going on to study?"

"If you can't be what you want to be, you mean?"

"Yeah. Why would we do all those years of study or training, if they can make you go and sweep roads or something?"

I thought of Mr Jacobs in that work gang, and how at school he had taught me to look for the writer's mind below the pages. I wondered what job they would make a vet do — sell chemicals, maybe. Grind corn?

"If we can't have some say in our future, then what's the point of anything?" said Rebekkah.

I looked at her as she stared up at the sky. "What do you want to do?"

"I came home from university when Mum got sick," she said. "I want to go back. I don't ever want people to own my working hours the way they do here."

She turned and shone the torch down the steep slope we had to go down. "My dad wanted me to be a running star. Imagine that."

I looked at the land the torch revealed. The trees were gone from this slope and only rocks remained, tumbled against each other, some bigger than a horse.

"We have to be careful on our feet." Rebekkah lit up the stony mounds. "There's too much here to fall on to."

We heard grunting behind us in the bush and took off. My boots slid on the wet grass. I used clumps of turf to slow me down and sometimes an outstretched hand against a rock. We both jumped the last metre down on to a sheep track and started laughing with sheer relief.

Though the moon was only a sliver, the sky had a radiance of its own and our puny beam only made the air seem darker. Rebekkah put the torch in her pocket and we ran. Soon her back was moving further and further away from me. I think her dad was right about the running.

As we ran round the curve of a hill, the concrete cylinder of the surge tower rose up before us, like some kind of lighthouse weirdly displaced in a paddock.

"Hell," said Rebekkah. She bent over with her hands on her hips and sucked in oxygen like me.

"I reckon."

"I knew it was tall, but I didn't think it went straight up like that."

We kept to the sheep track and ran again, down and on to a wider path, rutted by tyre marks. We followed it to the base of the tower and stood by one rounded side, out of the chill of the wind, and looked up at the steel rungs.

"Maybe you should have brought a safety rope?"

"And perhaps everyone should have voted

differently at the last election," said Rebekkah. "What's here is here." She handed me the torch. Before she had got six rungs up, her jacket was flapping so badly in the wind she had to come back down. When it was zipped, she put her hand up on a rung to start again.

"You're really brave, Rebekkah."

"I don't feel it," she said. "I'd rather be at the movies."

I pulled the hood of my own jacket closer and watched her climb. It was like the bush again — one foot, heel to toe, and then the next.

"Shine the torch up the rungs," she called down. I aimed the beam upwards and her bare hand reached into the circle of light.

There was a cough, somewhere behind me. I switched the torch off and stood there, my heartbeat suddenly accelerating in my chest. And then another cough.

"Oh, it's just a sheep!" I called up.

"Bloody sheep!" called Rebekkah, her voice more distant now, and started to climb again.

Beyond the tower and way, way down there was the sea. It stretched out glittering, brighter than the hills, brighter than the paddocks humped with the remnants of fallen trees and, now that I knew they were there, the bobble shapes of sleeping sheep.

Down there, by the edge of that sea, was Arapiko. And sleeping in a bed in our house, was my sister, next to my own empty room. And up the road in her house, Rachael was sleeping, if she wasn't just lying there, texting friends other than me. And further up the road, in a close-cropped paddock, was my own Lancelot — eating or sleeping, or maybe, with one hind foot resting, he had his ears pricked forward and was looking at the mountain.

I squinted up at Rebekkah. She was about three storeys up and nearly there.

There was an echoey bang as the first steel rod went into the mouth of the tower, then another bang and another and another.

"Victory!" yelled Rebekkah.

And then she fell.

SIXTEEN

I could have chosen any other poem instead of that rabbit one. Other lines came flying into my mind right then, like a rope across the waves . . .

"*Once the days were clear*
Like mountains in water,
The mountains were always there
And the mountain water . . ."

She screamed as she fell, and when she landed I heard the crack of bone breaking. A shocking sound over the keening of the wind. Last night it had rained so the earth and grass were softer for her landing than they might have been. I ran and crouched over her.

"My leg. Do something," she said. "I think the bone is sticking out."

I shone the torch on her legs. Her right shin had a lump sticking out under her trackpants.

"What should I do?" I wanted her to help me. She shut her eyes. "Okay, I'll take a look." I held the torch with one hand and, willing my stomach to remain calm, I pulled up the edge of her trackpants to see.

"Ahhh-h-h-h!" Her cry was louder than the wind — louder even than her cry of victory.

I took shallow breaths. The bone was so white. And there was gunky stuff that should not be coming out of it. I looked down at the grass, trying to think of natural things, like rain and sky and sun. Worms. Ohhh. I looked back up to Rebekkah's face.

"It's okay. I saw on a TV programme where someone broke their leg badly like this and the other person pulled . . . You'll be okay. It'll make you feel much better. I'll be able to do this."

I took a breath and blew out slowly while I studied the angle of her leg. Then I grasped her boot and, like I was birthing a calf or something, I pulled on her leg till the bone went straight. I eased her foot to the ground and took another breath.

She didn't scream — she was somewhere else, where she should stay for a few minutes longer.

I shone the torch around us. There were no

conveniently leg-sized flat boards lying about. There were thistles. A foxglove with spires of dried seeds. Sheep poop. I ran back up the track to where the fence sagged a bit. Now I could hear her moaning behind me. There was a broken fencepost on the ground. I took it back and placed it on the ground next to her leg.

"Rebekkah? I'm going to make a splint, sort of. To help you." I pulled off my jacket and laid it over her shoulders and stomach. Then I took off my sweatshirt. I bit into it. You can't just rip a sweatshirt. Not with your teeth. Not even when your friend's life almost depends on it. I chucked it down and pulled off my T-shirt instead. Same thing. Then my thermal, which at least was thinner and had arms.

The wind was like another presence on that mountainside — fierce and in my face. I put my T-shirt and sweatshirt back on before my skin started to ice up. Carefully, delicately, I got the long arms of my thermal under her leg and tied her shin to the fencepost.

"Sorry," I whispered as I moved her. She moaned. She began retching. I tilted her head.

"How's it feel now?"

She lay there with her eyes shut, not saying anything, just breathing. Then, after a while, "Bearable."

"Do you hurt anywhere else?"

"I got winded. My ribs . . . I'm okay."

I squatted next to her. The night stretched out almost insurmountable in front of me. "I'll go and get help," I said to her. "I'll get Andrea. Oh . . ." We both knew as soon as I said it that I couldn't. How could we trust Andrea? Look what she had done to me. And what would they do to Rebekkah if they found her like this — half their work already done for them?

"No, no. I won't get her."

"You've got to remember the big picture," said Rebekkah.

"No. I'll get help for you." I looked out at the coast, where Arapiko was, and doctors and nurses and hospital and painkillers and bandages. Short of running off the edge of the hill with a parachute, there seemed no way down that could help her.

"Got to get your mum," she murmured. "Before it's too late for her."

"I know." I looked up the hill we'd run down, and at the black bush beyond that. "I'll go and get

Mr A, and then we'll steal the van, and then we'll go and get Mum, and then we'll come for you. We'll do it."

"Okay."

"We'll come back for you. Are you warm enough?" Dumb question.

"My legs are cold."

I looked at her legs and pulled my sweatshirt off and laid it over as much of her jeans as I could. I rubbed at my bare arms. Now I really had to run. "See you, Rebekkah," I said softly. There was no answer. Her eyes were tightly shut against the pain.

I turned away from her and started loping up the track. I figured that, if a vehicle could come this way, then it must lead somewhere, it must intersect somewhere with a track to the camp. It was better than facing the dark bush and the wild pigs by myself.

My hands shook as I ran. I breathed, one-two-three-four, my legs following the wavery line of the torch and the wind hustling at my neck and unprotected back.

I thought of those steel rods on their own journey and wished for strong water to tumble them down through the hills to the generator. I thought of Rebekkah on the damp ground, with her white bone snapped and splintered. I felt the strength of my own legs and I willed them to keep on running.

SEVENTEEN

Sometimes when Mum was writing I would stop a moment outside her door. I'd hear the tap-tap-tap of the computer keys and think about the worlds that were being created. Rachael's mum, Mrs Berry, stayed home, too, to run their family business. Importing, or something. She ironed Rachael's clothes and went shopping for them. Rachael would come home and they'd be laid out on her bed.

Once I said, "Don't you wish you could go and choose them yourself?"

She said, "If I don't question her, she buys me even more."

All that time Rachael and I were out riding, Mistletoe and Lancelot racing neck and neck up the forestry tracks, or walking, heads stretched, reins in long loops, while Rachael and I talked —

all that time, her father knew about the drugging. He had to, if he was one of the top ones in power. He knew where the people with the cut-off hair were taken. He knew the shape of society he was aiming for — his own big picture.

The people who didn't fit into it were being taken away. And other people would see that the job was done — the ones who believed in that big picture as well. Like Donald Meads. And Andrea. The thought of them powered me up the next hill. They were taking our country to a stage where everything was mapped out and planned. Like someone choosing clothes for you. Like someone offering you a sanitised life, without flaws. But only doing this by taking away all your options. By taking away the option to be who you wanted to be — not just a cog in their wheel.

I got to the camp. The power was on still. The lights were on in the courtyard and off in the accommodation blocks. I stood panting next to a beech tree and checked the open area for security guards.

My arms tingled. The quick run had pumped heat through my body, but now I could feel this heat leave my shoulders, my arms, my fingers.

I hugged myself, rubbing my arms and blowing long breaths.

I could see the guards, two of them. Their torches flashed from side to side. They went past Red Block and shone their lights on to the vehicles in the bus shed. When they carried on, I stepped out of the shelter of the bush, picked up a handful of small stones from the road and ran over to the men's block.

Three windows from the corner, Mr Avison said. I threw a pebble and it missed the high window. I threw another one. This time it clattered with a small pop against the glass. How could that wake an old man? I looked around quickly then flung the rest of the pebbles up. They pinged on the glass.

I crept to the edge of the hall then ran across to the shadow of the bus shed. There were three buses, the van and a four-wheel-drive motorbike.

I waited in the blackness behind the second bus. There was a rustle in the corner and I wanted to swing my torch over and shine it there. A mouse, a rat? The wind had picked up again and it slammed against the shed in a sudden gust. I thought of Rebekkah by the tower. I hoped the cold would slow down the swelling in her leg. I hoped that it would help to take away the pain.

There were footsteps, three knocks on the metal of the bus. I clicked on my torch and shone it at the ground. The black figure came towards me — it was more solid, much taller, than Mr A.

"Anthony," I whispered.

"New plan," he whispered back. He waited. "Where's Rebekkah?"

"She broke her leg. She's all right. We'll just have to get her later."

"Oh no! Are you sure she's okay?"

"She fell off the tower. She'll be cold now, but she was talking when I left."

The wind had brought cloud, and it billowed and shredded past the opening of the bus shed.

"I gave her all the clothes I could," I said.

He reached out and touched my arm. "You're freezing." He shrugged off his jacket and I put my arms into the warmed-up sleeves.

"Here's the plan that Edward and I worked out. You and me, we go down to the mine, running. You up for it?"

Another run? I nodded.

"We get your mum and whoever else is there.

Bring them back, hide, send another stone signal to Edward and, that way, when we start the van — we just get out of here, no mucking around."

"Okay."

"And then we get Rebekkah. Ready?"

Anthony carried the torch as we ran. It was a relief to follow him, just to watch that small light and hear the sound of his footfalls on the gravel as well as mine. The road was broad — smoother than the farm track and all downhill.

We stood on the rise, looking down at the mine houses on the road to the mining compound.

"The drugged people came out of the second house," I said. Just then, an owl called its lonely cry across the forest. We crept down to the back of the house, my foot slithering once on the gravel. The streaming cloud made me feel as if we were bandits in the mist.

The back door was locked. We stepped back and surveyed the house. I pointed to the louvre windows of the toilet.

Once, at home, Mum had locked me out by mistake and I had taken all the louvres out of our window and wriggled through. They'd been a pain to put back in.

"Okay," whispered Anthony. I looked up at him. He was taller, stronger, braver than I felt, but he wouldn't fit through that opening. It was me who got lifted head-first into the darkness.

I stood in the bathroom of the house, listening. Was it even the right one? What if I walked into a room full of sleeping security guards? I tried to pick up the sound of breathing, but my heart was pounding so loudly it wasn't just in my stomach or throat, it was in my ears and head as well. I flicked the torch around. A bath, a toilet, a shower, three towels. I opened the door into the hall.

Another door opened. Someone in grey pyjamas came out. I just stood there, my heart yammering through my body.

"Mum?" I knew that shape.

"You're up early, Lorna."

"It is me. We're not at home, Mum." I took her hand and held it to my face. Her palm was hot against my freezing cheeks.

"You've been riding in the dark again," she said.

"Mmmm. Mum, we have to do this really important thing. We have to go for a walk in the dark. We have to get out of here. It's not safe."

Mum looked back at her room slowly.

"There's something in there," she said.

The adrenalin in my body leapt up a level.

"Paper," said Mum.

"Paper?" Oh. "I'll get it, Mum. I'll take you out to my friend. He's going to get us back to Amanda.

"First I'll sleep."

"Soon, Mum. We'll just do this walk first." I looked down at her feet beneath her pyjamas. They were bare. She padded up the hall with me to the door.

"Is there anyone else in the house, Mum?"

"Simon says," she said.

I unlocked the back door and Anthony took Mum's arm. She leaned against him.

"I think Simon's here," I whispered.

"I'll find him. You get going."

"I have to get something first." I went back to her room and shone the torch round till I found the closely written pages hidden under her mattress. I crammed them in my jeans pocket. Now for something warm. I picked up her shoes, a cardigan and the blanket off the bed and took them to the porch.

Mum was still leaning, eyes shut, against

Anthony. I bent down to put her shoes on.

"You'd hope," I whispered, "that, if we ended up like this, someone would come for us."

"Someone stupid enough to." He took the torch from me and went back into the house.

I got Mum as far as the shadow of the trees before the shout came — long and drawn out. A light went on in the house.

EIGHTEEN

A yellow haze from the window shone into the misty yard. I stood with Mum by the trees, not knowing what to do. Minutes ticked by. I scrunched and unscrunched my toes, watching that window of light. Instead of thinking about anything else, I thought about food. First, the food I had eaten at camp — cabbage soup, broccoli soup, celery soup, porridge for breakfast. Curry, soya beans and, that last meal — thin mince on rice, the mince so runny it was like brown soup with lumps in it. I'll bet whoever made up that menu had fun.

No other lights were on, no one came running. It was like a normal house, with someone up making coffee. The quiet gave me some hope. But what was happening to Anthony? Mum leaned against me. The blanket went round both of us, and it was the closest to resting I'd had all night.

How about food I wanted to eat? Hot sausages and tomato sauce — and I don't even like sausages that much. Avocado on rye bread. Mum's homemade French bread and slabs of cheese. A hot decent coffee with heaps of sugar in it.

"Come on, Anthony," I whispered into the night. "Come out of the house."

"Simon always shouts," Mum said, startling me. I had thought she was asleep on her feet. "They'll just give him something."

The house light went off again. I pulled the blanket tighter around us. The wind was blowing the mist past us in horizontal shreds, but it kept the frost and ice away. My boots were so damp my socks were wet. My feet shifted about, squelching in the moist succulence. Mum snored.

The door opened and a shape came out of it. It was Anthony with the blanket-wrapped bundle of Simon draped over one shoulder. My shoulders slumped with relief. He staggered slightly on the step then ran slowly towards the trees. He was safe, and now there were four of us.

"I got into his room and when I spoke he went completely bonkers," Anthony whispered. He was labouring under his burden as we walked up the road.

"We heard him."

"Far out, man. That was close. I just got under the bed before the nurse came in. But at least he's quiet now." Anthony stopped and took a breath, then shifted Simon's weight on his shoulder.

"Lucky he's a puny student," I said. My torch pointed relentlessly uphill.

"Yeah, lucky it's not you I have to carry."

"As if."

We trudged on, one step after another. Mum's weight against me made me feel the warmest I'd felt for days. Now and again, my arm knocked against Anthony on my left. I heard his breath coming in long, harsh but regular breaths, as if he was matching it to his steps to keep on going.

We went up and around a corner and into a smell of wet rock and fern so strong it was like walking into cold, stone-flavoured air. I took a big sniff. Water rushed under the road and tumbled out of a drain into the bush. A few more steps and I couldn't smell it any more.

Suddenly, I thought about what still lay ahead — how we had to get back into camp, how we had to take the van and how we had to go and get Rebekkah. My thoughts wavered. What if . . . what if . . . ? There was so much that could go wrong. For a moment, I no longer thought about where to put my feet, and my left ankle suddenly lurched into a hole.

The pain was so intense it was almost joyous. I stopped and Mum stopped with me. For a moment, a thought spread through me like a soothing warmth — this is it, now I cannot go on. I would have to stay on this gravelly road in a forest in the night, and whatever would happen, would happen. It wasn't up to me any more.

I felt the burden of the future shift from me to Anthony. If he failed, it wouldn't be my fault. My ankle had saved me. I held it up off the ground. The pain beat like struggling wings inside my skin.

Anthony stopped. He breathed in and out, resting for a moment before asking, "What's up?"

I couldn't say that I'd hurt my ankle. It sounded so weak when I thought of Rebekkah, who lay by herself on a rain-soaked hill, her bone exposed to the sky. "Are you okay?" he asked.

I lowered my foot to the ground and leaned some weight on it. Actually, it wasn't that bad. "Yeah. Just enjoying the amazing scenery and atmosphere."

"Cool, eh? Shine the torch up into those trees." I looked along the beam as it picked out black branches and the white mist creeping through them.

"It's like walking into Hades," said Anthony.

"Hades?"

"Through the gates of hell. I'm going to paint it just like this."

"I know what Hades is. I do read. But I'd hoped we were walking out of it, not walking into it."

Then we were both quiet.

"Are we going hunting?" Mum asked.

"No, Mum. But there might be hunters around. Are you warm enough?"

"So warm," she said.

Anthony shifted Simon again and we walked on, me favouring one foot. Mum kind of shuffled while Anthony took weight-driven steps that made dull, thuddy slaps on the gravel. Up above us, the wind shushed and flustered the treetops.

EIGHTEEN

An owl called and there was an answering call from way across the valley.

Mum peered round the blanket at the dark, dripping bush. "We're not supposed to be here, are we?"

"That's not the half of it," I said.

NINETEEN

Halfway up the slope, Simon kicked out with his leg, nearly hitting my face.

"Hey, man, take it easy," said Anthony. He half slumped, half dropped Simon on the road. Simon yelled out again and Anthony held him in a bear hug while Mum crooned to him. We staggered on like that.

"How come you paint your dad on the buses?" I asked.

"He was on the work bus and he had a heart attack. They wouldn't get him any help."

"Do you think they could have saved him?"

Anthony stopped and Simon leaned against him, like Mum leaned against me. "What do you think?" he said.

"It's six years next week since my dad died. I

think it suits them when people get hurt. It means one less they might have to control."

"Well, now they've got us."

"Yeah. They don't know what they've done." I smiled across at Anthony.

We reached a fork in the road. It was Anthony's idea that I go on alone. One way led up to the camp, the other way led to town. One of us had to go up and get Mr Avison and the van and, as I didn't have the strength to hold Simon, now that he was coming round from whatever they gave him, that person had to be me.

I didn't want to leave the little group huddled under the trees. There was my long-lost mum. And I kind of liked the company of Anthony. I didn't know much about Simon, except that he had a loud voice and a fast foot.

Mum held me and kissed me on the forehead. "Run like the wind," she said, remembering me in some other race, lined up, about six years old. I hobbled away as fast as I could; the wind had dropped to a flustery breeze, but it was still no contest. I poked the torchlight through the ragged clouds that roamed the road and took one small step after another.

Lights still blazed in the camp courtyard and there were lights on in the office block. I stood beside yet another black, furry trunk and contemplated the dark windows of Red Block. It was probably midnight. Three hours since I had abandoned Rebekkah.

Stepping into the light is always a dangerous proposition. It means being noticed. I bent down for the handful of gravel and straightened up.

An arm swooped up behind me and grabbed my wrist.

"Now what?" said Barry Drew.

"Don't be stupid," I hissed at him. I pulled my wrist back but his hand clamped tighter.

"Let me throw it!" I kicked down hard on his foot behind me and he dropped my arm. I bent it back to throw the stones and he cuffed me across the ear. Hot tears spurted from my eyes.

"You don't know what you're doing," I said. "Let me throw . . ." But he grabbed me around the middle and started hauling me towards the trees.

"What have I done?" I hissed. "What's the matter with you?"

"Because of you," he hissed back, slinging me from side to side. "I lost everything."

I kicked out and tried to throw my weight forward.

"I lost my job. I lost my house."

"I'm sorry. Whatever I did, I didn't mean to hurt you."

"And now they've sent me here, where they can beat me!" He pushed me so hard, I fell face first on the gravel. I grovelled forward on my knees, my hand still clutching stones, and threw them upwards and across, so that they fell against the building but nowhere near the windows.

"Can we talk?" I pleaded. "But out of the light."

He grabbed my jacket and pulled me up and back so that I fell again. My chapped hands were cut and bloody on the stones. I rolled into a ball. It was all I could think of. Like a hedgehog.

"Even if I smashed you," he said above me. "Even if I kicked you till your back looked like mine, it wouldn't make a difference."

"I'm sorry," I said from under the shelter of my arms. "I thought I was doing the right thing." And I really did hope Dana had thought that.

"I saw your name on the witness statement — Dana Dixon. But why did you say that about me? I wasn't stealing."

"I know that now." If I kept on agreeing with him, maybe he would relent. What had happened in that shop? If Dana thought he was stealing and he wasn't, then camp was a big punishment for nothing. I tried to keep my voice calm. "I'm sorry you lost your job."

"Well, it's too late." His boot slammed into the gravel near my head. I waited, crouched. I summoned every bit of energy I had, ready to leap up. I was going to fight back. I was not going to get kicked into the ground when there were things I had to do.

"Barry," I said. "You will get another chance. You'll be out of here soon."

"I'm not a thief," he said. "I had a good job."

"And I'm trying to help you."

He didn't answer. I unfurled my arms from my head. He was running across the yard and into the shadows. My arm was numb and my palms bled, my cheek, too. I put my fingers to it. For that moment, I only thought about myself. And when I sat up and looked across the yard, two security guards were standing there, watching me.

They put me in the white room. I sat on the bed and looked up at the light bulb, still glowing with electricity. My palms stung. I peered at them and rubbed a chip of gravel out of a graze.

For some reason that made me cry. Stupid tears, blipping down on to my jeans. My knees hurt, too, and were probably bleeding. Nothing like as much as a broken leg. At the thought of Rebekkah, I almost doubled over. I grabbed at my stomach and held on.

She was out there, lying as still as she could. Mum was out there, too. Mr A could still be asleep. Even if he was up, he wouldn't know where any of us were. Only I knew, and I was locked up with the guards on their way to get Andrea.

Was I locked in? I got up and wrenched at the door, but it stayed shut. The door, the bed, the painted-over, barred window, the walls — I walked three paces from one end to the other and back again.

I had my photo. I pulled it out of my back pocket and sat down, smoothing it on my knee. It had been everywhere tonight — down the mountain, up the mountain, through the black bush, running. I sat on the bed and stared at Lancelot's wild, shaggy head. Just like the picture Anthony drew. I turned my left hand over — not a trace of biro left.

And there was my young face in the photo. What was going to happen to me? They could take me away. They could blank my mind until one day I didn't remember Lancelot or who I was or why I came here. My poetry book would be thrown in the rubbish and all those pages that reached out to Dad and reached out to me would be gone.

Where were words now when I needed them? I tried to think back over every gem of wisdom I'd learned at camp.

"Escaping is pointless." Andrea.

"One person isn't worth risking the bigger picture for." Rebekkah.

"It's not clean until the job's finished." Flossie.

"A cup of weak tea and sugar will see you right." Mr Avison. Oh, Mr Avison. Had he heard my stones?

"Art gives people motivation." Anthony. And how was he getting on with Mum and Simon?

"The time for talk has passed." Rebekkah. Yeah. It had gone right past that.

"Good food is for nourishing people. It's not to make them sick." Flossie. Right in this room.

"The main thing, Dana, is that you stay safe." Mr Jacobs.

I tossed my head at that bit of memory. Where did staying safe get you when you wanted to make changes? I wasn't safe from the moment I got here — no, from the moment Mum disappeared. I hadn't been safe from the day they took my dad away from me.

I could hear a vehicle; car lights flashed against the window. I went over to it and listened. Two doors slammed shut. Andrea, then. And someone else. I sat on the bed and held my arms tight.

What would Dad think about this? Would he think I'd failed him?

I thought I could do everything. There was

Michael in town, trying to stop me coming. And Mr Jacobs right in camp, wanting to take over. And as usual I thought I knew best. And now Rebekkah was . . . and Mum in a cold, dark forest.

What about when the morning came? What would happen then? I walked up and down the room again.

The lock clicked and the door opened. The guard motioned me out. I walked towards him. He had tomato sauce on the collar of his overalls. He smelled of deodorant.

Down the corridor was the door to the outside. A wooden door painted white. The guard shoved my shoulder to push me the other way. Past one door, two doors, up another corridor. He knocked on the third door and, when Andrea called out, "Yes", I glanced once more up the corridor the way I had come.

She had a teapot on a tray on her desk and when I entered she turned and smiled at the man next to her. "Was that one or two sugars, Donald?"

"Two," he said. And they don't know how much that warmed me inside, thinking of Mr Avison.

Andrea poured the tea while I stood there

waiting. I thought about those rocks in the forest, lit up by our torchlight. How they were ancient and strong. How they were immovable.

When Andrea had sipped her tea she looked at her laptop screen.

"So, the father's a truck driver with a history of minor misdemeanours. More of a lout than a stirrer. The mother, well, she doesn't amount to much. And then there's you, Dana." She looked up at me. Donald Meads looked at me, too, and I kept my head down and tilted sideways so my long fringe fell across my cheek.

"It's one o'clock in the morning." Her eyes took in all of me. "So why are you in the state that you're in?"

I looked down at my muddy boots, the wet hems of my jeans. My hair no doubt had leaves in it and Anthony's jacket had a rip in one sleeve. I looked as if I'd been thrown on gravel after wading through a dark forest.

She picked up her cup and sipped it again. It was a white china cup with blue flowers on it. Her fingers hooked into the curly white handle.

"We'd like to believe that this was all about your hormones. I mean, here's a camp full of men, and you were seen in the courtyard with one of them. If that's what this is about, Dana, it's time to tell us now." She leaned forward to look at me. I could feel Meads staring at me, too. I just had to say — yeah, me and Barry Drew, we've got this thing going on.

What would I get? Isolation? I could risk being sent back to my room with a week of twelve-hour shifts, starting in the morning.

But, if I spoke, Meads could recognise me. I had to stay silent. And I'd been asking about Sheila Wilcox. If he knew it was me, Lorna, then he'd know it was Mum I was looking for. And I had her writing in my pocket. What would he do with Mum if he found her? A well-loved writer he'd had taken away and drugged? He'd make us both disappear.

"We find that people who don't fit into camp life are better off somewhere else," said Andrea. "What we want are people who do what they're told, who work hard and show they will change. Are you a person like that, Dana?"

I wanted to yell at her. Tell her you can't buy a quiet life with the freedom of others! Does mindless obedience make life better? I pressed my fingernails hard into my grazed palms instead.

My thighs were shaking from standing still. I felt my cheeks heat up in the warm room and I began to sweat in Anthony's heavy jacket.

"If she's smart, she'll tell us what we want to know," said Meads. "She reminds me of that young man, Simon. It's a pity. He could have had a great future."

"If you don't tell us, Dana, we will have to assume you were attempting to run away. Or to do something worse."

"I think we could try another way," said Meads.

Sweat trickled down my sides. My throat had that squashy, choked feeling. I thought about my dad and suddenly remembered the night he read a poem called "Victory" to me, after he lost his job.

"*It comes to this,*" he said, "*in plain words,*
You will be defeated."

I thought about the door behind me. The corridor. The next corridor. The desk that was between the two of them and me.

"Yes, I agree," said Andrea. She leaned forward and smiled at me. "It's what's best for everyone, Dana — that's what I have to keep in mind. And sometimes I have to take actions that will ensure the correct results. The white room, I think, Donald. In the morning, we'll move her out."

She pushed her chair to stand up, and at that moment everything went black. The rods had found their home at last. Before Andrea and Meads could get around the desk, I'd found the door and started running.

TWENTY-ONE

My hands banged the outside door open and I ran out into the wild night air. My mind was careening like my legs — dodging the side of the block, round the side of the kitchen. Where to? Where to? I heard the office block door crash open and shut behind me.

The bus shed? I didn't want my pursuers to follow me there. Through the bush? They'd come for me with torches. I ran round the back of Blue Block. No. I saw a guard in the mist in front of me. I turned and ran back towards the office block where the road was. A figure slipped through the main door and saw me.

"Lorna! Lorna!"

I stopped, chest heaving, and Anthony ran to me, grabbed my arm and kept running with me.

"The van is waiting down the mine road," he

said. We ran through the mist, the road showing up one stride at a time. I saw the back of the van, like a hunched-up animal. The door was open. We leapt in and Anthony slid it shut.

"Go, go!" he urged. Mr A let the brake off. We started rolling. I fell into a seat, next to Mum.

"Oh, Mum!" I clutched at her. "Mum!" She laid her head on my shoulder and sighed. Simon was slumped in the seat behind us.

"Which way to Rebekkah?" asked Anthony.

"Downhill, where it's farmland. I'll tell you when." I hugged Mum's arm. "How did you get them to the van?"

"With great difficulty," he said.

The mist drifted and parted as the van picked up speed. I stared out the windscreen trying to see the road. Mr A corrected the swerve of the van away from the trees and when we got down to the turn-off, he switched the headlights on, crunched into second gear and planted boot.

"I hope you were a rally driver in your former life," said Anthony.

"I was a shoe salesman." The van swung around a corner and Mum fell in to me.

"Andrea got me," I said to Anthony.

"That's what I thought. I waited for as long as I could."

"What were you doing in the office block?"

"I told him you were there," said Mr A. "I saw you taken away."

I looked across the aisle at Anthony. His eyes met mine and he winked.

"Did you hear my stones?" I asked Mr A.

"I heard everything. I was waiting for you. I saw that guy tussle with you. I saw the guards. I thought I'd better get to the van and await the outcome."

"And while he was waiting, he dealt with the buses and the motorbike," said Anthony.

"Hey, Mr A, how did you do that?"

"Never you mind. I've got more tricks up my sleeve than sugar."

"Sugar is sweet, my love, but not as sweet as you." Mum started up singing.

"And the car? The one Mr Meads and Andrea came back in?"

Silence. I swivelled round to look for headlights out the back window.

"Yeah, it is a problem," said Anthony, and he glanced back, too. "It's got the speed to take us on those straights before town."

I grabbed the back of the driver's seat to steady Mum and me as we curved round a long bend. The black trees suddenly gave way to farmland.

"There's a farmer in the anti-campers. He's the first driveway as we come out of the pine forest further down. A square letterbox, on the right, without a name," I said. "If we can get up his drive in time, we'll be safe."

And then my stomach clenched up with a sickening heave. How would we have time to stop and find Rebekkah? How would we even have time to move her?

"Is this nearly the place?" Anthony looked out the window.

"I think so. If I was out there, I'd recognise the hill shapes."

"I'm going to go get her," said Anthony. "You guys get down safe and call the hospital and a helicopter."

"You won't find her," I said. "I know where I left her." I leaned over Mum and untucked the camp blanket from her legs. She opened her eyes and looked at me and smiled briefly.

"Little mother," I said and laid my sore hand

against her forehead for a moment.

"I'll come with you then," said Anthony.

I wanted someone to shine the torch and share the dark. If something went wrong, though, there was only Mr A to drive.

"I wish you could. But someone has to help here. Now! Stop now!" The van slid to a stop and I pulled the door back. I looked at Anthony.

"Please take care of my mum."

"Take care of my sister." His hand grabbed mine and for a moment we held on. I clutched the blanket to my chest and jumped out.

The van accelerated around a corner and the night was dark again, with me alone in it. And probably a hundred wild pigs. I stood on the road, which at least I knew led somewhere. Then I turned my torch on and climbed through the barbed wire fence.

Weird shapes loomed out of the mist at me. My torch found foxgloves, bracken, rocks and great beasts of trees felled and scorched a hundred years ago. I saw the prow of a canoe in them, antlers from a giant deer, a clawed black hand reaching. It was a desolated forest and long grass and thick creepers grew tangled in it. Not a track in sight.

I remembered how once Lancelot and I came out on a ridge and I didn't know where we were. The sun had already gone down and light was fading. I urged Lancelot down a track and our shortcut brought us right up to a padlocked gate. Behind me lay kilometres of darkening forest tracks to get back to the road.

"You can do it," I told my pony. He had to; it was the only way forward. He cantered bravely at the big wire gate and then we were lifting up and up over it.

There was a speech Mr Jacobs taught us in English. "Accept the challenges so that you may feel the exhilaration of victory." Thanks, General Patton. My mind flew up the hill briefly to Mr Jacobs, asleep at the camp.

"Come on," I said to Lancelot. Even if he was just a photo in my pocket. Up and over the first log we went. Even if the van was going on to safety without us. Even if there was a car racing down the gravel road after it. Even if there were guards spreading out through the camp and the bush, their torches raking the undergrowth. Rebekkah was nearby and the night was damp and chilled.

TWENTY-TWO

"Are you all right? Did you manage to sleep?" I bent over the still shape in the grass.

"Have you tried sleeping with a broken leg?"

I was so happy to hear her voice that I almost kissed her.

"I've peed myself," she said.

"That's the least of our worries." I started lowering the blanket over her.

"If you so much as move a fraction of my leg, I'll probably die," she said.

"Probably." I shone the torch at the damp grass, then lay down beside her. Immediately, the cold leapt out of the ground at me.

"You should have this jacket on as well," I said.

"Nah, no point in us both suffering from hypothermia."

"Okay." I lay there, taking small breaths and

letting the damp grass absorb me. When I turned the torch off, the tower dominated my line of sight. I didn't actually want to look at it. I turned my head to look where downhill would be if I could see it.

"Tell me something good," said Rebekkah.

So I told her how Anthony and rally driver Mr A would get everyone safely to the farmer's house. And he would call a helicopter and then an anti-camper doctor would come and get Mum and Simon and take blood samples to prove they had been drugged. And they'd get a journalist to break the story, especially about Mum, the children's writer who nearly disappeared.

"Will they publish how we cut the power off to save the day?"

"Might not be a good idea. Just in case we want to stay anonymous," I said. "For now. And then there'll be a big enquiry about the drugging. And meanwhile, because of the power disruption, the camp will have to stay shut. And people will see that life is just as good without the camp."

"And at the election they'll all vote another way and everyone will get their jobs back," Rebekkah said. "And all the lost people will be found."

"This is all true," I said. "And, meanwhile, I'm freezing my butt off here."

"Mine went numb a while ago. Have you got any chocolate in your pocket?"

"I've got a photo of my pony. And some writing of my mum's."

"Okay. Read me a story then."

So I got out the pages and my torch, and I started to read her the story of us.

The birds called up the morning. The sky lightened and lightened until it was glowing. The mist had lifted and the sea was flat and shiny, mirroring the sky. I propped myself up to look across at the far mountains, rising up dreamy and blue from the sea.

"That is the most beautiful sight I have ever seen." I told it all to Rebekkah.

"It's called freedom," she said, lying there, looking straight up at the sky.

And then I heard a noise that was as welcome as Lancelot's rumbly whicker on a frosty morning — the sound of helicopter blades pulsing through the air, coming closer.

The 20 British Prime Ministers
of the 20th century

Wilson

PAUL ROUTLEDGE

HAUS PUBLISHING · LONDON

First published in Great Britain in 2006 by
Haus Publishing Limited
26 Cadogan Court
Draycott Avenue
London SW3 3BX

www.hauspublishing.co.uk

A CIP catalogue record for this book is available from the British Library

ISBN 1-904950-68-X

Designed by BrillDesign
Typeset in Garamond 3 by MacGuru Ltd
info@macguru.org.uk

Printed and bound by Graphicom, Vicenza

Front cover: John Holder

Contents

Introduction: Morning Departure

In the mid-morning of 16 March 1976, the teleprinters chattered into life all around Fleet Street with a message on the Press Association tapes. Unusually, the copy was printed in red capitals, a form reserved for events of the greatest importance. It read: HAROLD WILSON RESIGNS. Consternation ensued. At *The Times*, there was disbelief, until the story was confirmed by the newspaper's political staff in the House of Commons.[1] At Westminster, confusion reigned. Shock gradually gave way to belief, and then suspicion. Why had a reigning Prime Minister, apparently in good health, and enjoying a relatively secure parliamentary majority, chosen to walk away from the greatest prize to which a British politician can aspire? All previous premiers had been thrown out by the voters, or forced out through manifest ill-health. There was no precedent in the 20th century, except for Stanley Baldwin, who had been almost ten years older and worn out by the cares of office.

Officially, the Downing Street version was that Wilson had some time previously decided to retire on reaching the age of 60. That date had arrived five days previously, and he was simply implementing his long-standing decision. Sceptical political correspondents, many of them Wilson-watchers over several decades, held that this was too straightforward to be true. One called it 'another characteristic confidence trick, a final brilliant act of legerdemain'.[2] Wilson probably enjoyed that sally. Even his close political ally, Barbara Castle, wondered what he was up to, concluding that there must be more to it than Wilson's official explanation.

Her suspicion was justified. In public life, the Labour leader had been anything but guileless. Quite the opposite. He was famed, if not notorious, for twists and turns, almost invariably to his advantage. In the previous year, he had led the nation into a successful referendum to stay in the European Union, after consistently opposing the same idea when it was politically convenient. There was no body of thought known as Wilsonism, but the journalistic adjective 'Wilsonian' was a catch-all term for cunning, duplicity and even deceit. What, then, was he up to? More to the point, what had he done that must now be covered up by a hasty departure from Number 10?

The newspapers thrashed about in a feeding frenzy, dredging up old stories about possible scandals relating to women, particularly his most confidential aide Marcia Williams, ennobled by Wilson as Lady Falkender. There was also speculation about his left-wing origins, and possible connections with the Soviet Union, where he had strong business links at the height of the Cold War in the 1950s. Nothing emerged that would give credence to any of the conspiracy theories, though that did not prevent them from circulating for many years. Indeed, 30 years later, they are still not quite dead.

It is always hard for the media to accept the obvious solution, because simple truths do not sell papers anything like so well as conspiracies. There is nothing like a good plot, and the word itself fits marvellously into a headline. But from the vantage point of the 21st century, with a plethora of memoirs available from the dramatis personae of the period, the initial verdict has to be that Wilson was, for once, being straight. When he walked into the Cabinet Room at 10.30 on that fateful morning, he was fulfilling the promise he had made to himself, to quit while he was ahead at the age of 60. That he was ahead, there is no doubt. His success in persuading the British people that their destiny lay in Europe had crowned victory in four of the five elections he had contested as Labour leader, a record in his time and unlikely ever to be overtaken, as the example of Tony Blair demonstrates. Having climbed these peaks, there was not much more he could do, except more of the same in Downing Street and simply being Prime Minister did not motivate him as it had done 12 years earlier.

Those close to Wilson had known for some time what was in his mind. Like anyone in a demanding top job, occasionally he wondered aloud whether the game was worth it, almost as soon as he arrived at the summit. The musing became serious as early as 1970, when, according to his press secretary Joe Haines, he went into his first general election against Edward Heath thinking of his retirement. Had he won, 'he would have stayed a couple of years,' argues Haines. At that stage, he would have won three elections in a row, a feat unequalled until Blair 35 years later, and would have gone only four years before his eventual departure. In a conversation with Roy Jenkins before polling day, Wilson even put a date – 14 June 1973, when he would have served longer than Asquith – on his putative retirement.

Later that year, Wilson confided a very similar message to Tony Benn at a Christmas party. On this occasion, he talked of going after three years. Benn was unsurprised, but equally unconvinced. In July 1971, when his leadership was under threat from malcontents in the Shadow Cabinet, he again raised the prospect of going – as early as October that year. To Benn, the indefatigable recorder of conversations, he growled that *they can stuff the job*, a characteristic Tyke (slang for Yorkshireman) snarl. He hinted again at resignation to Barbara Castle at about this time, and before the 1974 election set another prospective date, 1 March of that year, if he lost the 'Who rules?' election called by Heath during the miners' strike.

So, if his hints were not strewn as thick as the leaves of the brooks in Vallombrosa, they were copious enough to give a strong indication of his state of mind. And though it is in the nature of politicians not to believe until they see, Wilson's colleagues must have known that their man was not for staying. After his success in the October 1974 election, the hints turned to firm guidance. He was orchestrating his own political requiem. By the end of 1975, he had told Roy Jenkins. Harold Lever found out, probably after Wilson blabbed at a dinner for press barons given by his advisor, Lord Goodman. Lever passed on the information to Jim Callaghan, the Foreign Secretary. The Chancellor, Denis Healey, is very likely to have been similarly informed. Merlyn Rees, the reliable Northern Ireland Secretary, was aware of what was going on, and Barbara Castle certainly knew two weeks ahead of the announcement, as did Benn. Wilson's 'Kitchen Cabinet' in Downing Street had been party to discussions on the timing

A leading figure on the left of the Labour Party, Tony Benn (b. 1925) first entered Parliament in 1950. The son of Viscount Stansgate, he campaigned to be allowed to renounce his peerage to continue in the Commons, which was allowed by the 1963 Peerage Act. After serving as Postmaster General and Minister of Technology in the 1960s and Secretary of State for Industry and for Energy in 1970, Benn unsuccessfully stood for the deputy leadership of the party in 1981 and for leader of the party in 1988, losing to Neil Kinnock. In 2001 he retired from the Commons to 'devote more time to politics'.

for several months, and he had discreetly informed the Queen at his regular meeting at Balmoral in September 1975. This was not a *démarche*: it was a carefully-prepared handover. For perhaps the first time since he assumed the mantle of power, his leadership was not in question. His rivals sensed that he was going, and waited as calmly as the situation allowed for events to take their course. It was assumed, rightly, that Wilson wanted Callaghan to succeed him, though there would inevitably be a struggle not merely for the crown but for the political direction of party and government.

Before the fateful Cabinet meeting on the Tuesday morning, and mischievous to the end, Wilson called Callaghan into the lavatory outside the room moments before ministers took their places. He told him what he was about to do, and then told him a second time in his study at a less informal gathering with Healey and Ted Short, the Lord President. Healey, a fellow Yorkshireman more given to the wrath of his county, was allegedly livid at this preferential treatment, almost an anointment in the toilet. Quite why he could be so angry, when only minutes were involved and Wilson's choice of successor was well known, is mystifying. He and Healey had never hit it off. In any event, they were all round the Cabinet table at 11.00 a.m. on 16 March when Wilson announced that he had a statement to make. Once he intimated that he had just come from the Palace, there could be no doubt about its contents. Even for those in the know, it was an historic moment. For those who had been kept in the dark, it was a shock to the system.

Wilson cited four reasons for retiring: his length of service, which had exceeded Asquith's record. He had been an MP for 31 years, mostly on the Labour front bench, party leader for 13 years, member of the Cabinet for 11 years and coming up for eight as Prime Minister. Second, he wished to give someone else round the table an opportunity to become premier and party leader, who might be over 60, a clear indication that he was making way for an older man. Callaghan was almost 64. Third, he wanted to give his successor time to prepare for the next election. Fourth, he did not wish to go on making the same decisions in different circumstances. Anticipating the storm of incredulity that would break over his head, Wilson insisted that these reasons were *the total explanation* for his decision. There were no impending problems that were not already in the public domain.

With a mildly theatrical flourish, Wilson circulated signed copies of the statement round the table, pointing out that he had presided over 472 such Cabinet meetings. He was upbeat about the economy, and adamant that his successor should adhere to Britain's commitments *to our allies and partners overseas*, which ruled out endorsement of any candidate from the Left. For himself, the war was over. He would go to the Commons back benches, and refuse any jobs in industry or academia. With a few tips to his successor on how to be Prime Minister, particularly the need to know what is going on, he ended a life in politics. Ted Short broke the awkward silence, remarking on what an appalling shock and blow this was, while Callaghan paid a personal tribute, thanking Harold 'for all you have done for us'. Wilson gathered up his papers and left the room. Minutes later, he was discovered in his office with his pipe and half a pint of beer.

Does the initial verdict stand the test of time? Barbara Castle was both cross and suspicious after the drama in Number 10. For Harold to do this 'so gratuitously and so apparently senselessly' in the middle of a perfectly reasonably successful terms of office almost looked like frivolity, she confided to her diary. 'Has one the right to throw one's party into turmoil for no apparent cause, to face them with a fait accompli because one knows they would plead with one to stay if they knew in time? What exactly was Harold up to? More than had met the eye, I had no doubt.' Indeed, what if there was an 'apparent cause', but apparent only to Wilson and the denizens of the secret state that had harried him for years?

Within two months of resigning, the newly ex-Prime Minister was seeking to provide a fuller account of the 'Wilson Plot' hatched by dissident elements in MI5 to get rid of him and his government. He gave the story to two investigative journalists, Barry Penrose and Roger Courtior, whose book, *The Pencourt Affair* appeared the following year. A decade later, in 1988, David Leigh, probably the leading investigative journalist of his generation, published *The Wilson Plot*. In it, he claims that Wilson had been informed of high-grade security gossip at a weekend house-party in Oxfordshire, at which his friend the historian Martin Gilbert had been present. So too was an MI5 officer who had 'spoken very freely', and the *Daily Express* journalist Chapman Pincher, who had strong links with the security services. The gist of the conversation was that MI5 suspected the existence of a 'Communist cell' in Downing Street, and certain officers were determined to oust Wilson. This information was relayed to Wilson over lunch early in August 1975 by his publisher and friend, George Weidenfeld. According to Leigh, a furious Wilson called in Maurice Oldfield, the head of MI6, the rival secret service, and asked him if he was aware of any 'plots' against him by members of MI5. The MI6 chief admitted that he did. A section of MI5 was 'unreliable' and engaged in a subversive campaign led by Peter Wright, an obsessive agent whose subsequent memoirs, *Spycatcher*, finally disgorged details of the plot years later.

An enraged Wilson then summoned Sir Michael Hanley,

the head of MI5, to Downing Street and confronted him with
the allegations, citing Oldfield as confirmation that there was
a rogue element operating with the domestic secret service.
Hanley gingerly admitted that there was a group of 'young
Turks' (they were mostly of late middle age) in his office, who
were evidently preoccupied with Wilson, partly out of frustra-
tion with their inability to find a top-level mole within MI5
itself. The suspect in this case was none other than Sir Roger
Hollis, Hanley's predecessor, who was (wrongly) suspected of
being a Soviet agent.

Wright and his friends, who included the even more
paranoid and sinister James Jesus Angleton, a highly-placed
CIA operative, saw Russian spies everywhere. Wilson was
probably a spy, because he had sold Rolls-Royce jet engines
to the USSR in the 1940s, had regularly visited the Soviet
Union as a business consultant to timber merchant Montague
Meyer in the 1950s, had opposed American policy in Vietnam
in the 1960s, and befriended Jews from Eastern Europe all his
life. On top of that, he might well have been responsible for
poisoning Hugh Gaitskell to drive the Labour Party to the Left
and shackle Britain to the wheel of international socialism.
There was nothing so trivial that it could not be prayed in aid
in the Wilson Plot. A perfectly innocent photograph of him
with a woman was regularly trotted out to 'prove' that he had
been compromised by a honey-trap Natasha in Moscow.

Interviewed in 1987, Penrose disclosed that Wilson had
told him: 'Hanley had been forced to confirm that this group
of right-wing officers existed with the service, within MI5,
and they'd been up to no good as far as Wilson had been
concerned.' Hanley had further admitted the existence within
MI6 of another officer linked to the dissident MI5 group, but
insisted that the position had been cleared up 'and that was
the end of it'. Plainly, it was not. 'Immediately after his con-

frontation with Hanley, he [Wilson] decided to resign, and began to prepare the stage for his departure' wrote Leigh.[3] However, he is less confident that Wilson's disgust and alarm about MI5 altered the timing or increased his determination to go. That, he argued, was still an open question.

In 1991, Stephen Dorril, a recognised expert on security issues, and Robin Ramsay, editor of *Lobster*, a journal devoted to intelligence matters, published *Smear! Wilson and the Secret State*. This book went thoroughly over the whole ground of the Wilson Plot, and established that the facts supported its existence. There had been a very long campaign by anti-democratic elements in the security services. Though small in number, working in collusion with right-wing allies in the media and the political establishment, they had been able to create a public perception of Wilson as 'a crook, a red, a union stooge, unpatriotic, a Walter Mitty and a threat to the British way of life', whereas in real life he was essentially a Liberal whose radical tinges were more than balanced by his love of the monarchy and the unwritten British constitution.

However, Dorril and Ramsay did not finally answer the 'open question' as to whether Wilson's retirement was determined by the subversive operation against him. The question may well remain open for ever, because Wilson himself clammed up following his initial excursion into the subject with Penrose and Courtior. Their verdict, for what it is worth, was that Wilson painted to them a disturbing picture of his premiership in those final months in Number 10. He had been affected by rumours and suspicions, and a statesman whose outstanding quality for years had been strong leadership of those around him had suddenly lost control. But the loss had surely been gradual, rather than sudden. The madness of MI5 and MI6 could have proved the tipping point. The files, if they are ever opened, are unlikely to give an honest account.

Harold Wilson was never the kind of man his enemies portrayed him to be. He was quintessentially English, middle-class and unashamedly middlebrow. He preferred Gilbert and Sullivan to Benjamin Britten, and eating at home to dinner at the Savoy. His politics, like those of his party, owed more to Methodism than Marx (he claimed never to have got beyond page two of *Das Kapital*) and his ideas of public service were modelled on Baden-Powell rather than *noblesse oblige* or revolutionary Socialism. He brought to the national stage a discomforting breeze of Christian Nonconformism, common in the Pennine hills that gave him birth, and it is there that his springs of action should be sought.

Part One

THE LIFE

Chapter 1: England Made Me

Rievaulx is a tiny hamlet almost hidden in the steep-sided, wooded vale of the River Rye in the north Yorkshire moors. Its scattered pantile and limestone cottages, dominated by the magnificent ruin of the 12th-century Cistercian Abbey, are a far cry from Harold Wilson's vision of a hi-tech 20th century. When he took the title of Lord Wilson of Rievaulx, the choice entertained cynical observers, who assumed that the old man was seeking to cash in on one of his home county's most celebrated cultural landmarks.

There was nothing 'Wilsonian' about the decision. His family originated there, and the parish registers are full of Wilsons going back generations. The first reliable evidence of his roots lies in the records of Helmsley church, where his great-grandfather John Wilson was baptised in 1817. He was a cobbler in Rievaulx, and also farmed the land as his forebears had, but he later took charge of workhouses, first in Helmsley and then in York. Harold's grandfather James, born in Rievaulx around 1843, forsook agriculture and went into the drapery trade, initially in York and then in Manchester, where he flourished, to the extent of marrying Eliza Thewlis, the daughter of a Huddersfield millowner. This was a step up in the world, not merely socially, but politically. The Thewlis family were well known in northern Liberal politics. Herbert, Eliza's brother, an umbrella manufacturer in Stockport, became Lord Mayor of Manchester.

James and Eliza were blessed, as his Congregationalist fellow-worshippers would no doubt have put it, with six children. The eldest, Jack, showed the earliest signs of political interest, twice acting as Keir Hardie's election agent at the turn of the century. Harold's father, James Herbert, was born in Manchester in 1882. Despite showing a prodigious memory and intellectual precocity, particularly in maths (traits that would reappear in his son), he left school at 16 and went to work in Levinstein's, a local dye factory. He qualified as an industrial chemist, and in his spare time flung himself into the family's political activity. At the age of ten, Herbert (as he was invariably called) was giving out handbills for the Liberals, but in 1906 he worked for John Hodge, of the steel smelters' union, who won the Gorton constituency. This was the year of the 'Lib-Lab Pact', a secret anti-Tory agreement that brought in the first wave of Labour MPs.

Herbert has been described at this stage as 'a radical, but certainly no socialist', and in his choice of a wife, he found a political and religious soulmate. Soon after that historic general election, he married Ethel Seddon, a big, strong-minded lass, a schoolteacher from Openshaw and the daughter of a white-collar railwayman on the Manchester, Sheffield and Lincolnshire Railway. Ethel may have shared Herbert's strict Nonconformist Christian views, but they also had in common a zest for life and 'getting on'. In 1912, the couple moved to Milnsbridge, a mill village outside Huddersfield in the Colne valley, where Herbert had found work as an industrial chemist. He was a departmental manager in a synthetics factory, and his £300 a year salary was paid by cheque, a sign of his arrival into the middle class. The Wilsons were not proud, being Christian Dissenters, and they were not well off.

But they were not poor, like the workers in Herbert's charge. In later years, Harold Wilson liked to stress his humble origins. The riverside streets about him may have been lowly, but his family circumstances, though sometimes straitened by Herbert's unemployment, were not. The family lived first at 4 Warneford Road, Cowlersley, a respectable three-up and three-down stone terrace with a bathroom, rented for 12 shillings (60p) a week. The Wilsons were stalwarts of their local Baptist chapel, there being no Congregationalist place of worship. Herbert ran the Scouts, and the amateur dramatics while Ethel saw to the Girl Guides and the Women's Guild. The couple were organisers, not the organised.

James Harold Wilson was born in the mid-morning of Sunday, 16 March 1916, in the middle of the Great War, the couple's second child. His father had been exempted from military service because he was engaged in vital war work, and his firm was flourishing, in large part from the manufacture of TNT. Harold, as he always called, after an uncle who was an electrician, dates his first memories to the house where the Wilsons moved when he was a toddler, at 40, Western Road. Even Harold, always at pains to stress his humble origins, admitted this was a substantial, stone-built terrace partly detached from its neighbour by a ginnel (an alleyway), though in his memoirs he omitted to mention that his father bought the property for £440, paying half the price from cash savings. Towards the end of the war, Herbert Wilson moved jobs, to an acid-manufacturing firm, where he was paid £425 a year. In the company of Tories, he remained defiantly 'working class', but in truth he was a quite senior manager, with chemists and process workers under him, charged with sacking employees, a duty he found distasteful and only to be invoked where drink or carelessness was involved.

Young Harold was despatched to the local New Street

council school, a terrifying experience with a schoolteacher, Miss Oddy, whom he later identified as *incompetent or a sadist, probably both*. She was probably no more of a dragon than most of her kind in those post-war years. His earliest recollection is of being required to write on the board the longest word he knew: 'committee'. He culled it from the cover of his exercise book, printed with the legendary West Riding Education Committee. His precocious memory was already beginning to impress, even if he was not regarded as particularly brilliant. At the age of seven, Harold underwent an appendicitis operation, memorable chiefly for urging his parents as he recovered from the anaesthetic to go off to vote for Philip Snowden, Labour's first Chancellor, that evening. That he should demonstrate such early political development was unusual; that he should retell the anecdote was not. By his own admission, Harold had *a very provincial upbringing*, but unlike most of his classmates, he visited London and posed for a memorable photograph outside 10 Downing Street, a bashful eight-year-old in short trousers, his face almost lost under a wide flat cap.

He was not above making the most of his experiences, even as a child. At the age of nine, his mother took him to Australia for six months. Ethel was keen to see her father, who had emigrated, perhaps for the last time. The Seddons had flourished 'down under'. Ethel's brother Harold became a state legislator (though for the conservative Liberal Party) and was eventually knighted. Young Harold travelled to Kalgoorlie into the outback, and on his return wrote *A Visit to an Australian Gold Mine*. The article was rejected by *Meccano Magazine* and *Scout*, but published in his secondary school magazine and he gave a polished talk on his experiences. Harold was a keen scout, winning a *Yorkshire Post* competition on 'my greatest hero' – Baden Powell – at the age of 12.

He also took a full part in Chapel activities, in a straightforward, decent way, unencumbered by religiosity, that would easily be misunderstood in today's satirical, agnostic world. Growing up in the 1920s, he was surrounded by poverty and unemployment, and the Christian message had a practical, though not yet socialist, meaning. His upbringing found echoes later in the nurture of Gordon Brown.

In 1927, Harold won a county minor scholarship to Royds Hall Grammar School, Huddersfield, a school opened six years earlier across the valley and geared to strongly academic education. Pupils dressed in brown uniforms with blue piping, and the curriculum was demanding. Initially, he failed to shine, not entering the 'A' stream until his fourth year. The headmaster, E F Chancy, found him no better than the average intelligent lad, but possessed of an inquiring mind and 'determined to make a success of anything he tackled'. Surprisingly, perhaps, in view of his later taciturnity, he was also popular with his schoolfellows.

Just as he was making academic headway, Harold caught typhoid from milk he drank on a scout camp. Six of his fellow scouters died, and if Harold had not knocked over his glass, the nation might have been deprived of a future Prime Minister. As it was, he hovered close to death and emerged weighing only four and a half stones. He returned home from the isolation hospital in January 1930 'like a skeleton' to find that his father was another victim of the Depression spreading across Britain. It was two years before he found work again, at a chemical works in Cheshire. The family moved across the Pennines, and Harold entered Wirral Grammar School, Bebington, even newer than Royds Hall; so new, in fact, that he was the only sixth-former and enjoyed one-to-one tuition from senior masters. Frank Allen, his classics tutor, was a socialist, and according to Wilson, had more influence on his teenage political development than anyone else. The intensive instruction paid off. In 1934, he won an open scholarship to Jesus College, Oxford, worth £60 a year. Harold learned of his success when his father read out the examination results from the *Manchester Guardian*.

Success with girls had hitherto eluded him, but now, aged 18, he chanced upon the woman who would share his life. At a summer tennis event where his father was engaged in a mental arithmetic contest, Harold's eye fell on Mary Baldwin, the daughter of a Congregational minister in nearby Rockferry. They both attended the same church, and had not met because he went in the morning and she in the evening. They were soon 'walking out', and Harold announced that he was going to marry her. He also vouchsafed that he would become an MP, and Prime Minister. Mary was a quiet girl, and might have had second thoughts had she known he really meant it.

Before any of these hi'falutin notions were put to the test, young Wilson had to get a degree. At Jesus College, he was a Stakhanovite student, at his books for as many as 46 hours a week, including Saturdays. He lived sparingly, not smoking, and drinking only *the occasional glass of beer*. He switched from History to Philosophy, Politics and Economics (PPE), the coming subject, and began to make an academic name for himself by winning the Gladstone Prize with an 18,000-word essay on 'The State and the Railways in Great Britain, 1823-63'. He claimed to have read 400 books on the subject, and to have found Gladstone's draft Bill for nationalising the railways when he was President of the Board of Trade – a portent of things to come.

Politics were not a consuming passion during his under-graduate days. Despite efforts later in life to portray himself as a budding socialist, keen to convert liberal-minded fellow students to the Left, Wilson actually rejected socialism in favour of the Liberal Party, of which he was a member for most of his university career. He claimed never to have read Marx after failing to get past a (non-existent) long footnote on page two of *Das Kapital*, and spurned the University Labour Club after attending only one meeting. He subsequently rationalised his dislike by claiming that it was dominated by public-school Marxists who knew nothing of the way of life of the proletariat they professed to be in the business of liberating. His rebuff to Labour was something of an embarrassment in later life, when he tried to gloss over his early adherence to the Liberals as the product of *ignorance and vanity* that he might convert them to his middle-of-the-road Colne Valley outlook.[1]

Wilson's first known political statement comes in a letter to his sister Marjorie, seven years his senior, in October 1934, recording attendance at a Jesus College discussion group of the Anti-War movement, when he tried to counteract *the Labour element* with Christian arguments, advocating closer co-operation with the churches and similar bodies. It must be said that the undergraduate Wilson comes across as rather priggish in his social outlook, and cautious in the extreme in his speeches to the annual conferences of university Liberal Societies. He was an efficient treasurer of the Liberal Club, restoring its financial fortunes, but he made virtually no political impact during his time at Oxford.

However, his relationship with Mary prospered. She wrote to him regularly, and came to Oxford once a term to see him. The rival pleasures of undergraduate life in the late 1930s evidently had little appeal for him, and there were no others. He duly got his First in PPE, the best of his year (as he never ceased to remind people) and won the George Webb Medley Senior Scholarship, worth £300 a year. Academia beckoned, and they planned to marry. Mary would have liked nothing better than being married to an Oxford don. But an early marriage was ruled out when Harold's father again lost his job, and Wilson had to supplement his parent's exiguous income with some of his scholarship money. Like millions of his less fortunate countrymen, he was obliged to look for work.

Finding it in the late 1930s was no easy task. On the advice of his tutor, Wilson sought employment in journalism. The *Manchester Guardian* offered him a summer vacation job, writing leaders. This could have led to a permanent appointment, but he felt the Webb Medley scholarship had given him sufficient financial security to look for academic posts. It is otiose, but interesting, to speculate what kind of journalist Wilson would have made. He was undoubtedly brilliant, but he lacked the common touch and the intense human curiosity needed to make a good reporter. He would probably have preferred the ivory-tower anonymity of the leader writers' office, and we should have been deprived of a politician of the first rank.

Sir William Beveridge (1879–1963), creator of the modern Welfare State, was born in India and served as director of the London School of Economics and Master of University College Oxford. His report on *Social Insurance and Allied Services* was published in 1942 and argued that the government should fight the 'five giants' of 'want, disease, ignorance, squalor and idleness'. It proposed that people should pay a national insurance contribution in return for a welfare state and benefits to the most vulnerable. His arguments were widely accepted, and after the War Attlee's government set about creating the welfare state he envisaged.

Instead, Wilson became research assistant to Sir William Beveridge, who gave his name to the report that founded the

British welfare state. Beveridge, an outstanding academic of his day had just become Master of University College, Oxford, was on the lookout for a bright young man and Wilson fitted the bill admirably. Technically, he was engaged in a PhD entitled 'Aspects of the Demand for Labour in Great Britain'. The thesis was never written, but it did give Wilson hard labour for many months, some of it at Beveridge's cottage in rural Wiltshire where he was expected to put in two hours' work before breakfast. He also found part-time work lecturing at Oxford, and as Beveridge's protégé secured a fellowship in University College in 1938, worth £400 a year.

About this time Wilson came into contact with G D H Cole, also a Fellow at University College but a much more well-known and influential figure most emphatically of the Fabian Left. Cole, Wilson insisted later, was a substantial intellectual lever in his conversion to the Labour Party. There is little evidence to substantiate the claim, or of his active involvement with the party, membership of which he dates from this period. Wilson stood aloof from the famous 'appeasement by-election' of September 1938, when the socialist Master of Balliol, Sandy Lindsay, stood on a Popular Front ticket against the Tory, Quintin Hogg. The campaign attracted progressive students right across the political spectrum from Denis Healey, then a Communist, to Edward Heath, Wilson's future Tory rival at the Despatch Box. Hogg won. In his memoirs, Wilson does not even mention the event, memorably described by the communist historian Christopher Hill as 'good against evil, democracy against fascism, Balliol against All Souls'.

Bigger events were taking shape, however, that would put his fledgling academic career and political vacillation into a harsher context. Having spent the summer with his head buried in labour market statistics for a book on the trade cycle, to be written jointly with Beveridge, Wilson drove to Dundee in late August to attend a meeting of the British Association. Its proceedings were rudely interrupted on 1 September by news of Hitler's invasion of Poland. Wilson delivered his paper on the trade cycle to the roar of departing car exhausts, and set off south. He was probably in chapel with his future in laws in Fleetwood, Lancs, when Chamberlain made his momentous announcement two days later that Britain was at war with Germany.

Aged 23, and unmarried, Wilson was a prime candidate for the call-up. He was not in a reserved occupation, and had no obvious physical defects. His childhood illnesses seem not to have stunted his physical development, indeed he enjoyed cross-country running, the sport of the solitary intellectual. Wilson presented himself at the local labour exchange on the date appointed for his age group, to register under the Military Service Act. However, he did not strive officiously to enlist, preferring to remain at Oxford until his considerable talents could be employed in the wartime civil service. Classified as a 'specialist', he was soon given work as a £3-a-week temporary clerk in the Potato Control section of the Ministry of Food, which had been evacuated from Whitehall to Oxford. The job was not onerous, and he was able to retain links with his college.

The outbreak of war crystallised Harold and Mary's intentions. They married on 1 January 1940, in the chapel of Mansfield College, and planned to honeymoon in the Scilly Isles, where he would spend so much of his leisure in later years. Wartime travel restrictions put paid to their plans, however, and they went instead to the Old Swan at Minster Lovell, but only for five days, Wilson's imperious patron Beveridge insisting that that was quite long enough to consummate a marriage. The couple were granted a flat within University

College, and settled down for the war. Their discreet married bliss was not to last for long.

In April 1940, Wilson was plucked from potato control to the Ministry of Supply in Whitehall, working once again under Beveridge in the statistics department on the problems of wartime manpower supply. The work moved to the Ministry of Labour later that year, where Wilson became head of the Manpower, Statistics and Intelligence Branch, at the age of 24. He scarcely looked his age, despite having grown a moustache to make himself look older. Wilson persuaded his minister, Ernie Bevin, that the manpower needs of the armed forces should not be permitted to curtail munitions production.

Having made his mark at Supply, Wilson was promoted to the Mines Department of the Board of Trade in August 1940. Here, his statistical skills were put to good use drawing up regular, reliable coal production figures and a much-needed manpower strategy for the industry. He soon became convinced of the need for public ownership of the mines, based on a rational assessment of the nation's needs rather than political ideology. But he also came into close contact with the National Union of Mineworkers, substantial power-brokers in the Labour Party, and impressed them with his abilities.

When the Mines Department was floated off to become the nucleus of a Ministry of Fuel and Power, Wilson became director of economics and statistics, on £1,150 a year with 350 staff under him. He spread his wings further in 1943, working for the secretariat of the Combined Chiefs of Staff planning the Allied landings in France. He was responsible for ensuring the coal stocks were in the right place at the right time, especially the landing ports. This job also took him to the United States, negotiating for mining machinery and other supplies. He congratulated himself that his Yorkshire accent and direct style had impressed the Americans, while taking the opportunity to replenish his wardrobe and stuff himself with food unavailable in wartime London. For his war work, Wilson was given an OBE in the New Years Honours List of 1945. It was a deserved recognition of his self-driven commitment to public service, a virtue that would remain with him for the rest of his public life, very often to the detriment of his family life.

Chapter 2: Honourable Member

It was late in the war before Wilson's interest turned seriously to politics once again. His experience of the war effort had by this time turned him away from Liberalism towards a socialist planned economy. He was also conversant with the House of Commons through his work at the Ministry of Fuel and Power. The arcane procedures of Westminster held no terrors for him. He saw parliamentary politics as the straightforward marshalling of facts and figures in rational pursuit of a utilitarian objective. It was obvious that he should seek a political career.

Wilson began writing papers for the leftish Fabian Society, sketching out policy for the coal industry and nationalisation of the railways for adoption by a post-war Labour government. He was elected to the Society's executive, and was proud to appear on a platform with Herbert Morrison and Ellen Wilkinson. His transition to Labour was under way, though Wilson also debated the shape of a new Britain with Gwilym Lloyd George, his Liberal Minister of Fuel and Power and son of the First World War leader he much admired, while V1 flying bombs rained down on the capital in 1944. Early that year, he was recommended to Transport House, Labour's HQ, by his ministry's parliamentary secretary, Tom Smith, an ex-miner, and his name was placed on the list of potential parliamentary candidates circulated to constituency parties. It was almost as simple as that.

With so many Labour hopefuls still away fighting, the party was looking for new blood at home. From a embarrassingly rich list of options, Wilson chose Ormskirk, the potato capital of Lancashire. It was a widely-dispersed constituency, much of it unbroken agricultural land, with pockets of white collar affluence towards Southport and areas blighted by the declining coal industry in the east near Wigan. Croxteth and Ormskirk were the largest towns, and there were also rising numbers of urban Liverpudlians squeezed out of the war-damaged city. The constituency was regarded as a Tory marginal, having been won only once before by Labour, in 1929, but the MP had gone in with Ramsay MacDonald's National Government. In the war years, Ormskirk was represented by the faintly exotic figure of Commander Stephen King-Hall, a well-known broadcaster, and by coincidence a friend of Wilson in his capacity as a propagandist for raising coal production. King-Hall, standing as an independent supporter of Winston Churchill, was opposed by the Tories, thereby splitting the anti-Labour vote in the fateful summer election of 1945.

The nation was still at war, with millions of men under arms, many of them serving abroad, and the election in Ormskirk was an uneventful sideshow. Wilson's speeches were painfully dull and larded with statistics. Having, perforce, resigned from the civil service as soon as he was adopted, he spent much of his spare time writing his first book, *New Deal for Coal*, which was well received by the party hierarchy and contributed to the nationalisation of the industry. In a throw-forward to his 1960's image as the man of white-hot technological revolution, Wilson told voters that the war had triggered *a great industrial and technical revolution*, and only Labour could harness this change to the service of the people. He also took (at least) his share of the credit for the

Beveridge revolution which would bring about the welfare state. He excoriated the *tired old men* of the Tory Party, and the voters were inclined to listen. On 26 July, he was declared the winner, by a margin of 7,022 votes over the Conservative. King-Hall ran third, but took enough votes to deny a Tory victory.

Wilson arrived at Westminster as one of 393 Labour MPs, in the Attlee landslide that was to reshape British society for the next 40 years. It was no easy task. The post-war Labour government faced enormous challenges of expectation from a nation victorious but exhausted, working with an economy battered by the *Luftwaffe* and skewed almost exclusively to military production. Many MPs arrived at Carriage Gates in uniform, still adapting to civilian life. Despite being only 29 years old, Wilson the Whitehall insider had a head start. He could have been forgiven if the notices of his arrival had gone to his head. The *News Chronicle* called him 'outstanding'. In a government dominated by Labour veterans, a surprised and flattered Wilson was immediately appointed Parliamentary Secretary at the Ministry of Works. His swift elevation clearly owed much to five years working in the back office of government, but he had the good grace to admit in later years it was probably not unrelated to Attlee being a University College man.

At Works, Wilson had responsibility for the housing programme, which he found – like so many of the country's homes – in ruins. Production was way behind wartime government targets, and most of programmes were based on hopelessly inadequate planning. He immersed himself in the job of speeding up construction, attracting praise from his civil servants. Wilson found less admiration from his fellow MPs. Among his housing responsibilities was the rebuilding of the House of Commons, badly damaged by bombing, and it was impossible (as it still is) to satisfy the accommodation demands of his fellow parliamentarians. Had he not been a minister, Wilson's profile would have been no higher than any other backbencher. His speeches were lacklustre, and he took no part in Labour's ideological warfare.

After little more than a year, Attlee took him out of the front line to head the British team taking part in the launch of UN Food and Agriculture Organisation in Washington. Another job for 'organisation man'. It was not the most opportune time to champion feeding the world, since Britain could not feed itself: Labour had recently put bread on the ration before he left for the USA in October 1946. Wilson started with a clean sheet on the subject, in that he knew nothing about farming and not much more about the politics of food. He threw himself into the job with characteristic verve, working 12-hour days for three months and produced a report for Parliament that not only occupied 17 columns of Hansard but earned the approval of the Prime Minister. So much so, that when another managerial job came up, this time *holding Ernie Bevin's hand* after the Foreign Secretary had a heart attack in Moscow, Wilson was despatched to negotiate a trade agreement with the Russians. With the plane ride came promotion to Secretary for Overseas Trade, in March 1947, and an increase in his ministerial salary to £1,500, on top of the MP's salary of £600. He was now going places.

The first place he went was the British Embassy in Moscow, where Bevin was delivering a breakfast harangue to American service chiefs on the devious Russians and their plans for strategic advancement. The importance of Wilson's involvement with trade and the Soviet Union cannot be over-estimated. In later years, his supposed closeness to the Russians and alleged sympathy with Soviet communism came to play a key role in the attempts to subvert both him and the Labour government. At the time, his skill in negotiating marked him out as a prospective President of the Board of Trade and member of the Cabinet with eyes on the party leadership and, ultimately Downing Street.

In Moscow, Wilson parleyed with Anastas Mikoyan, later to become president of the USSR. It was the Armenian carpet seller, a Machiavelli among negotiators, versus the cunning Yorkshireman who only lost his temper for show and concealed his cards better than Cool Hand Luke. They established a mutual respect, not least via Wilson's unexpectedly strong stomach for vodka, if his protestations are to be believed. Britain wanted timber and grain, while Russia sought engineering equipment, particularly rails and rolling stock for their war-ravaged transport system. Talks dragged on throughout the summer and came within sight of a comprehensive deal but finally broke down in late July.

Diplomats praised Wilson's 'great skill and firmness', insisting that he was 'fully a match' for Mikoyan, compliments that very nearly became his obituary when his plane crash landed on returning home, injuring other passengers and thoroughly shaking up the carpet seller's tormentor. His boss, Stafford Cripps, observed: 'Things some ministers will do to get publicity!'[1] Attlee took a less jaundiced view, and in late September 1947 gave him Cripps' job as President of the Board of Trade (BoT). He was a Cabinet minister at the age of 31, the youngest since 1900, and the only one, commentators noted, born in the 20th century. The Prime Minister felt moved to justify his appointment to King George VI on grounds of 'great ability' and 'exceptional' performance at international conferences.[2] Wilson himself avoided expressions of surprise on

'Things some ministers will do to get publicity!'

STAFFORD CRIPPS

this occasion, but Mary offered gloomily: 'I shall see less of him than ever.'[3]

Happily, she was wrong. The job kept him more at home than Overseas Trade, and on his Cabinet salary of £5,000 a year, he could now afford to buy a decent family house, 10 Southway, in Hampstead Garden Suburb, one of the more agreeable parts of north London. The property, bought on the recommendation of a Tory MP, cost them £5,100, and they moved in at the beginning of 1948 shortly before the birth of their second son, Giles. Robin, the first, had been born in London in December 1943. In 1953, the family moved next door to Number 12, which remained their home until they went to live 'over the shop' in Downing Street in 1964. Their new neighbourhood was, if not a hotbed, then a warm patch of political activity. The Jays, the Pakenhams, the Gaitskells and the Gordon Walkers all lived within walking distance, as did the parents of a future Blairite Cabinet figure, Peter Mandelson. Unlike them, however, Wilson had no time for the socialist dinner-party circuit, and in any case devoted much of his waking hours to the BoT grind, even to the extent of installing a camp bed in his private office.

Wilson took over a ministry somewhat diminished by

Son of a Conservative MP, Stafford Cripps (1889–1952) joined the Labour Party in 1930 and became MP for Bristol East in 1931, serving as Solicitor General. Expelled from the party in 1939 after advocating a popular front against Fascism with the Communists and anti-appeasement Liberals and Conservatives, Cripps was sent to Moscow as the British ambassador in 1940. He served briefly in Churchill's War Cabinet, and rejoined the Labour Party after the war. Cripps was appointed Chancellor in 1947, becoming known as 'Austerity Cripps' before health problems forced him to retire from Parliament in 1950.

Cripps' appointment as overall supremo as Minister for Economic Affairs, but it was still an awesome task. He was responsible for the entire gamut of controls and incentives for private industry, which had developed into a virtual state within a state during wartime. As the minister for promoting exports and rebuilding industry at home, Wilson favoured making capitalism work, rather than nationalising all and sundry. His style, denounced as 'unashamedly capitalistic and chauvinist' by hard-left critic Paul Foot, was a forerunner of the New Labour attitude towards business. In the circumstances of an economy still recovering from six years of total war, it is hard to see what else he could have done. The nation was in the middle of a crippling economic crisis that threatened to extinguish the UK's gold and dollar reserves until Marshall Aid came on stream. Besides, his accommodating nature was more inclined to pragmatism than ideological experiment. Wilson was placed on the Left by those who wished to see him there, rather than by any natural political instinct. He was, however, genuinely attracted to the great standard-bearer of the Left, Aneurin Bevan, the fiery Welsh Health Minister.

Wilson's businesslike outlook chimed with improving times. Exports went up, and the Commonwealth, for which he cherished a special fondness from his childhood visit to Australia, supplied an increasing share of imports, particularly food. Two months after assuming office, he was back in Moscow, reviving the trade talks with Mikoyan, this time successfully. One side effect of this drawn-out process was Wilson's conversion from cigarettes, which he never inhaled, to a pipe, which enabled him to puff away while stalling negotiations. The pipe would become a political trademark, a comforting symbol of sagacity. The Russian grain deal he brought back saved the livestock industry, but attracted severe criticism from the Tories, not unmixed with some suspicion, even among Cabinet colleagues, that Wilson might he too friendly with the Reds. The world was slipping imperceptibly into a Cold War.

Such notions of unreliability were quickly dispelled by the performance of the British economy in 1948 which, in part inspired by Wilson, expanded rapidly. The balance of payments moved out of the red and unemployment fell sharply. At home, Wilson began a difficult but popular process of lifting post-war rationing, starting with children's shoes, and on Guy Fawkes Day that year lit a 'bonfire of controls' on commerce. With a canny eye to publicity, he had himself photographed tearing up his own ration book. While never, up to this point, a commanding presence in the Commons, Wilson proved a capable minister, taking legislation through the House on export guarantees, monopolies and industrial development. Barbara Castle, inherited as his PPS, found his speeches 'dreadfully dull', and being a more extrovert Tyke, told him so. Together, they worked on his debating style, which improved, though he was never in the Bevan league.

Otherwise known as the 'European Recovery Plan', the Marshall Plan (after the US Secretary of State George Marshall) was the American-funded programme to reconstruct countries that had joined the Organisation for European Economic Co-operation after the end of the Second World War, including Britain, France, Germany and the Benelux countries. Although the Soviet Union was invited to take part, Stalin refused. Approximately $13 billion was given by the United States in aid, which was paid for by increasing US taxes. When the plan was completed in 1951 all the economies involved (with the exception of West Germany) had grown to above pre-war levels.

The first full-scale political crisis to hit Wilson grew imperceptibly from the spring of 1949. As early as March, economists in the BoT were arguing for devaluation, following a sudden dip in the nation's trading fortunes. In Cabinet, ministers began forming up for and against devaluation of the pound against the dollar. But Cripps, now Chancellor, was too ill to take command of the crisis, and was despatched for treatment to Switzerland in July 1949, leaving his deputy Hugh Gaitskell, increasingly Wilson's main rival for power, holding the fort. Gaitskell, a pro-devaluer, Wilson and Douglas Jay, another Treasury minister, were hastily formed into a three-man team under Attlee to resolve the crisis. Sterling came under increasing pressure from speculators (later to be excoriated as *the gnomes of Zurich*) and, as Wilson subsequently recalled *the argument began to change from* whether *we should devalue to* when *we would have to do so.*[4]

A contingency plan to devalue from $4.03 to $2.80 was prepared, with Attlee's imprimatur, and Wilson was entrusted with delivering this hugely-sensitive document to Cripps in his hospital bed in Zurich. The Chancellor had been deeply hostile to devaluation, but to Wilson's astonishment did not dispute the economic logic of the step this 'inner cabinet' proposed to take. He did, however, suggest a general

The argument began to change from whether we should devalue to when we would have to do so.

WILSON

election before devaluation, prompting Attlee to describe him as a 'political goose'. As the crisis deepened, Wilson's own position had been ambiguous, supporting the principle of devaluation but nervous about the timing and offering no clear lead. Gaitskell and Jay, both speedy devaluers, suspected him of seeking political advantage by his equivocation. Their scepticism was later confirmed by leaks to the press from Wilson's own ministry that he had fought for devaluation from the outset while Gaitskell and Jay prevaricated. Whatever the justice of the case, this passage of events marked Wilson's emergence as a truly political animal, rather than a souped-up civil servant managing a branch of government. At the same time, the episode also laid the foundation for decades of wariness. Jay, for one, never trusted him again.

Born into a mining family in Monmouthshire, Aneurin ('Nye') Bevan (1897–1960) was a trade union official before he was elected to Parliament as MP for Ebbw Vale in 1929. Bevan was appointed Minister of Health in the first Attlee government, and played the key role in the creation of the National Health Service. He resigned as Minister for Labour in 1951 over the decision to introduce prescription charges in order to pay for the Korean War. He lost the leadership to Gaitskell in 1955, and became Shadow Foreign Secretary. He was elected Deputy Leader of the party in 1959, but died of cancer the following year.

In the event, devaluation to $2.80, so long foreshadowed, took place on 18 September without immediate danger. But the austerity measures introduced by Cripps to 'balance the books' laid the basis for the next, and more far-reaching, political crisis for Wilson. The Chancellor proposed legislation permitting prescription charges of one shilling (5p: the current charge is £6) if a 'fair and workable' scheme could be devised. To Bevan, no such scheme could ever be fair: the free NHS was untouchable. Amid dark threats of his resignation, the government was plunged into a general election in February 1950 for which it was singularly ill-prepared.

Wilson had been one of a handful of ministers urging Attlee, unsuccessfully, to go to the country a year before. His contribution to policy preparations was a paper to Attlee urging development of the state's ties with industry, rather than further nationalisation, though he made an exception of ICI which he felt should be taken into the public sector. His views did not greatly endear himself to Labour hardliners, but did cause a fright among right-wingers such as Jay and Gaitskell who saw his attitude as a lurch to the Left. Their hostility merely served to drive him into the arms of the Left.

Pleading ministerial pressure of work and the problems of serving a sprawling constituency, Wilson had already abandoned Ormskirk for the next-door constituency of Huyton, a safer (but not safe) seat. During the campaign, the Tories hammered Wilson for his alleged softness on Communism, a throwback to his long nights with Mikoyan, and employed for the first time the wounding charge that he was a self-deluding 'Walter Mitty'. He won by a margin of only 834 votes. Ormskirk fell to the Tories on a massive swing, which, repeated across the country slashed Labour's Commons majority from 186 to six. Wilson returned to the Board of Trade in a government run by tired and often sick men at the top, the very charge made by Labour against the Tories in 1945. He was discomfited by the appointment of Gaitskell as Minister for Economic Affairs, rightly seeing in it a block to his ambition to succeed Cripps as Chancellor. When Cripps resigned on health grounds eight months after polling day, Gaitskell took his place. Through gritted teeth, Wilson congratulated him as *the right man for the job* and pledged his support. The promise was not bankable.

International events, in the shape of the Korean War, supervened in Labour's burgeoning civil war. The Americans wanted an increase in Britain's military spending, and in January 1951 Gaitskell dutifully proposed a rise in the annual defence budget from £3.4 billion to £4.7 billion. Wilson argued that such a dramatic leap was neither justified nor practical, because industry simply could not cope. Furthermore, Foreign Secretary Bevin was calling for German rearmament in the face of a perceived threat from the USSR. On both issues, Wilson was at odds with Cabinet heavyweights. Simultaneously, the threat of prescription charges re-emerged as Gaitskell looked for way of increasing revenue to meet the arms bill. Wilson always argued that the ensuing confrontation was, on his part, driven by the defence budget, whereas his resignation from government is still popularly believed to have been over 'teeth and glasses'. And in politics, it is often the case that perceptions count more than reality. In this instance, Wilson's political reputation was the beneficiary.

Labour MPs took sides in the arms budget quarrel, and Wilson became closely involved with a group around Bevan (now Minister of Labour) agitating against Gaitskell's plans. A war of threatened resignations ensued, with Bevan going public in a speech in the East End of London, pledging that he would never remain in a government that charged NHS patients. The Chancellor ploughed on, introducing charges for teeth and spectacles in his April Budget. Attlee, ill in hospital, urged caution on his ministers, though Wilson opined later *he was fed up with all of us*.[5] Bevin, encouraged by Wilson to believe that the whole affair was a plot by his mortal enemy Herbert Morrison, tried to mediate. His intervention was cut short by sudden death.

All the gladiators in this contest knew that the government was on its last legs, and a general election could not long be postponed. Conflict was a luxury that Labour could not afford, but the burgeoning political egos of the next generation of leaders were not to be restrained. Bevan resigned when the Finance Bill was tabled. Wilson heard of his departure by telephone during a speech to the Great Yarmouth Chamber of Commerce. Outwardly placid, he stayed overnight in

Yarmouth, and affecting the calm of Sir Francis Drake, played a round of golf the next morning before returning to London. Bevan urged Wilson to stay, but he demurred, arguing that honour compelled him to go, and quit ministerial office on 23 April.

On this occasion, honour concurred with ambition. Wilson later insisted that he was not putting down a marker for the leadership, indeed he suggested that it might be an act of political suicide. John Freeman, who quit with him, judged that resignation offered Wilson the best route to the top, as Bevan's natural successor. This obvious conclusion could not fail to have occurred to a calculating politician like Wilson. Voluntary departure from high office is never easy, but at his age – he was still only 35 – he could expect to resume his ministerial career in a future Labour government. No less a figure than Sir Winston Churchill, the practised resigner, said he had done the right thing, while Mary and his parents privately lauded his courage and sincerity. If you have to go, having the battalions of the good on-side is a comfort.

Meanwhile, Wilson had to survive a nightmarish general election, in which the Catholic Bishop of Leeds publicly denounced 'crypto-Communists' – shorthand for Bevanites in the Labour Party. Huyton had a large population of Catholics, some of whom resigned in protest from the party. An ailing Attlee lost the election of October 1951, which brought Churchill back to Downing Street at the age of 79, but Wilson hung on in Huyton, with his majority marginally increased to 1,193. He had resigned to fight another day.

Chapter 3: Struggle for Leadership

Few had trod the path that now lay before Wilson. Since 1945, he had never sat on the back benches, whether or not his party had been in government. He began his parliamentary career as a minister, moved into Cabinet and only after six years as an MP did he taste the uncertain pleasures of obscurity. It was an unusual trajectory, to say the least.

Wilson's most immediate task was to plug the financial hole left by his departure from office. He had a mortgage, and both sons went to fee-paying schools. He later claimed to have been offered, within hours, posts that would have given him in total £22,000 a year, making him a rich man by the standards of the day. But some of the jobs would have curtailed, or even prohibited, his political career. He chose instead to become a £1,500-a-year part-time economic adviser to a firm of timber importers, Montague Meyer. Much of the company's trade was with Russia, and Wilson could fairly claim expertise in this field. Meyer also took on his secretary and gave him an office in the Strand, a useful a base outside Westminster. His vague job description allowed Wilson to develop a broader interest in tax regimes and trade law, and travel abroad. Using his old contacts in Moscow helped Meyer's land a contract for new methods of chipboard manufacture in the USSR and he won trade favours from the Romanians. All in all, he was a useful fellow to have around, and he often lunched with Meyer at the Savoy after a morning's consultation, before attending the Commons in the afternoon. He also threw himself energetically into the setting up of the charity War on Want, arguing the moral imperative of rich nations devoting 3 per cent of their annual GDP to poor nations. Moreover, the man whose boyhood scribblings had been rejected by *Meccano Magazine* was now in demand to write for the newspapers, particularly the pro-Labour *Reynolds News*. No wonder he wrote to a friend *it is wonderful to feel free after six years of the other life.*

Wilson did not move out of the political fray, however. He took the chair at Bevanite meetings, which Richard Crossman described as a group of MPs keeping alive 'real socialism' in the parliamentary party. Wilson was close to Bevan, while not always agreeing with him and sometimes privately appalled by his penchant for gesture politics. He defined himself as 'a co-belligerent, not a satellite'. Being identified with the Left did Wilson no harm in the wider party. He almost won election to Labour's National Executive Committee (NEC) in 1951, and succeeded the year after, ousting Hugh Dalton. But as early as January 1952, Wilson had clearly signalled his intention of returning to the front bench via the annual elections for the Parliamentary Committee, as the Shadow Cabinet was formally known. In the autumn 1953 poll of MPs, he failed by one vote, a result that was to haunt him, not because he failed but because his position as runner-up placed him in the line of automatic succession.

He managed to keep on side with the Left, opposing German rearmament and the American-inspired South-East Asian Treaty Organisation (SEATO) military pact, but also spoke with growing confidence from the back benches, with Attlee's approval, on economic issues. In April 1954, after a Commons spat with Attlee, Bevan suddenly resigned from the Shadow Cabinet. Wilson would automatically succeed to the vacant place. To avoid doing so, he would have had to resign upon taking up the position, which was not in his game plan, personal links with the tempestuous Nye notwithstanding. He rejected Bevan's plea to follow him into the wilderness, and struck out on his own. This decision, a natural obverse of his 1951 resignation, marked his final transition from a civil servant at Westminster into a politician. His brief was to shadow Board of Trade issues, for which he was almost uniquely fitted. Wilson later owned that this act of independence was *a watershed* in his political life, though only in the sense of bringing him back into the mainstream of his party. In fact, it was much more than that. He was now part of the Establishment. Gaitksell invited him to a reconciliation lunch and made him an honorary member of his Kitchen Cabinet.

Despite earning the undying resentment of Bevan, the move boosted Wilson hugely. He came top of the poll among constituency parties in the NEC elections six months later, and was able to begin discreetly distancing himself from the Left. He no longer identified himself as a Bevanite, while insisting that his policies had not changed. He began to throw his weight about in the party, pioneering marginal seat politics, so much a part of campaigning today but then a less understood science. His rapprochement with Gaitskell flourished. Wilson could see in Gaitskell a future Labour leader, with himself as deputy and potentially Chancellor. *Number Eleven will do quite well*, he once told his teacher in Huddersfield.[1] Indeed, if anything untoward happened to Gaitskell (as it did), he would be the obvious heir apparent, not those tired old war horses, Herbert Morrison and Nye Bevan. This crystal gazing may be regarded as looking too far ahead, but a sophisticated number-cruncher of Wilson's star quality cannot have failed to make the necessary calculations.

Meanwhile, he kept in good stead with the Left, rescuing Bevan from expulsion from the party in the spring of 1955 over yet another ill-tempered Commons revolt on defence. Wilson, who on this occasion loyally supported the Shadow Cabinet line on Britain's nuclear 'deterrent', employed adroit delaying tactics to avoid a damaging split in the run-up to another general election where unity would be paramount. He still feared that the incident was a calamity, which played into the hands of Anthony Eden, Churchill's successor. And so it proved. Eden duly went to the country in May 1955, determined to exploit Opposition divisions. Wilson himself benefited from the continuing influx of Liverpudlians to Huyton, and doubled his majority to 2,558. No longer a minister, he had been able to give more time to voters' problems, and was now regarded as a good constituency MP. He would never be troubled about his electoral powerbase again. He also had a new personal secretary, Marcia Williams, aged 24, a former typist in Transport House who he poached from Labour's HQ on a generous salary of £15 a week. In years to come, she would play of role of inestimable importance in his life. For now, she simply hero-worshipped him.

1955 was also the first general election in which television played a substantial role. Wilson took part in a Labour Party broadcast with Edith Summerskill as a man and wife bemoaning the high cost of food under the Tories. Old party hands dismissed the new-fangled intervention, and Wilson was not an instant star of the small screen, but it went down well with housewives. Not well enough, however, for Eden was returned with a Commons majority handsomely tripled to 59.

Wilson was more than ever convinced that Labour must skip a generation and make Gaitskell leader. Following a joint broadcast with him after the annual conference that year, Wilson confided frankly to his longstanding enemy that *you're the only possible leader*. He believed that Bevan's behaviour had ruled him out, and pledged his support – and continuing loyalty – *when Attlee goes*. That date could not be long in coming, for though the Labour leader had hung grimly on (with the unacknowledged but avowed purpose of averting a Morrison succession), his failing health pointed to an early leadership contest.

Leader of the Labour Party from 1955 until his death in 1963, Hugh Gaitskell (b. 1906) was first elected to the Commons in 1945. He rose quickly through the ranks, serving as Minister for Fuel and Power from 1947–50 before being appointed Attlee's last Chancellor. In 1955 he defeated Nye Bevan for the leadership following Attlee's resignation. After failing to remove Clause IV (about public ownership) from the party's constitution, he was under constant pressure from the Left over unilateral nuclear disarmament. His sudden death in 1963 inspired the conspiracy theory that he was killed by the KGB enabling Wilson to become Prime Minister.

Gaitskell and Wilson worked as a team, opposing the Eden government's autumn Budget. This was an emergency package of measures designed to restore the tax cuts of the Tories' vote-catching pre-election Budget. Gaitskell's mauling of the Conservative Chancellor, Rab Butler, together with Wilson's skilful supportive role, convinced Attlee that it was safe to hand over the reins of power 'now those two are working together'. He quit on 7 December 1955, triggering a three-cornered contest fought between Morrison, Bevan and Gaitskell. The prospect of a Gaitksell/Wilson hegemony naturally infuriated Morrison, who still fondly imagined himself as the king across the Thames. Quite how far he – and Bevan – were out of touch with the new PLP was reflected in the voting: 157 for Gaitskell, 70 for Bevan and a derisory 40 for Morrison, the ladies' man with the quiff and the ear of the press. Wilson, who briefly contemplated standing but wisely let it be known that he backed Gaitskell, once observed of Morrison that *the press were not present, but Herbert Morrison was, so they were saved the journey*.[2] The old guard was out, and the new men were in.

The press were not present, but Herbert Morrison was, so they were saved the journey.

WILSON

Gaitskell immediately appointed Wilson Shadow Chancellor, a move that was greeted with satisfaction rather than ululation. In the Budget debate, Wilson had scored a palpable hit against the government by defeating the Finance Bill on a technicality, gaining for himself what he admitted to be an entirely unwarranted reputation for parliamentary brilliance. His tactical victory did not prevent the Conservatives getting their measures through, but it did put fresh heart into troops whose morale had been torpedoed by the election result. He enjoyed a fresh respect from backbenchers and the whips, a sentiment shared by his new adversary, Harold Macmillan, selected as the new Chancellor to replace the fading Butler. Wilson swiftly established a personal rapport with the clubbable Macmillan, with whom he shared affable conversations in the Commons Smoking Room. In the chamber, their sallies brought out Wilson's engaging, even humorous, side, which enlivened debates on economic legislation. MPs were impressed, voting him top of the poll for the Shadow Cabinet, and Gaitskell was pleased with his performance. Wilson's memory of these halcyon days may have been rose-tinted. Class was a much greater issue then, and the patrician

Macmillan was said to have viewed him as a rather common little man. Either way, the double act made good Westminster theatre. The cartoonists dubbed Macmillan 'Supermac', while Wilson chose the less flattering sobriquet *Mac the Knife*.

This cosy world was shattered in October 1956 by Britain's invasion of Egypt in response to the nationalisation of the Suez Canal by President Nasser. The military action, undertaken jointly with France and Israel, brought international condemnation down on the government's head and UK–US relations plunged to an all-time low. Risking public obloquy at a time when 'our boys' were in action abroad, Gaitskell took a principled stand against the invasion. Wilson, whose pro-Israel sympathies were well-known, shared his leader's uncompromising views, but played very much a secondary role. In the Commons, he stressed the economic consequences of the Suez fiasco, as it turned out to be.

The greatest personal loser of the Suez affair was Prime Minister Eden, whose failing health was exacerbated by the awesome burden of going to war on a pretext. He was compelled to resign on health grounds in January 1957, and was succeeded by Harold Macmillan. The days of Harold vs Harold at the Despatch Box were over, though as Wilson soon detected, Macmillan continued to run the Treasury from Number 10. Incapable of doing anything more than watch in furious admiration, Wilson saw 'Supermac' play the economic cycle like a violin maestro. In the two years after Suez, Macmillan stimulated the economy through tax changes, and put household goods within the reach of working people, many for the first time, with the introduction of hire purchase. Voters with recent bad memories of rationing and shortages under post-war Labour responded enthusiastically to his slogan 'you've never had it so good!' Britain suddenly seemed a more fun place to live. Even the first motorway opened, albeit only eight miles long round Preston. Why change?

Why indeed? Sensing the public mood, Macmillan went to the country in October 1959, after a spring Budget bulging with tax cuts and measures to increase consumption. At the head of a united party, with Bevan happy in his role as Shadow Foreign Secretary, Gaitskell had buried the devils of the contentious past. Yet he was far from confident about winning, despite offering more of the same that the Tories proposed: lower purchase tax and increased public spending, but no tax rises – as if Labour's slogan was 'it might be good with them, but it will be better with us!' Opinion is divided on Wilson's share of the blame for this maladroit strategy. Some held him equally culpable. The faithful Marcia thought he had 'doubts'. Wilson's own subsequent silence speaks volumes.

The voters swiftly saw through Labour's charade, and returned the Conservatives with a majority almost tripled to 99. Wilson's own majority continued its upward track, reaching 5,927, and his local paper reported the view of a councillor that he would be 'a very early Prime Minister'. Local politicians, even national ones, are prone to say this kind of thing in the heat of an election, but the prediction began to have a solid feel about it. Gaitskell, humiliated by the poll result, cast about for scapegoats: the party's failure to modernise ('renovate' was the word he used), and in particular its adherence to the outdated Clause IV, which promised nationalisation of the means of production, distribution and exchange. He retreated into an inner circle of right-wing allies, excluding Wilson from the post-election inquest and planning for reform. All the old Bevanite slurs were now dredged up to damage Wilson. He was too ideological, too cold and unfit to be Shadow Chancellor. In turn, Wilson felt that Gaitskell, by seeking a symbolic victory against the Left over Clause IV, was reverting to authoritarian instincts and endangering the very unity which was the keystone of his loyalty to the leader.

Wilson hung fire on the ensuing Clause IV controversy, neither supporting Gaitskell nor the *status quo*, until February 1960. His instinct was to find a way of sustaining unity, preferably by a conciliatory statement on nationalisation that would settle the party down but not frighten the voters. His compromise route was eventually adopted, and Wilson kept his Shadow Cabinet job, but it was not long before Gaitskell chose another issue on which to stamp his authority. Once again, he turned to defence as the *cause célèbre* on which to make his name as the moderniser, much as Neil Kinnock was to do in later years.

The Campaign for Nuclear Disarmament (CND), established in 1958, had made strong inroads into Labour's socialist cadres, and Gaitskell saw this as a golden opportunity to gain advantage with the wider electorate. Besides, his own instincts were strongly in favour of the Bomb. Wilson shared his rejection of unilateralism, but with characteristic distaste for division, did not go along with his high-profile denunciation of a growing minority within the party. Ominously, Frank Cousins, a CND supporter, was now General Secretary of the Transport and General Workers' Union (TGWU). The largest single party affiliate and Bevin's old union was moving towards the unilateralist left. For Gaitskell, slaying the union barons and his own left-wing was of greater political importance than party unity, and at the Scarborough conference in 1960 he famously promised to 'fight, fight – and fight again' to reverse his party's drift into unilateralism. Wilson chose to smoke his pipe during the leader's speech, and ostentatiously failed to join the ovation. Relations between the two were back in the deep freeze, and the Right made fresh attempts to have Wilson sacked in favour of Roy Jenkins, though Callaghan manoeuvred for the job, too.

It was a most difficult juncture. Bevan had died in July 1960, and his widow, Jennie Lee MP, a genuine darling of the Left, now urged Wilson to stand against Gaitskell in the annual leadership election, which should have been a formality. Initially, he refused, but on hearing that if he did not stand, then the louche figure of Tony Greenwood would, made *the most miserable decision I had ever had to take*[3] and changed his mind. If he stood, he faced charges of treachery – or worse, being a Communist stooge. If he did not, then Gaitksell would represent his position as an endorsement of his leadership in all its aspects. He stood, and was soundly beaten by more than two to one: 166 votes to 89. But it was a creditable performance, and Wilson buoyed himself with the conviction that Labour now had two standard bearers.

In 1961, Gaitskell secured his reversal of unilateralist policy, and peace broke out with Wilson

The Campaign for Nuclear Disarmament (CND) was founded in 1958 after an article by J B Priestley, criticising Labour's abandonment of unilateral disarmament. Michael Foot was among its founder members. CND campaigned primarily for the abolition of the British nuclear programme, staging demonstrations and using acts of civil disobedience such as sit-ins as a protest. In September 1961, 1,300 CND members were arrested in Trafalgar Square, and 350 at Holy Loch in Scotland. Membership has declined substantially since the end of the Cold War. Today the group focuses on lobbying of MPs and at international conferences, and on tracking and publicising shipments of nuclear materials.

once more. He was offered, and after overcoming suspicions of a trap (Wilson always saw traps, even where there were none), accepted the post of Shadow Foreign Secretary. He reasoned that if he made a success of the job, it would advance his claim on the leadership, and if he failed, well, failure might bring up him against the final boundary of his abilities. In fact, after a flashy and unworthy start, he proved very much at home in a challenging role that brought him to close quarters with the rising issue that would dominate politics for generations to come: Europe. Gaitskell, bored with the topic, eventually came out against British membership of the EEC, as it then was, and at the 1962 conference in Brighton fulminated against Europe in terms far more strident than Wilson would have used. However, since the Europhiles with Roy Jenkins at their head were scarcely Wilson's friends, he saw no reason for a public quarrel. He also felt his stock had risen enough to challenge George Brown for the deputy leadership that November. Brown beat him, by 30 votes. It was another marker for the future.

Weeks later, Gaitskell fell mysteriously ill and in January 1963 went into hospital. After sounding out the Whips, Wilson went ahead with a lecture tour of the United States, but kept in regular touch. On his way back by car from the United Nations to his hotel in New York on 18 January, he heard the news of Gaitskell's death. He returned to London the next day, and as Tony Blair was to do two decades later, decided in a car from the airport to stand as leader. It was a peculiar election, with campaigning frowned upon and no overt manifestos. The Parliamentary Labour Party (PLP), however, prided itself as being the most sophisticated electorate in the world. Its 258 MP voters had three of the most unsophisticated candidates from which to choose: George Brown, a former trade union official and a drunk; James Callaghan, another former union official, the son of an Irish-born naval petty officer who, like Brown, had not been to university; and Harold Wilson, the pipe-smoking lad from Huddersfield who despised the dinner-party circuit.

As was to be expected, with the stakes so high, it was a dirty election. To all the old smears about Wilson's supposed softness on Communism and suspicious links with Russia were added new ones about the alleged shakiness of his marriage and Marcia being his mistress. Even godlessness was invoked, strange for a man of quiet but firm Christian adherence. But the real flaw in the 'Stop Wilson' campaign was the failure to stop two candidates from the acknowledged Right of the party splitting the anti-Wilson vote. Brown and Callaghan each refused to give way to the other. Both were vying for the support of the Gaitskellites, and their *amour propre* gave Wilson a head start. In the first ballot, he picked up 115 votes, with Brown taking 88 and Callaghan 41. Callaghan dropped out, and on the second ballot Wilson emerged a convincing winner, with 144 votes to 103 for Brown. Wilson may not have had the warmth of the PLP, but he had its respect, and the value judgement that, of the two, he was the more likely to win a general election. After 12 years in the political wilderness, that was what counted. At the age of 46, Wilson was leader. He had convinced his MPs. Whether he could convince the voters was still very much an open question.

Part Two

THE LEADERSHIP

Chapter 4: First Government

At the point of Wilson's succession, a general election could have been virtually imminent. The two previous Conservative governments had lasted four years, and this period was up in October, only eight months away. But luck, and events, were on the new leader's side. The Profumo scandal was breaking, Kim Philby, MI6 agent and Soviet spy, was shortly to disappear behind the Iron Curtain, and Macmillan, in failing health, was no longer the 'Supermac' of the cartoonists. He had been badly wounded in the First World War, and the strain of office during a succession of security crises exacerbated his old injuries. He was also suffering from an inflamed prostate, which would eventually force him from Number 10 during the Conservative Party autumn conference, compelling the jaded Tories to look for a new leader of their own. They chose Lord Home of the Hersel, a skull-faced aristocrat whose arrival from 'the Other Place' was welcomed by Wilson in the fond belief that voters in the 'Swinging Sixties' would not be attracted to an obscure Scottish earl more at home on the grouse moor than the campaign trail. His confidence was to prove almost fatal.

First, he had to stamp his authority on his own party without provoking fresh internal tensions. He had little need to placate the Left, which had voted for him en bloc but carried little weight in the Shadow Cabinet. He did, however, feel obliged to conciliate the Right. Callaghan continued as Shadow Chancellor, while George Brown took on the Home Office portfolio, fortified with vague promises from Wilson that he would get something bigger in an actual government, perhaps even Foreign Secretary, a job that Patrick Gordon Walker, an intimate of the new leader, now shadowed. Denis Healey, the brilliant but maverick right-winger, took on Defence, but otherwise the top team was much as it was under Gaitskell. Wilson confided to an ally that it was *like running a Bolshevik Revolution with a Tsarist Cabinet.*

Elected to Parliament as MP for Belper in 1945, George Brown (1914–85) challenged for the Labour leadership after Gaitskell's death, but was beaten by Wilson. He served briefly in the Attlee government as Minister of Works, and rose steadily through the ranks in opposition before becoming deputy leader of the Labour Party after Nye Bevan's death in 1960. He held onto the post until losing his seat in 1970, also serving as Minister for Economic Affairs and Foreign Secretary under Wilson. He left the Labour Party in 1976 and his consistent drink problem meant he was not very high-profile after joining the SDP.

He also dusted down plans for two new ministries, for Technology and a Department of Economic Affairs (DEA), a super-ministry designed to break the stranglehold of the Treasury over economic strategy. Overall, Wilson pursued a policy of conciliation, offering leadership on the issues of the day that could command the widest possible support in the party. Not too much of this, not too little of that, whether on defence, nationalisation, Europe or industrial relations. He famously characterised the Labour Party as a stagecoach, whose occupants were exhilarated or too seasick to cause trouble if it went at speed. He kept the coach rattling along, throughout the summer, keeping the party happy and impressing the public with frenetic activity.

His perpetual motion culminated in a speech to the autumn party conference in Scarborough that still resounds to this day. His vision of a second industrial revolution, driven by *an alliance of science and socialism* that would galvanise industry, secure full employment, transform education and bring about a planning utopia. In this brave new world, there would be no room for Luddites. Change, technology and automation would usher in a new Britain *forged in the white heat of this revolution*. There would be no place for restrictive practices or outdated methods on either side of industry. For the first time, voters heard the mantra of *the many, not the few*, which was to reappear as New Labour's slogan 30 years later.[1]

Wilson's speech electrified his audience, and woke up the media to a genuinely new force in British politics. He was Labour's first prophet of modernisation, speaking to an electorate open to ideas of change. Harold Wilson may have been born in the First World War, but he captured the mood of the 1960s. The speech was an instant success. On the BBC, academic pundit Robert Mackenzie, responded enthusiastically: 'Harold Wilson has moved the Labour Party forward fifty years in fifty minutes.' In the *Daily Herald*, James Cameron whooped 'here is the twentieth century'. Even the right-wing press hailed his courage and inspiration.

A new Britain forged in the white heat of this revolution.

WILSON

Less than three weeks later, Macmillan was gone and the Conservative Party had chosen Lord Home, the last leader to be selected by the undemocratic 'magic circle' of anonymous nabobs. Home, translated to the Commons in a quickie Perthshire by-election, proved a more formidable figure than

Wilson had expected. *I thought I was going to have the time of my life with him in the House, but I was proved wrong*, he admitted. Wisely, the Tories spun out the parliament to the bitter end, giving time for them to regroup – and, they hoped, to expose Wilson as a charlatan.

The election was not called until 15 October 1963. Labour began the campaign ahead in the polls, and Wilson stumped the country tirelessly, offering his vision of a new Britain in precisely the same way that Tony Blair was to do in 1997. It was not a one-man band, but virtually so. If it worked, he would be the hero of the hour. If it did not, he risked being the most short-lived party leader on record. In the event, it did neither. As polling day approached, the Conservative government regained ground, and the race became neck-and-neck. Labour made gains in the marginals, but not enough to replace Home's majority of almost 100 with a similarly healthy lead. Wilson and Mary left Liverpool in the early hours of 16 October to claim a triumph at Transport House. They had to wait until three in the afternoon before Labour won the seat that confirmed Wilson as the next Prime Minister. His overall Commons majority was a perilously-low four, sufficient to take office but almost certainly insufficient to rule for a full parliament. Labour had actually won fewer votes than in 1959, and as his first biographer Leslie Smith noted 'complete stalemate had been averted by only a handful of votes'. It was, indeed, a half-hearted endorsement of the white-hot vision.

Wilson had no alternative but to soldier on as though he had a secure working majority, even though his fragile hold on power was almost immediately diminished by the loss of a safe London seat by Patrick Gordon Walker, the Foreign Secretary designate seeking to re-enter Parliament after losing his Smethwick constituency. The energy that carried Wilson through his first year as Opposition leader continued in office. He built his Cabinet largely round the Shadow version, making George Brown DEA Secretary and, effectively, deputy prime minister. He also brought in Barbara Castle to head an expanded Ministry of Overseas Development and Dick Crossman, his maverick intellectual backer, as Housing Minister. He made good his word to set up a Ministry of Technology to harness scientific advance to the needs of the nation, but contrarily brought in a dyed-in-the-wool, left-wing trade union leader, Frank Cousins of the TGWU, to run it. Cousins, never at home in the Commons, eventually quit. After Gordon Walker's inglorious defeat, Wilson appointed the sepulchral but dependable figure of Michael Stewart as Foreign Secretary.

Almost as important as the real thing, Wilson established a Kennedy-style 'Kitchen Cabinet' in Number 10, composed of his secretary Marcia Williams, political cronies, including George Wigg, his eyes and ears in the Westminster political underworld, economics adviser Lord Tommy Balogh, Peter Shore, his PPS, and later press spokesman Gerald Kaufman from the *New Statesman*. They were more of a comfort zone than an instrument of policy planning, for despite his

MP for Blackburn 1945–79 and a Bevanite, Barbara Castle (1910–2002) served in Wilson's governments as Minister for Overseas Development, Minister of Transport (introducing seat belts and the breathalyser), and Secretary of State for Employment and Productivity, where she produced *In Place of Strife* and introduced the Equal Pay Act 1970. From 1974–6 she was Secretary of State for Health and Social Services and set up the Child Benefit scheme. Sacked by James Callaghan, she left Parliament in 1979. She was an MEP 1979–89. Created a baroness in 1990, she spent her last years fighting to re-establish the link between pensions and earnings.

protestations to the contrary, Wilson was not a man for the long term. Outside this cabal, the Prime Minister listened most to his Cabinet Secretary, Burke Trend, a quintessential mandarin, indeed the kind of civil servant that Wilson might once have become.

In the short term, grave economic difficulties faced the fledging government. On the day he took office, Wilson was told the annual trade deficit was £800 million, twice the estimated figure. Devaluation of the pound looked a distinct possibility. Abroad, Khrushchev had just been deposed in Moscow, the Chinese had exploded an atomic bomb, and America's involvement in Vietnam threatened to turn into a nuclear war. Psychologically, Wilson, closely involved in the devaluation of 1948, could not afford to be seen as leading the party of economic weakness. He successfully resisted the pressure, but at a cost (in Barbara Castle's words) of putting the government in a straitjacket for the next three years.

Nevertheless, it was a bold first Queen's Speech, abolishing prescription charges, scrapping the Tories' Rent Act, establishing an Ombudsman, allowing a free vote on hanging, nationalising the steel industry and reviewing the whole field of social security. Callaghan's first Budget improved pensions and benefits, increased income tax and, to the consternation of the City, introduced a capital gains tax and corporation tax. There was an instant run on the pound, and Wilson faced the wrath of the governor of the Bank of England, Lord Cromer, who demanded savage cuts in government spending. He won this confrontation, threatening to go to the country on a 'bankers versus democracy' ticket if the Bank did not back down. The nuclear option worked. But Cromer had to secure a $3,000 million loan to protect sterling, and Wilson realised now (if he had not before) that international financiers would prefer that his summer holiday home in his beloved Scilly Isle of St Mary should become his permanent residence. He was never to have any rest from 'the gnomes of Zurich.'

Wilson moved quickly shore up what he called the *close* (rather than 'special') relationship with the USA. The Johnson administration accepted that he represented mainstream Labour feelings, but had doubts about this 'cold' man. He was not admired in Washington, particularly after rejecting the President's request to send troops to Vietnam. 'Not even some of your Scottish pipers?' asked Johnson, only to be rebuffed.[2] Wilson invariably gave formal policy support to America over Vietnam, but never to the extent of military involvement. With ideas above Britain's station in the matter, he hankered after a peacemaking role, perhaps via the USSR, only to be thoroughly disabused by the Americans. Foreign affairs, in the shape of the Rhodesia (now Zimbabwe) crisis, further intervened as Wilson celebrated his first hundred days as Prime Minister. The minority whites, led by the wily, astute Ian Smith, a wartime Spitfire pilot and the colony's Prime Minister, was determined to forestall black majority rule, even if it meant a unilateral declaration of independence – UDI. This duly came in November 1965, prompting Wilson to impose sanctions.

By this time, Douglas-Home had succumbed to the inevitable political pressures that follow defeat and resigned the Tory leadership. His successor Edward Heath was a complete break with Conservative tradition: a grammar school and Oxford man, much in the mould of Harold Wilson. The two great parties now had 'classless' men at the helm, Heath literally so, as he was a keen yachtsman. The next general election, which could not be postponed for very long, would be between leaders of similar background, class and even broadly similar outlook. Like Macmillan, Heath had been on the side of the angels in the famous 1938 Munich by-

The Special Relationship

'Though the names of those who came to question and in some instances oppose his policies in Vietnam included men as influential as Senators William Fulbright and Mike Mansfield ... and numerous leaders from abroad, including ... Harold Wilson, no one reading Johnson's Vietnam tale could have guessed the nature of their misgivings and even less the policies that they advocated.' The special relationship, which had still existed between Kennedy and Macmillan, when the President had at least listened to the Prime Minister who had urged him not to invade Cuba 'until I speak again with you' (22 October 1962), had evaporated. Misgivings were noted by Johnson, but his policy decisions were not swayed by Wilson.

'While Johnson represented his responses to North Vietnam, including his later bombings of Hanoi and Haiphong as the necessary responses to their acts of aggression, comparable to those taken against the North Koreans in 1950, he believed he was avoiding the mistakes Chamberlain and others had made in the 1930s – seeking peace through a mistaken policy of appeasement ... Johnson wrote self-righteously of what he and his advisers did, never admitting error, but never seeking to shift the blame to those who served as his principal collaborators.

From the time he used the attacks on the US destroyer as the excuse for securing the Tonkin Gulf Resolution from Congress, which authorized him to take 'all necessary measures' to 'repel armed attacks against the forces of the United States and to prevent further aggression', the president told only very partial truths. Senator Wayne Morse, one of only two senators to vote against the resolution, insisted that the *Maddox,* the destroyer in question, had been escorting South Vietnamese patrol boats in their raids on North Vietnam, but Senator Fulbright categorically denied the truth of the allegation, as did McNamara. In fact, it was true. So, also, a reported second North Vietnamese attack on the destroyer never occurred, and the president knew this but said nothing; it was acknowledged decades later, in 1995, by Robert McNamara.'[Stephen Graubard, *The Presidents* (Allen Lane, London: 2004) pp 458ff] election in Oxford, when the Master of Balliol, A D Lindsay stood, unsuccessfully, as the anti-appeasement candidate against Quintin Hogg. Despite his much-touted right-wing credentials, Heath was a One Nation Tory, passionate about Europe, just as in many ways Wilson was a one nation Labour man. This was discernible in his handling of the one old-fashioned nod towards socialism in the manifesto, steel nationalisation. With a parliamentary majority down to three, and the bankers at his heels, Wilson could claim that it was inopportune to pursue this radical measure, especially as no powerful industrial case had been made out in favour. Two Labour backbenchers threatened to vote against any nationalisation bill, and Wilson prevaricated, searching for a compromise that would give the state control if not ownership. The idea was abandoned from the 1965 Queen's Speech, prompting disquiet among the Left about Wilson's true political direction. The penny was finally dropping that 'their' man was not a socialist in the ideological sense, but a fair-minded pragmatist: above all a Christian socialist intent on doing good, and doing nothing where doing something might do harm.

Meanwhile, the heat was going out of Wilson's white-hot revolution. He had under-estimated the cunning and staying power of the Treasury, whose long-range role was to have been superseded by George Brown and his DEA. With a great media fanfare, the DEA finally published to its much-vaunted National Plan in September 1965. It was a hugely optimistic document, full of good intentions and offering targets for industry and a vision of Great Britain plc powering ahead towards a great society. Unfortunately, it was based on predictions of trading surpluses that even then looked unduly rosy, and never materialised. By then, in the real world, the economy was in trouble and the Treasury was piling the pressure on Wilson for a statutory prices and incomes policy. In late July, Callaghan was compelled to bring in an emergency Budget, cutting public spending and reimposing prescription charges. In the autumn, the Prices and Incomes Board was given powers to 'vet' increases and to Wilson's relief the Labour conference voted to support incomes policy legislation by 3.6 to 2.5 million votes. This decision sent a signal to speculators, and put off the pound's evil day yet again, but this hand-to-mouth regime, sustained by a parliamentary majority of three could not continue indefinitely. Wilson had always argued, *pace* Churchill, that 'a majority of one is enough', while knowing that at Westminster it is most emphatically not. In between trumpeting the achievements of his first session – 65 Acts, twice the normal rate of parliamentary production – he began to plan for a second general election to rescue his government from calamity. On the way, he rejected private approaches from the Liberal leader, Jo Grimond, for a Lib-Lab pact.

This time around, the election would be at a moment of his own choosing. A by-election in January 1966 in Hull North almost stayed his hand, but a Labour victory, assisted by the promise of a suspension bridge over the Humber, persuaded him that the time was ripe. He had but recently reshuffled his Cabinet, bringing Roy Jenkins in as Home Secretary and promoting Barbara Castle to Transport, to be replaced by Anthony Greenwood. Wedgwood-Benn, as he still was, was made Postmaster-General, but not of Cabinet status. In the last months of Wilson's first government, Labour was ahead in the polls. Wilson's own standing in the country was equivocal. His award of MBEs to the Beatles in the July Honours List 'for services to exports' attracted contempt as well as admiration. His establishment of the Open University, by contrast, was greeted with unqualified praise. It had its origins in the

Soviet Union, where he noticed that a high proportion of scientists received long-range tuition. The institution sent down deep roots, and has benefited the lives of millions.

Wilson determined upon a spring election, and immediately had to face down the threat of a national rail strike on St Valentine's Day. The myth of 'beer and sandwiches at Number 10' was born from this confrontation in Downing Street with rail union leaders. With the aid of Barbara Castle, and the provision of thick sandwiches and pies after the men in boiler suits complained about the quality of Whitehall's refreshments, he prevailed on them to call off the strike and accept a pay and not-very-onerous productivity deal. His intervention set the stage for a campaign based on ability to deliver industrial peace at home, improvements for the old and those in rented property, and an economic record which, if not enviable, was at least not catastrophic either. Unlike his hero Attlee, he could not claim to have slain Beveridge's five giants – want, disease, ignorance, squalor and idleness – but he had killed a few lesser Tory dragons and laid the foundations for a fully-fledged Labour government. He had kept Britain out of an unwinnable Asian war, and he had dealt firmly and honourably with a white colonial revolt.

The most successful pop/rock group of all time came from Liverpool and its members were John Lennon (1940–80), Paul McCartney (b. 1942), George Harrison (1943–2001) and Ringo Starr (b. 1940). Their innovative music and films, their interest in the peace movement and eastern religion helped define the Sixties. Lennon and McCartney are the most successful composers in popular music history. Lennon was murdered outside his flat in Central Park, New York and Harrison died of cancer.

Polling day was set for 31 March. Callaghan eschewed the opportunity to stage an election Budget, but did announce

help for home buyers, to be bankrolled by a tax on gambling. Labour's manifesto, *Time for Decision*, stressed industrial harmony, voluntary incomes policy, and economic and social planning (the National Plan had gone down surprisingly well). Nationalisation of steel reappeared, but the line on Europe was non-committal. Even more than in 1964, Wilson sought to present a presidential image to the country, urging voters to give him the opportunity to get on with the job. Mary Wilson, in a new set of clothes, appeared more often at his side, to remind voters that they were a happy family whereas Heath was a solitary bachelor.

Labour began the campaign nine points ahead, and, it appeared, could only throw the election away by a return to the public squabbling that had helped to keep them in the wilderness for 18 years. There was none. His MPs had tasted power, and it was to their liking. On the stump, Wilson's practised speechifying ran him streets ahead of the wooden Heath, even to the extent of capitalising on a boy who hit him in the eye with a stink bomb. *With an aim like that he should be in the England eleven*, he quipped. He did not, however, take up the Conservatives' proposal of an American-style televised debate, suggesting that his confidence was more apparent than real. It was born out when the votes were counted. On a slightly reduced turnout, Labour took 48 per cent of the popular vote, gaining 46 seats and winning an overall Commons majority of 97 – almost the total obverse of Macmillan's result in 1959. His own majority at Huyton was almost 20,000. For the first time in history, a Labour leader had won a higher majority for an incumbent Labour govern-ment. Wilson was back in power with sufficient authority to deliver whatever he put to Parliament. What would he do with it?

Chapter 5: Second Government, Second Devaluation

The scale of Wilson's victory was a surprise not entirely to his liking. He would have preferred a majority of around 30, large enough to govern but small enough to rein in his hard Left backbenchers. He joked to the visiting Pakistani premier Ayub Khan that his handicap had gone up from three to 97. Nor did he feel inclined to bring any of the intelligent Left, most prominently Michael Foot, into government. The ideologues in the PLP, whose ranks had been swelled by Labour's unexpected successes in 'unwinnable' seats, were not slow to grasp early signals that Wilson's second government was no more likely to be overtly socialist than the first.

His Cabinet stayed substantially the same, though the promising Richard Marsh was brought in at Power to nursemaid the nationalisation of steel and George Thomson took over the Duchy of Lancaster with responsibility for Europe. Wilson did not have a master plan for Britain and the Common Market, but wanted to demonstrate that the issue was moving up his agenda. He had intended to flag up a renewed bid to negotiate entry to the EEC in the 1965 Queen's Speech, but was dissuaded by Crossman. This elephant in the room could not be completely ignored, however, and Thomson's appointment was a sign of future moves towards Europe.

At the beginning of May, a restive Callaghan, becoming prone to the George Brown disease of resignation threats, brought in a deflationary Budget, increasing corporation tax and imposed a Selective Employment Tax to encourage manufacturing rather than service industry. By far the greater challenge to Wilson's economic strategy, however, was a seamen's strike that gradually brought the nation's overseas trade to a standstill from mid-May. The National Union of Seamen (NUS), for decades virtually a tool of the shipowners, now had a more left-wing leadership elected on an aggressive wages policy. Wilson berated this *strike against the state, against the community*. When a court of inquiry and his own intervention failed to break the dispute, he angrily denounced NUS leaders in Parliament as *a tightly knit of politically-motivated men* pursing the aims of Moscow rather than the wishes of their members. MI5 had been shadowing the union's executive, and warned Wilson that a number were Communists or extreme Left-wingers, in clandestine contact with Bert Ramelson, industrial organiser of the Communist Party of Great Britain.[1] This was certainly true. It was also true that the strike had been solid, and the men had a very good case. After Wilson's outburst, which sickened some of his own ministers, morale among the strikers plummeted, and the dispute was called off after 47 days. By then, however, his voluntary incomes policy had been exposed as feeble, and speculators moved against the pound, creating the first big sterling crisis of his second government.

Wilson determined that there should be no repeat of this debacle, and in July introduced the Prices and Incomes Bill, containing a statutory incomes policy. Frank Cousins resigned on the spot, and was replaced by Tony Benn. But legislation was not enough to stem pressure on the pound, and Callaghan, backed by a group of ministers across the political spectrum, wanted to devalue. The alternative was deflation on a much greater scale than the May measures. Devaluation would also aid the UK's bid to enter the Common Market. While the crisis raged, Wilson was actually in Moscow, pursuing his pipe-dream of acting as honest broker with the Russians in the Vietnam War. His trip came to nothing, but he believed that abandoning his travel plans would create even more economic uncertainty. By this stage, he genuinely saw himself as, if not the fount of all wisdom, then certainly greater than the sum of all the parts of Cabinet. His self-confidence was not misplaced, in the sense that ministers invariably gave way to his wishes. On his return, Wilson, as ever mindful of his own reputation defied the pro-devaluation camp and insisted on a massive £500 million deflationary programme. The July Measures, which he presented to the Commons himself (Brown being in resignation mode yet again), cut public spending, restricted high-street buying and imposed a six-month freeze on wages and prices, to be followed a further six months of 'severe restraint' on wages.

Cabinet ministers complained that Wilson had missed a golden opportunity to devalue, but they grumbled in private. None dare raise his head too far above the parapet for fear of Wilson's revenge, and while Brown, Callaghan and Jenkins all believed they could do the job better than him, none of them thought one of the others could do so. Wilson's aim of 'creative tension' between the DEA and the Treasury may have turned out to be a joke, but the inspired stress he set up among his would-be heirs worked very much to his advantage. With a smile, he occasionally confided satisfaction at these divide and rule tactics to trusties such as Barbara Castle. In the make-believe world of the Westminster village, his attitude was understandable. Outside, in the harsher world of jobs, votes and party loyalty, the July programme began an

De Gaulle and Soames

'Someone needed to "get through" to de Gaulle, to read his mind better, to cosy up to France, to try and replace an arid defensiveness with intimations of something warmer.' So Wilson supported the appointment of the Conservative politician Christopher Soames as ambassador to Paris. Soames took up his post in September 1968, but it was not until 4 February that de Gaulle received the ambassador and his wife, Winston Churchill's daughter Mary, at lunch at the Elysée Palace. On the menu was 'a monologue, in which the General described the kind of Europe he would like to see developing. This would be a very different "Europe" from the EEC, a looser yet broader construct, with more members and wider tasks, yet liberated from some of the supra-national pretensions and invasions of national sovereignty that so offended Gaullist France. Such a Europe, de Gaulle speculated, would be led by the powers that possessed serious armies: France, Great Britain, West Germany and Italy. When Soames commented that the arrangement took little account of the existence of NATO, de Gaulle portrayed it as something necessary in anticipation of the day the Americans departed, and Europe had to look after itself. He did not, he said, conceive the idea as anti-American. But he did propose a radical alteration in the concept of what "Europe" meant, and who should be allowed to constitute it. Ireland, Norway and Denmark would obviously belong, but most important was Britain, now offered not only membership of the group but a seminal role in discussions leading up to its possible formation. For what the General seemed to be proposing was a series of secret bilateral negotiations between Britain and France, to be followed, if they succeeded, by a British launch of the grand plan, which France would then be heard to endorse, and others invited to join.' When Soames' account of the lunch reached London it caused immediate consternation. To John Robinson, as head of the Integration Department, 'de Gaulle's proposition constituted nothing but a devilish trap. Whichever way you looked at it, it presented Britain with ruinous options. [Hugo Young, *This Blessed Plot* (Macmillan, London: 1998) pp 200ff] inexorable drift of support from trade unionists and activists that would sap support for Labour in the months and years to come. Voters seeking cheer looked instead to England's footballers, who won the World Cup, beating Germany in the final 4–2.

Wilson could not disguise the impact that these savage measures were bound to have on Labour's dreams of an expanding, science-led economy. Indeed, to US President Johnson he made a virtue of their severity, arguing that Britain was at last facing up to its economic responsibilities. The assertion went down well in Washington better than at home. Wilson's standing was diminished, as was his own physical stature. Observers remarked that he looked fatter, smaller and even more hunched than normal. His hunched demeanour hid a steely resolve. Wilson suspected a 'July plot' to supplant him, and though this was more a product of his conspiratorial brain than a reality, his reaction was aggressive. *I know what's going on. I'm going on*, he told his kitchen cabinet.[2]

> *I know what's going on.* I'm *going on.*
> WILSON

In August, Wilson reshuffled his Cabinet, sending Brown to the Foreign Office and Michael Stewart to the DEA, now nearing the end of its less than useful life. Crossman was made Leader of the House to handle the PLP, an appointment that mystified other ministers who felt he had no man-management skills. The team was much the same, but the captain had reminded them who decided on their positions. Election year wound up with a combative performance by Wilson at the TUC and Labour Party conferences. Delegates accepted the pay freeze, but car workers protested outside the hall and delegates called for work-sharing rather than redundancies. Unemployment was rising ominously, and Wilson was hard put to work his old magic with the delegates.

He could not, however, pull off the same trick with Ian Smith, the rebel premier of Rhodesia. The new Commonwealth Secretary, Herbert Bowden, flew to Salisbury (modern Harare) in November 1966 to test hopes that the recalcitrant whites might be ready to forsake UDI. The response was sufficiently encouraging to set up full-scale talks between Smith and Wilson aboard the cruiser HMS *Tiger* a mile offshore from Gibraltar. It was almost a rerun of the Mikoyan meetings: two of the most artful politicians in the business facing each other across the negotiating table. Wilson had the card of UN mandatory sanctions to play. Smith had the colony virtually in his pocket. A draft settlement was drawn up, and approved by the cabinet in London on 4 December, but rejected by the Smith regime the next day. Wilson had been outfoxed. UN sanctions followed, and Wilson withdrew the *Tiger* offer in favour of a declaration of NIBMAR – No Independence Before Majority African Rule.

In the 1964 general election, Shadow Foreign Secretary Patrick Gordon Walker had been defeated in his constituency of Smethwick in Birmingham (held by Oswald Mosley for Labour 1926–31) by the Conservative Peter Griffiths in a racially-charged campaign on the subject of immigration. Griffith's party workers were accused of spreading the slogan 'If you want an nigger for a neighbour, vote Labour'.

At home, interests rates were eased back as the unions knuckled under to voluntary pay restraint, though ostensibly operated by the TUC rather than legislative fiat. Callaghan's April Budget struck an appropriately seamanlike 'steady as she goes' note, with only mild stimulus to spending. Wilson was increasingly preoccupied with the prospect of entering the EEC as a solution to the nation's problems. Privately, his view had turned almost full circle, from committed anti-European to lukewarm enthusiasm. His enthusiasms were often like that: apart from rare flashes of anger, such as his denunciation of the Tory victor against Patrick Gordon Walker as *a parliamentary leper*, Wilson did not exhibit public emotion.

He and Brown toured European capitals to sound out opinion, and brought the prime ministers of EFTA, of which the UK was a member, to London for talks. The success of this peripatetic endeavour rested solely on De Gaulle, however, and he received the pair of supplicants coolly. A measure of Wilson's new-found earnestness was found in the Commons in mid-May, when the government, seeking all-party backing, tabled a resolution in support of Britain's application to join the EEC. It was carried by 488 to 62, the biggest majority of the century. About 30 Labour MPs voted against, less than one in ten of the PLP. De Gaulle, deeply suspicious of the UK–US relationship was unimpressed, and six months later vetoed the application. Wilson sought to shrug off the reverse, but did not try again while De Gaulle remained in the Elysee Palace.

The Six-Day War between Israel and Egypt, resulting in massive defeat for Nasser, fortunately did not require Wilson's close involvement, and was barely raised in Cabinet, though there was no question where his sympathies lay. The same could not be said of intense pressure from Labour MPs for Britain to withdraw, or at least, dramatically scale down, her forces 'East of Suez'. Washington was flatly opposed to a military exit from Asia, and had in the past tied help for the ailing pound to a supportive presence in the East. Wilson envisaged a draw-down of troops and facilities beginning in 1970 to be completed within five years.

This timetable was almost acceptable to the Americans and Britain's allies in the theatre. But the ink was barely dry on Denis Healey's Defence White Paper when the government was once again assailed by economic perils, deepened by losses in by-elections and a lurch to the Left in the labour movement. The election of Hugh Scanlon, with Communist support, as president of the traditionally-moderate Amalgamated Engineering Union came as a shock to all but those who had watched the unions drifting leftwards at shop-floor level. In the TGWU, Cousins retired, making way for Jack Jones, a republican veteran of the Spanish Civil War from Liverpool, and another powerful figure on the Left. Between them, the 'terrible twins' shifted the political balance of the TUC, and began to undermine the leader's long-standing reliance on the union block vote at conference. Wilson had responded to public disquiet about strikes and the power of the unions by setting up a Royal Commission under Lord Donovan, a judge and former Labour MP, but it was not due to report until 1968. As it debated, strikes proliferated, in the docks, on the railways and the motor industry.

The Six-Day War was fought between 5–10 June 1967 and was the result of a pre-emptive Israeli strike, after Egypt blockaded the Straits of Tiran and deployed troops near the Israeli border. Jordan and Syria were also involved. Claims were made by the three Arab countries that Israel was receiving support from Britain and the US, although both denied this. Later, Arab countries announced an oil embargo because they refused to believe Israel could have won so decisively without such support. Israel gained control of the Gaza Strip, the Sinai Peninsula, the West Bank, and the Golan Heights, affecting the geopolitics of the region to this day.

Meanwhile, the Arab-Israeli War and the closure of the Suez Canal, coupled with a civil war in Nigeria, had increased the cost of imports and driven up oil prices alarmingly. Financiers were not impressed by the results of Wilson taking direct control over the DEA. The department was technically under the control of Peter Shore, but Wilson called the shots and his moves to stimulate employment and High Street spending alarmed the bankers. They also noted that beer and sandwiches in Number 10 were no longer a panacea for industrial disputes. Jobless figures reached half a million, the highest since the dark days of 1940. Pressure on the pound intensified through the summer, prompting the first discussion of devaluation at Chequers on 22 July 1967. Wilson again defied the logic of this dramatic step. The industrial climate worsened, interest rates began to creep up again and the balance of payments swung back into the red. Adding fuel to the flames, the EEC proposed Britain's abandonment of sterling as a reserve currency as the price of European entry.

The full crisis erupted on 4 November 1967, when speculators moved against the pound. Callaghan's advisers recommended virtually immediate devaluation, which ministers discussed four days later. But the government temporised. It was not until 13 November that the decision to devalue was taken by Wilson and Brown, sitting in full evening dress in the Cabinet Room of Number 10, having just returned from delivering an upbeat speech on the economy to the Lord Mayor's banquet. The move was approved by senior ministers the next day, and on 16 November by full Cabinet. Two days later, the pound fell in value from $2.80 to $2.40, or by 14.3 per cent.

Whatever his inner turmoil, Wilson presented to the world at large a confident, almost serene, face. Critics might have said that, with so many to choose from, it did the job as good as any. And the repercussions would not have been so bad had not Wilson made a public relations blunder of such magnitude that even his friends feared for his mental equilibrium. Presented with a draft of his Prime Ministerial broadcast by the Treasury, Wilson homed in on a phrase that devaluation did not mean that 'the money in our pockets is worth 14 per cent less'. This he honed into political-speak as: *From now on, the pound abroad is worth 14 per cent or so less, in terms of other currencies. That doesn't mean, of course, that the pound in your pocket or purse or in your bank has been devalued.*[3]

That doesn't mean, of course, that the pound in your pocket or purse or in your bank has been devalued.

WILSON

He did concede that prices would rise because the cost of imports would go up, but his words were at best disingenuous, at worst deliberately deceitful. Unquestionably, they were the remarks of a man who would now be described as 'in denial'. The British housewife, who he had duplicitously sought to reassure with warm words about the pound in her purse, would foot the bill. If he had a tenuous hold on the public's trust before that fateful Sunday evening television broadcast, he had none at all thereafter. Breathtakingly, Wilson sought to portray the collapse of his economic strategy as a springboard for recovery, despite a humiliating $3 billion loan from the International Monetary Fund and the central banks, and swingeing cuts in public spending that he was also forced to announce the day after his broadcast.

Wilson's effrontery, as much as the devaluation itself, unleashed a torrent of reproach. Lord Cromer, the former Bank of England governor now in the Upper House, mauled Labour for the humiliation that the pound and the country had been made to suffer. Ted Heath accused Wilson of misleading the public about price rises. Tony Benn thought the broadcast absurd, and the Queen, watching it at Windsor with Crossman sitting next to her, remained silent for some time before offering that such a speech was 'extraordinarily difficult'.[4] Not, perhaps, as difficult as sustaining the government's authority. An unhappy Callaghan immediately tendered his resignation, but not wanting a rival of his stature on the back benches, Wilson gave him a straight swap with Roy Jenkins at the Home Office. It fell to Jenkins to introduce necessary but painful post-devaluation measures, initially in January 1968 and then a year later. The plan to raise the school leaving age to 16 was shelved for two years, prescription charges came back and public spending, particularly housing, curtailed in cuts totalling £900 million. Withdrawal from East of Suez was also brought forward, and the purchase of American F111 aircraft cancelled, to the anger of Washington. Wilson's political management problems were eased, rather than compounded, by George Brown's 18th and final resignation some weeks later, ostensibly over the Prime Minister's 'presidential' style of government but actually over not being consulted on yet another, short-lived, sterling crisis. There was considerable substance in Brown's charge, and his views were shared by other Cabinet ministers. Wilson managed the feat of appearing to be the most collegiate of premiers, while invariably getting his own way, and it rankled.

He was less adroit in his handling of the media. The D-Notice Affair in February 1967 exposed a bullying side to his nature, and made him unnecessary enemies in the press. The *Daily Express* ran a story that the security services were intercepting international cables, which Wilson denounced as a breach of the D (for defence of the realm) Notice system under which newspapers self-censored stories that could be a threat to national security. It emerged that Colonel Sammy Lohan, chairman of the D-Notice Committee which liased with editors, had consented to publication, and an inquiry of Privy Councillors headed by Lord Radcliffe came down on the side of the *Express*, not the Prime Minister. To the consternation of his ministers, an infuriated Wilson put out a White Paper repudiating the Radcliffe Report. Lohan was effectively sacked, and relations with the press went into deep freeze for the rest of the parliament. The BBC also felt the brunt of his disapproval, and his paranoia about Cabinet 'leaks' intensified.

Controversy had followed controversy like Pelion mounting upon Ossa in 1967. The arms to South Africa debacle that ensued late that year touched on Wilson's genuine hatred of the apartheid regime, and prompted him to a rare moment of mobilising backbench Labour opinion against right-wing ministers. Military collaboration had continued, *sotto voce*, but the pending sale of helicopters that could be used to put down civilian unrest angered MPs. The Cabinet was split over the issue, and Wilson, while ambivalent about the embargo on grounds of lost exports, stood his ground and maintained the embargo. His steadfastness only encouraged the Right to conspire against him, and soundings in favour of Jenkins, the favourite, and Callaghan escalated in the summer of 1968. The coup plotters appeared to have won a highly-placed ally in Cecil King, publisher of the Labour-supporting *Daily Mirror*, who in May ran a leader proclaiming 'Enough is Enough' and demanding a new leader. King, a megalomaniac in the old Fleet Street tradition, was also a member of the Court of the Bank of England. He warned that 'the greatest financial crisis in history' was about to break, and the government did not have the reserves to meet it. But King, having discreetly sounded out Lord Mountbatten, the Queen's uncle, as the potential head of a 'national government', had overplayed his hand. He was obliged to quit his Bank job, and his intervention helped to kill off what became known as 'the July plot' against Wilson. Jenkins was afraid to wound, much less to strike, and Callaghan followed suit.

1968, the year of turmoil in France that eventually brought down de Gaulle and of the Prague Spring in Czechoslovakia when Alexander Dubcek's 'human face of communism' was ground into the dirt by Soviet tanks, ended with Harold Wilson still firmly in the saddle.

Chapter 6: In Place of Harmony

It had been a favourite theory of Wilson that his erstwhile rival Hugh Gaitskell deliberately set out to find dragons to slay, in order to consolidate and advance his position. 'Saint Harold' now mounted his own charger in search of enemies whose subjugation would enhance his standing as a legend in his own lifetime. There being no fire-breathing monsters in the vicinity, he alighted on the next best thing: the trade unions.

It was an extraordinary gamble for a politician of such a cautious nature, but Wilson could plead a growing economic imperative. The government's wage freeze powers, which had worked, were gradually eased down during 1967, though compulsory notification procedures remained in place. In March 1968, Chancellor Jenkins promulgated a 3.5 per cent 'norm' for pay rises, which could only be exceeded through self-financing productivity deals. To beef up this concept, the old Ministry of Labour was transformed in April 1968 into the Department of Employment and Productivity, and Barbara Castle, Wilson's close ally, took the 'bed of nails' over from Ray Gunter, a right-wing drunk. She inherited from the crumbling DEA the task of holding the line on prices and incomes, at a time when support for the policy was on the wane, though not disastrously so. In 1967, the party conference had backed the government, and as late at May 1968, left-wing MPs opposing any form of statutory policy could not muster four dozen votes in the Commons.

Events outside Westminster gathered pace. The Donovan Report, published in June, noted a significant shift of collective bargaining from national to factory level largely in the hands of shop stewards. It proposed a Commission on Industrial Relations to promote best practice in industry, and measures to curtail unofficial strikes, while stopping short of criminal sanctions against unions or strike leaders. These measures, proposed after three years of exhaustive consideration, were plainly too little, too late for a problem that was getting out of hand. In the year to August 1968, 3.5 million working days were lost through strikes, mostly unofficial. The Tories latched on to public disquiet about industrial disruption with proposals for a tough framework of legal discipline, *Fair Deal at Work*, based on the ideas of Conservative lawyers. Wilson did not fully share their enthusiasm for draconian curbs on union freedoms, but he knew a dragon when he saw one. Never having been a trade unionist, or held down what many of his electors in Huyton would have called 'a proper job', he was frustrated that these leviathans born in Victorian times could still exercise such power over industrial change and economic growth. Perhaps he was also tiring of his beer and sandwiches peacemaking role, which unions like the railwaymen had come almost to expect as their due.

The plates in the labour movement began to shift dramatically that autumn. At the party conference, ex-minister Frank Cousins of the TGWU led the charge against legal constraints on pay bargaining and secured a majority of almost six-to-one against the government. A confrontation was inevitable, and in the Queen's Speech Wilson signalled his intention to act. Barbara Castle was tasked with producing a White Paper on the reform of trade union law, loosely based on

Donovan. Just how loosely became clear when she proposed compulsory pre-strike ballots, ministerial powers to order a 28-day cooling-off period before a strikes could begin and a Commission on Industrial Relations (CIR) whose rulings in disputes could be enforced through fines against employers, unions or strikers themselves, possibly through attachment of wages. The pill was sugared with provisions for recognition of trade unions and the granting of bargaining rights. Inevitably, interest would focus on the 'penal clauses'. Castle moved fast, presenting her White Paper, *In Place of Strife* (the title was suggested by her *Mirror* journalist husband, Ted) to ministers, the TUC and the Confederation of British Industry (CBI) before its approval by Cabinet on 14 January, by ten votes to six. Among the dissenters were Callaghan, a former official of the tax collectors' union, and the ex-miner Roy Mason. The Home Secretary's role would prove pivotal.

As a package, *In Place of Strife* was nothing short of revolutionary. A Labour government proposed to shackle the very people whose voluntary organisations had founded the party that put Wilson and his Cabinet into power. Although some union leaders were attracted to the positive aspects of the package – statutory recognition, for instance – they could not publicly accept sanctions against shop stewards, the front line of industrial organisation, no matter how troublesome they could sometimes be.

The TUC general council rejected sanctions, sending the acting General Secretary Vic Feather (the outgoing General Secretary, George Woodcock had a heart attack when the proposals were unveiled and subsequently accepted appointment as chairman of the CIR), to negotiate with the government. Feather was conciliatory, but tied by his brief. Moreover, the trade union group of 137 Labour MPs, then (as now) the largest in the PLP, did not like the White Paper. Callaghan had been stirring the pot vigorously. In a Commons debate on 3 March 1969, 53 Labour MPs voted against the White Paper and 39 abstained – almost three-quarters of the trade union group and easily enough to defeat a Bill unless the Tories supported the government. Opposition also surfaced on the party executive, where miners' leader Joe Gormley pushed through a resolution rejecting legislation based on the White Paper.

Among the rebels was Home Secretary Callaghan, whose leadership of the revolt swiftly became public knowledge, further undermining the government's position. Wilson claimed to have slapped down his awkward squad, invoking the rule of Cabinet responsibility. In reality, he seemed incapable of dealing with union mulishness or his own ministers. By mid-April, he had watered down the package, removing pre-strike ballots – the one element that could genuinely be described as 'democratising the unions' – but still failed to sell a short, interim Bill to a sullen PLP despite claiming that it was critical to the government's continuation in office.

Meanwhile, the TUC, after flatly rejecting any move to bring the criminal law into industrial relations, had been busy drawing up an alternative strategy based on Donovan, to be called *Programme for Action*. It called for joint, voluntary steps by the government and both sides of industry to tackle unofficial strikes. Under pressure, Wilson tacked further towards the unions, offering to delay the penal clauses while the TUC finessed its ideas. The unions called a special congress for 8 June to draw up battle lines, stimulating Callaghan to propose a delay until after that date. The whole sorry business was unravelling fast. Hostility in Cabinet to the Home Secretary's public disloyalty was strong enough to make him offer his resignation. Wilson urged him to stay and *be convinced*.

Callaghan was convinced, but not of the strength of Wilson's position. Next for the axe was the cooling-off period, or conciliation pause, which Bob Mellish, the hard-line new Chief Whip, offered to abandon. In the background, the July Plotters were busy again (it being almost that time of year), with much the same pusillanimous results. With the Prime Minister virtually a political hostage to the unions, neither Jenkins nor Callaghan felt it wise to move against him

Wilson did not give up hope, holding a top secret summit at Chequers on 1 June, where over roast duck he pleaded with Feather, Jack Jones and Hugh Scanlon not to place him in history alongside Ramsay MacDonald and Dubcek. His final scolding to the AEU president, *I'm not going to surrender to your tanks, Hughie*, was leaked to the press under the defiant headline *Get your tanks off my lawn!*[1] The Croydon Congress duly repudiated sanctions against unions, and Wilson decided three days later to go down with all guns blazing,

Get your tanks off my lawn!

WILSON (ATTR.)

or, at any rate, with the possibility of them being fired at some unspecified later date. Penal clauses would be in the Bill, but they would go on the back burner while the TUC formalised its measures to curb wildcat strikes. On 17 June, Wilson accepted a diluted form of the conciliation pause, while angrily refuting suggestions of capitulation, fortified by several stiff brandies at a Cabinet meeting in the Commons.

His red line was credible action against unofficial strikes: a TUC declaration of intent would not do. Overt and secret talks, with Feather smuggled in and out of Number 10, continued for several days, with resolve on the government side unwinding until Wilson suggested a *solemn and binding undertaking* on the part of the TUC to mediate in factory walkouts. Unions failing to get their members back to work when the disputes procedure had not been exhausted would be reported to Congress, with the ultimate sanction of suspension.

To the man in the street, and particularly the trade unionist on the shopfloor, this was a toothless punishment, a petty restriction that would not deter militants. In *The Times*, columnist Bernard Levin derided 'Solomon Binding', and the cartoonist Garland in the *Daily Telegraph* showed Wilson and Feather as two dazed boxers in the ring exchanging documents, one entitled '*In Place of Action*' and the other '*Programme for Strife*'. That was about right, but Wilson insisted on proclaiming a famous victory, calling a press conference at which, with Feather and Castle beside him, he lauded his agreement with the TUC. A relieved, silent Cabinet endorsed the deal, and it was gracelessly supported by the PLP. Wilson even told Healey that the classic trade union fix *gives us all we wanted*.[2] It did nothing of the sort, and 18 June 1969 went into history as the day of Wilson's most humiliating defeat, suffered at the hands of his so-called comrades. In truth, he never understood them, and they knew they had the measure of him.

With the benefit of hindsight, Wilson's proposals were about right. And by frustrating his – by today's standards, modest – reforms, myopic union leaders merely postponed the day of reckoning to a time when a Conservative government with a majority as big as Labour's was then could impose much more far-reaching legislation, and make it stick. Fortunately, this debacle occurred on the brink of the summer parliamentary recess, when politicians of every stripe are itching to get away from the febrile world of Westminster. The appetite for subversion was sated. Wilson was able to retire to the Scillies to lick his wounds, and come out fighting again in the autumn conference season. At the Portsmouth congress of the TUC, he was bullish about the economy and showed no contrition about *In Place of Strife*, urging instead that the unions respect 'Solomon Binding'. The party conference in Brighton took on a pre-election atmosphere, with delegates cheering Wilson's new-found conversion to the environment, which he identified as the burning issue of the 1970s. It did not have quite the same ring to it as the *white-hot revolution* slogan of 1963.

Technically, Wilson could have soldiered on until the early summer of 1971, after five years had elapsed, before calling a general election, but modern convention dictates that parliaments last only four years. Attention therefore focussed on alternative dates in 1970. Labour had been thrashed in a string of by-elections, losing 17 seats to nationalists and Liberals but mostly to the Conservatives. Swings against the government of 20 per cent were commonplace, though were now falling back to about half that level. The balance of payments was moving back into surplus. Under Heath, the Conservatives had made some headway, taking advantage of Wilson's humiliation over labour law to promise tough legislation of their own. However, as memories of his rebuff by the men in boiler suits receded, Wilson began to feel more confident about winning an unprecedented third term.

The steady return of a 'feel good factor' was shattered by events in Northern Ireland. A return of 'the Troubles' there had been foreshadowed on 5 October 1968, when the Royal Ulster Constabulary (RUC) batoned, water-cannoned and finally crushed a peaceful civil rights march in Londonderry. The marchers demanded votes, jobs and homes, all of which were in short supply in the province's second city because of gerrymandering, corrupt local government and employment discrimination by the ruling Ulster Unionists. The march was banned, and civil rights activists appealed to Wilson, then at the party conference, to intervene. He did nothing, and the demonstration went ahead. It was put down with singular ferocity, in traditional RUC style, but on this occasion the police violence was captured on television and was flashed round the world, creating grave embarrassment for the government especially in the USA's large, highly-vocal Irish community. To Wilson's alarm, three Labour MPs joined the Irish republican Labour MP, Gerry Fitt, on a fact-finding visit to the province.

As Prime Minister of the United Kingdom, Wilson could not avoid becoming involved. Indeed, he had shown more than a cursory interest in 'John Bull's Other Island', returning the bones of the hanged Irish traitor Roger Casement to Dublin in 1965, and promising social justice for the province. He regularly met Irish prime ministers, and abolished trade barriers between the two countries. But he had not been fully engaged with Northern Ireland, accepting at face value the Unionists' false pledges to reform. After the police siege of Londonderry, his policy of benign neglect would not wash. He summoned the province's premier, Terence O'Neill, to London on 4 November 1968 and told him in no uncertain terms that Ulster must reform itself on democratic lines. The Unionists who ruled Londonderry, a majority Catholic, Nationalist city, began hasty changes in housing allocation. Full local government franchise for all Catholics followed two weeks later, and repeal of arbitrary powers of arrest and detention were promised.

Once again, it was too little, too late. Civil rights agitation intensified, as did the quasi-military response of the authorities, particularly the hated B-Specials, a paramilitary police entirely composed of Protestants. The Catholic enclave of Bogside in Londonderry barricaded itself in, and IRA guns began appearing. By the summer of 1969, street warfare had engulfed the city. At a secret meeting with Callaghan (who as

Home Secretary, had Cabinet responsibility for the province) at the St Mawgan RAF base in Cornwall – the nearest secure venue to the Scillies – Wilson decided to mobilise the British army, following pleas from Ulster's new Prime Minister, Major James Chichester-Clark. The troops went in on 14 August. Initially, they were welcomed by the Catholics of Londonderry and Belfast as saviours from the brutality of the B-Specials, but applause gradually turned to fury when it dawned on Nationalists that the confused troops, behaving as though they faced insurgents in Malaya, were there to maintain the *status quo*. This had not been Wilson's intention. He saw the role of the army as restoring law and order, not buttressing a corrupt system. He wanted the B-Specials to be disarmed, and reform of the RUC, a change that would not happen for more than 30 years and then only half-heartedly. Talks with Chichester-Clark produced the 'Downing Street Declaration' at the end of August, designed to chip away at Unionist monopoly of power, employment and housing. However, any hint of reform only served to inflame Loyalist sentiment, and troops first used their guns on civilians against Protestants in Belfast's notorious Shankhill Road after the murder of an RUC officer. From that point, the descent into virtual civil war was inexorable, but voters were getting used to seeing television pictures of violence on the streets of Northern Ireland. As long as the war did not come to 'the mainland', it was far enough away not to impede normal politics at home. If anything, the engagement in Ulster bolstered Wilson's authority, restoring some of the leadership credentials lost in his battle with the TUC. He may have shrunk from conflict with the unions, but not with the Unionists.

In this atmosphere of returning boldness, Wilson scanned his diary for possible election dates, consulting his inner Cabinet of senior ministers in late April 1970. A minority argued for delay until the autumn, but Wilson plumped forcefully for 18 June, with a short, sharp four-week campaign designed to take the Tories, who were known to be planning a summer propaganda blitz, off guard. Encouraging results across the country in the May local elections closed the argument in Wilson's favour. He was raring to go. The opinion polls had moved decisively in Labour's favour, and his government had a positive narrative to put to the electorate. Wage increases were rising faster than inflation, and the national felt better off. Britain's balance of payments was running at a £600 million surplus. Men thrown out of work could expect redundancy payments from the state. Child allowances and pensions had improved. On the social front, Labour had chimed with the mood of the Sixties, partially decriminalising homosexuality, ending capital punishment and advancing the cause of women. *In Place of Strife* apart, it was a good record to put before the British people. Wilson wanted a 'doctor's mandate', claiming that his government were the best doctors the people had. Privately, he believed he would get back with a majority of around 20, and predicted a government victory in a letter to President Nixon. 'Dr Wilson' was definitely in charge of the campaign, which he sought to portray as a personal battle between an avuncular, trusted man who knew best and a barking right-winger who would plunge the country into industrial and economic chaos. Edward Heath did indeed offer a serious political alternative: tax cuts, an end to state aid for 'lame ducks' in industry, and harsh laws against trade union militancy. This platform, hammered out in the Selsdon Hotel in Croydon, invited the modern Conservative archetype of 'Selsdon Man'.

It was the very model of a modern general election, with political advertising on television and vast amounts of airtime for the leaders, which Wilson embraced avidly. It was a flaming June, perfect weather for electioneering, and Wilson used the antipodean trick of 'walkabout' to great effect. 'Anything but policy' seemed to be the watchword, and for three weeks the trick worked. Labour remained ahead in the polls, and a jaunty Wilson revelled in the prospect of four more years. However, Barbara Castle was haunted by the fear of a silent majority waiting to come out and punish the cocky Tyke who had dominated the campaign.

The economic good news tailed off. Bad inflation figures and an unexpectedly sharp rise in the Retail Price Index were compounded three days before polling day, when the trade figures showed a £31 million deficit, caused by the state airline's purchase of two Jumbo Jets. Wilson feared that changed voting habits, with more working women voting during the day, would hurt Labour. Furthermore, male morale took a beating when England was beaten in the World Cup quarter-finals by Germany, a reverse of the result in 1966. Two days before polling day, Labour's private pollsters predicted the unthinkable: a Tory victory. Turnout on 18 August was down to 72 per cent, the lowest since the war, and while Labour's share of the vote remained at a respectable 43 per cent, the Tory share shot up to more than 46 per cent, garnering an extra two million. Labour lost 60 seats, returning as the Opposition with 287, while the derided Heath won 330, a gain of 68. The Conservatives were in with a majority of 30. On the government side, George Brown was among the losers, at Belper in Derbyshire. As this author can testify, his first reaction was to tell his wife Sophie: 'This means we shall have to give up the flat in Marble Arch.'

Much more than agreeable accommodation had been lost, though the defeated premier did take refuge at Chequers for the weekend. 'Dr Wilson' had asked for a mandate, and the people had decisively rejected him. At the age of 54, with no obvious prospect of returning to Number 10, he looked finished.

Chapter 7: Locust Years

Having asked for a doctor's mandate, Wilson had suffered the indignity of the voters seeking a second opinion, and on the whole preferring it. Opinion about the impact of this rebuff was mixed. Some found him exhausted and bowed, physically shrunken, even: the stoop more pronounced, the hunched shoulders gathered in more closely. But Tony Benn thought he bounced back within weeks 'just like an India-rubber man'. In truth, his response was as mixed as anyone's. He could be blasé about the prospects for politics and his party, and depressed in virtually the next breath. What he could not do was blame anyone else. Amid subversive muttering about his 'presidential' style, Wilson had shouldered the entire burden of leadership during the campaign out of a conviction that he, and only he, could convince the electorate of Labour's fitness to continue in office. He had gambled on the value of his own charisma, and lost.

It was equally true that while there were aspirants for his job as Prime Minister, enthusiasm to oust him as leader of the Opposition was not so pronounced. This was unsurprising. Who would want to lead a party that was so deeply divided over the biggest issue facing the nation – Europe – and which at times seemed on the brink of an outright split? When the shrunken PLP met at Church House on 29 June, he was re-elected unopposed, after a pantomime scene in which Leo

Abse tried to challenge his coronation on the logical grounds that Labour had fought an election on the personality of the leader and must now ask whether it had the right leader. He found no support for this embarrassing question about the King's clothing. In a contested election Roy Jenkins was returned as deputy leader, a comfort to the pro-Marketeers. However, Michael Foot, the darling of the Left, signalled his arrival as a man of the future with 67 votes, and took responsibility for Fuel and Power in Wilson's first Shadow Cabinet. Healey took on foreign affairs and Callaghan remained at Home. In the party, the Left gained ground in the national executive elections, but serious rebellion would have to wait until the electoral bruises healed.

Wilson decided to anticipate the historians by writing his own verdict on his two governments. The project would serve a dual purpose: of pre-emptive rehabilitation, and of putting his finances, family and political, on a sound footing. Unlike the largesse delivered to Opposition leaders today, no state provision was then available. A number of rich friends, mostly Jewish businessmen attracted to this strong friend of Israel, contributed to a secret trust fund set up by Lord Goodman, and payments from Transport House helped to defray the £20,000 annual cost of running his office now situated in the Commons. High office had not made him a rich man. Wilson left Number 10 with an overdraft, but the sale of his house in Hampstead Garden Suburb yielded £14,000. In October 1970, he bought a house in the country, Grange Farm, half a dozen miles from Chequers and close to his favourite golf club at Ellesborough. To finance his country squire lifestyle, he worked tirelessly on his book, *The Labour Government 1964-1970*, throughout the winter. He had help, most noticeably from the historian Martin Gilbert, but the thumping great tome that emerged from his labours was essentially all his own work.

In those days, it was considered *infra dig.*, if not actually unlawful, to disclose the secrets of Cabinet so soon after leaving government, but Wilson knew that Crossman and Benn were both keeping diaries and intended to publish. He was determined to win the race to the printers with his half-million-word apologia. Wilson won a £30,000 advance from his publishers, and the *Sunday Times* agreed to pay £250,000 for serialisation rights. This was a gigantic sum of money for the time (probably in excess of £1 million today). He was understandably sensitive about being seen to profit so greatly from his years in power, and exploded on television when David Dimbleby asked him about the payments, claiming that the *facts* in newspapers had been *invented*. The facts in his 836-page book were certainly not invented. Nor were they assembled in a literary manner. It did not sell well, and could not have earned its advance. Wilson did not break major confidences, and the 'orgy of self-justification' as Cecil King described the book, failed to establish his political record as the pioneer of a 'white hot' revolution that had changed society. Given the nature of events on his watch, it could hardly have been otherwise.

Elected to the Commons for Coventry East in 1945, Richard Crossman (1907–74) held his seat until his death. He was a prominent figure on the left of the Labour Party and a supporter of Nye Bevan. A member of the NEC from 1952–67, he was briefly Party Chairman. Crossman was appointed Minister of Housing and Local Government in Wilson's first Cabinet, becoming Leader of the House of Commons in 1966 and Health Secretary in 1968. He resigned from the Labour front bench in 1970. His diaries, which came out in 1975, were the first ministerial diaries to be published.

Fortunately, he had real events to help sustain his position. Within weeks of becoming Prime Minister, Heath had to contend with a national dock strike. He declared a state of emergency, the first of five during his premiership, and all triggered by industrial disruption. Blooded in this first encounter with the unions, Heath moved swiftly to legislate against strikes. Shamelessly, Labour under Wilson fought the Industrial Relations Bill all the way through its parliamentary progress, even though its resemblance to *In Place of Strife* was unmistakable. Benn saw this process as 'a party purging itself of government'.

Wisely, Wilson played little part in the fight against the bill, much of which was extra-parliamentary including political strikes and the biggest demonstration in London since the Chartists. As a parliamentarian, he disapproved of industrial action for political ends, and indeed this form of syndicalism was largely foreign to Britain. It failed to gain universal backing, but the unions nonetheless opposed the Act from the day it received Royal Assent in August 1971. They discovered a relatively painless device to make it unworkable. In order to secure the modest collective bargaining benefits available under the law, unions were required to join a government register. The TUC boycotted the register, threatening affiliates with expulsion if they co-operated, eventually throwing out more than 30 unions for failing to toe the line.

The legislation did nothing to stem the rising tide of industrial warfare. In 1971, 13 million days were lost through industrial action, up two million on Wilson's last year in office. In 1972, the figure almost doubled again, but this surge was due largely to the first national miners' strike since 1926. In late 1971, having changed their rules so that a 55 per cent majority in a pithead ballot would be sufficient to call a strike, the National Union of Mineworkers (NUM) began a crippling overtime ban. It turned into an all-out strike in February 1972, lasting seven weeks.

Unlawful secondary picketing at the power stations turned off electricity supplies. The government responded with a state of emergency and a Court of Inquiry. Labour's National Executive Committee (NEC), on which sat Joe Gormley, the NUM president, backed the strikers. Wilson, the politician who 30 years earlier had argued passionately for a new deal for coal and miners, kept his head down. The Wilberforce Inquiry recommended huge pay rises, but the NUM held out for more and ended up getting virtually anything they asked for from Heath late at night in Downing Street. On this occasion, they drank the Prime Minister's whisky rather than beer.

Badly shaken by the success of the miners' insurrectionary tactics, and faced with knock-on claims, Heath did a U-turn towards Wilson's policy of a voluntary incomes policy. Negotiations with the TUC foundered, and the government was compelled to legislate in November 1971, freezing prices and incomes for six months, followed by stages two and three of limits on pay rises. In parallel, Wilson had been secretly negotiating with TUC general secretary Vic Feather for a 'social compact' (later upgraded to 'contract') between Labour and the unions for inclusion in the party's next election manifesto. With such an agreement in the bag, it was argued, Labour could present itself as the party of industrial peace. Negotiations took place in a new body, the TUC-Labour Party Liaison Committee, bringing together leaders of both wings in a corporatist instrument of power that consolidated the social partnership role of the unions. They liked that.

They did not, however, like the prospect of performing a similar role in Europe. The Labour's government's application to join the Common Market, lying moribund on the table after De Gaulle's veto, was revived when the General resigned in April 1969. Wilson appointed George Thomson as minister for Europe, and put out fresh feelers to the French. A White Paper on the benefits of entry had appeared in February 1970, but the election, in which Europe played virtually no role, put paid to Labour's accession initiative. Heath, easily the most pro-European premier of modern times, lost no time in picking up Wilson's uncertain baton.

Talks began directly after the election, placing Wilson in a dilemma. Practically, he favoured entry. Politically, he knew that opinion in the party was running fast in the other direction. His task, as ever, was to hold the party together. He would do this, whatever the charges of opportunism, however sinuous the twists and turns required, and no matter what the cost to his reputation. For Wilson, the paramountcy of keeping Labour intact as a going political concern was unarguable. If 100 per cent unity was not possible, then 90 per cent, and so on down to 51 per cent. There could be different opinions, but only one party. The American motto, *e pluribus unum*, from many, one, could have been his own. As the events of 1981, when the European wing split to form the Social Democrats, pushing Labour into the wilderness for more than a decade, were to demonstrate, his solidifying instincts were correct.

Wilson's most urgent mission was to prevent the Europhobes from committing Labour to outright opposition to the EEC, *in principle*. The 1970 conference voted by the narrowest of margin – 95,000 votes out of six million – not to oppose entry. He drew the teeth of hostility by making his support for entry conditional *on the right terms*. This was a perfect exit strategy that enabled Wilson to denounce the government's terms as a sell-out. Benn suggested a referendum on the issue, a stratagem initially offensive to Wilson, but one which began to gain ground in the party. It was assumed, quite wrongly, that public opinion, as expressed by opinion polls, would reject entry. When Heath's successful negotiating outcome was published in June 1971, Wilson duly rejected the terms. A special conference, at which an EEC official described the leader's speech as 'a man pouring shit all over himself', deferred a decision until October.[1] At that point, Labour formally rejected the terms but also spurned a bid to oppose entry on any terms. The door was still ajar, if not by much. Wilson took no part in the debate.

When the Commons finally debated the Heath package, Wilson reluctantly recognised the strength of feeling among MPs and the five-to-one vote at conference, and imposed a three-line whip against the government. Heath triumphed by 356 to 244. Led by his deputy, Roy Jenkins, 68 Labour MPs defied Wilson and voted with the Conservatives, and a further 20 abstained. A third of the PLP had snubbed their leader, over a stand in which he did not genuinely believe and had only adopted to secure unity at any price. The price was public obloquy. *The Times*, which once clamoured 'sooner George Brown drunk than Harold Wilson sober' thundered that Wilson must never be Prime Minister again, having sacrificed national interest to party interest, 'a crime for which a party leader can never be forgiven'. The denizens of New Printing House Square, who did not have to stand for election (and who later proved at least as two-faced on Europe) plainly did not understand party politics. The media consistently under-estimated Wilson. It was not fatal. He made a good living out of being under-estimated. Heath signed the Treaty of Accession on 22 January 1972, just before the lights began going out all over Britain. The French insisted upon holding a referendum on UK entry, instantly giving credibility to Benn's referendum idea. Wilson shifted his ground in favour, and won the backing of the PLP, prompting Jenkins's resignation from the Shadow Cabinet, a move described by his biographer Austen Morgan as 'probably the greatest rupture in the collective leadership of the party since the war'.

If so, it did not appear so at the time. Wilson reshuffled his Shadow Cabinet, giving Foreign Affairs to Callaghan and the Treasury to Healey. At the 1972 conference, Wilson won support for a 'consultative' referendum and again secured narrow rejection of opposition in principle. Everything was still to play for. Britain became a full member of the EEC on 1 January 1973, along with

'Sooner George Brown drunk than Harold Wilson sober.'

THE TIMES

Ireland and Denmark. Wilson had achieved the near-miracle of keeping the Labour stagecoach on the road, with the loss of only one high-ranking passenger.

Northern Ireland consumed much of what was left of Wilson's attention in this turbulent period, at any rate, when he was not engaged in burnishing his historical legacy. His record of government was to be followed by a second book, *The Governance of Britain*. For this *magnum opus*, his advance was considerably lower than his first work, at £5,000. If the sales of *The Labour Government* had disappointed, so perhaps did the portentous title of his new volume on how Britain is governed billed as 'unprecedented, the first on this subject ever written by a man who has had the supreme responsibility of government'. It was not to see the light of day until 1976.

Chapter 8: In Power Through Strife

While no politician blithely spurns the prospect of power, few Labour figures would have been as reluctant as Harold Wilson to be handed the premiership via industrial insurrection. After all, had he not faced down the National Union of Seamen, and was he not the only true begetter of *In Place of Strife?* However, the lure of Downing Street through violent picket lines was an enticing scenario when Britain's coal miners flexed their industrial muscles again in 1973.

The build-up to the second confrontation between the National Union of Mineworkers and the Heath government began in the spring, when coalfield branches began submitting their pay claims to their annual conference in July. Formally, they, like all other workers, were bound by Phase Three of the Conservatives' statutory incomes policy, which laid down a maximum 'norm' of 9 per cent from November. There was some wriggle-room under an 'anti-social hours' clause, deliberately inserted to mollify the miners. Heath did not want a rerun of the 1972 debacle.

This process was under way as Wilson sought to build up his party's image as the deliverer of industrial harmony, in contrast to Heath's confrontational style. In February 1973, the TUC-Labour Party Liaison Committee published a joint policy statement sharply critical of the Industrial Relations Act. Against Heath's best intentions, the National Industrial

Relations Court set up under the Act had jailed five London dockers the previous year for acting in contempt of orders to cease blockading a road haulage company. The dispute was of piffling industrial significance, but it brought dockers out on strike, where they were joined by other groups of workers including Fleet Street printers. The TUC was obliged to threaten a one-day general strike. The 'Pentonville Five' were freed on the orders of the Official Solicitor, a fairy godmother whose existence (to protect the rights of children and contemnors) was hitherto unsuspected, but the mayhem had served to highlight the high-stakes unworkability of the law.

Wilson agreed to repeal of the Act by a future Labour government, in return for union acceptance of an independent conciliation service – ACAS, which still exists – with powers to intervene in strikes. The powers were, however, voluntary. The rest of the document outlined a worker-friendly alternative economic strategy, and the whole caboodle would be wrapped up in a 'wide-ranging agreement' between the unions and a Labour government once in power. The Social Contract, quickly denounced as the 'Social Con-Trick', was born.

The various elements of Labour were at this time running on parallel lines, rather than twin-track. Militant groups like the miners spoke in Marxist tones of 'creating the concrete conditions' – i.e. ungovernability – for the downfall of Heath and the return of a Labour government committed to socialist policies. This was as much anathema to Wilson as it was to the Conservatives, but he nonetheless benefited politically from the firebrand rhetoric and did not go out of his way publicly to condemn it. Simultaneously, he was wooing the union barons (he had once snorted *they're dukes!*) into a political pact designed to gain maximum electoral advantage from the Tory government's discomfiture. Each group profited from the other, and Wilson pocketed the political takings. Privately, Heath and his ministers shared public unease about the debacle created by its labour legislation. Days lost through strikes had fallen since the *annus horribilis* of 1972, but were still running at seven million a year. Through his employment secretary Maurice Macmillan, Heath began secret soundings with the CIR to identify possible concessions that would make the Act more palatable to the unions, and hence at least partially workable.

When they met at Inverness in July, NUM militants adopted the union's biggest ever pay claim, amounting to £138 million a year. Lawrence Daly, the union's General Secretary, warned of 'a confrontation not of our own making, but of the making of "Benito" Heath,' even though he bore a stronger resemblance to Mussolini than did the Prime Minister. Encouraged by the quadrupling of Middle East oil prices in the wake of the Yom Kippur war, which made coal even more vital, they staged part two of their earlier strike, banning overtime from November 1973. Heath imposed a state of emergency and then put the nation on a three-day week. Mid-winter power cuts became the order of the day, and thousands of workers were laid off as secondary picketing once again disrupted generating stations. Despite the crisis, ministers judged it unwise to invoke the Industrial Relations Act, fearing an even greater slide into anarchy.

Wilson engaged in private diplomacy with Joe Gormley, the politically moderate but industrially militant miners' leader. The NUM president offered Heath a solution: if the National Coal Board paid the men extra for the time they spent going down the mine and returning home – the so-called 'waiting, winding and washing time' – then he would abide by the 9 per cent pay rise norm. Gormley went round to Lord North Street and informed Wilson of his peace feelers. Wilson accused the miners' leader of *pulling the government's irons out of the fire for them*, and scuppered the putative deal by going public on the secret deal.[1] Gormley, a member of Labour's NEC and canny politician in his own right, was incandescent. To have the Tories playing politics with an industrial dispute was bad enough, but to have his own party doing it was 'beyond belief'. He never forgave Wilson. The NUM secured a four-to-one majority for all-out industrial action in a pithead ballot, and on 5 February called a national strike.

Two days later, Heath, assailed on all sides by contradictory advice, called a 'Who rules?' election for 28 February. As the nation shivered in the dark, there had been rumours for several weeks that he would go to the country, but the Prime Minister dithered. The original date for polling day, 7 February, slipped by. Conventional wisdom opposed a single-issue election, because voters could not be relied on to give the right answer and would begin asking other, awkward questions during the campaign. Wilson had ordered contingency planning, just in case Heath's hand was forced. The Shadow Cabinet and NEC met in December to draw up a campaign document, which was put to the Liaison Committee twice, on 4 and 11 January before being approved by the unions. This document would form the basis of an election manifesto. It vetoed statutory incomes policy, the very issue at stake in the current crisis, and did not commit the unions to a voluntary arrangement.

Wilson had no great expectations of winning.[2] This was not his preferred ground on which to challenge the Tories. He had no taste for a campaign based on public support for striking miners, particularly after the NUM's communist vice-president urged British soldiers to disobey orders if called in to break the strike. He told the Shadow Cabinet on 30 January that McGahey's remarks had done *a great deal of damage* and 100 Labour MPs were deployed to sign a motion hostile to 'politicisation' of the dispute. Wilson and Callaghan rushed out a statement 'utterly repudiating' McGahey's remarks. Heath realised he had been dealt a potentially winning card, and went on television to say: 'We can't afford the luxury of tearing ourselves apart any more. This time, the strife has to stop. Only you can stop it. It's time for your voice to be heard, the voice of the moderate and reasonable people of Britain, the voice of the majority.' Had Wilson been in Number 10, not Transport House, it would be very easy to imagine him saying exactly the same thing. Much more than the seamen, the miners had influential communists and men of the hard left on their national executive.

Wilson claimed afterwards to have done his level best to avoid a strike, mediating between the NUM and the government, but Gormley's evidence suggests that his motives were at best equivocal, at worst cynically advantageous. There was no guarantee that Labour would win a 'Who rules?' election. Much would turn on the public view of who was more guilty – the Tories for precipitating the strike, or the Labour Party for being so closely associated with the unions, but particularly the NUM, whose president was on the party executive. As the country had lurched from one state of emergency to the next over the previous three years, Labour had enjoyed a lead in the opinion polls. Now, at crunch time, they were two points behind the government on 31 per cent.

Labour's manifesto, *Let Us Work Together*, stressed the virtues of co-operation in industry, a strategy enshrined in the Social Contract. Prompted by *The Times*, he even offered to extend the deal to the CBI, representing employers. Instead of being a mildly-fraudulent compact with the power-brokers of the labour movement, it was to be an umbrella under which all could shelter. And the man holding it would be the calm, avuncular figure of Harold Wilson, able to rise above the fray, in contrast to the class warrior who had turned the lights off. It was consummate Wilsonian positioning. In a speech in Nottingham, he urged the value of a social contract between the government and both sides of industry. The strategy had to be carefully nuanced, to avoid giving the impression that Labour was no more than the strikers' friend. Heath derided the idea, returning to the theme of a statutory incomes policy, though his current impasse in a strike of dimensions sufficient to put the economy on half-time scarcely recommended such a policy to voters.

On 21 February, Derek Robinson, an Oxford academic who was deputy chairman of the Pay Board conducting the inquiry into pit pay, briefed journalists with interim findings that the miners had slipped further down the wages league than had been calculated. Their claim was substantially justified. In the excitement, few appreciated that Robinson's father, a miner in Barnsley, was himself on strike. The story was front-page news. Heath, having already pledged to honour the board's findings, was dumbfounded. Wilson immediately accused him of calling a sham election. Worse was to follow. Trade figures for January came out, showing a deficit of £383 million, the mirror image of Labour's discomfiture in 1970. Two days before polling day, Campbell Adamson, Director-General of the CBI, told a conference of managers that the Industrial Relations Act ought to be repealed. He thought he was speaking privately, but his explosive comments swiftly leaked to the press and further damaged the government's case. In five short days, Heath's original pretext for the poll, his policy to defeat militancy and his economic credibility had collapsed. If that were not enough, on 26 February, Tory rebel Enoch Powell, whose inflammatory speeches about coloured immigration had won him a wide following, most notably among working-class voters, denounced the election as fraudulent and declared that he had voted Labour in his Wolverhampton constituency. He did so in support of Wilson's anti-Europe stance, which was itself more apparent than real. The move was co-ordinated with Wilson's office, a bizarre step even by the standards of this topsy-turvy election. In fairness, it must be said that Wilson's personality dominated the campaign, even though he tried to restrain his natural presidential instincts. He was mobbed in Huddersfield, and his 'masterplan', based on Cromwell's order of battle at Marston Moor – first week: containment of the Tories; second: attack; third, flank assaults on issues arising – went like clockwork.

The polling day that none of the politicians really wanted produced a dramatic result. Despite the wintry weather, turnout was up by three million votes, to almost 79 per cent, a figure that had not been reached since the 'never had it so good' election of 1959. Labour dropped half a million, taking 37 per cent of the popular vote, with the Tories losing more than a million to pick up a larger share at just under 38 per cent. Heath garnered more votes than Wilson, but Labour came out in front with 301 seats to the Conservatives 297. Whoever ran the country, voters decided, it was not the Tory premier who had called the election. Equally, Wilson had not been handed the keys to Number 10. He was 17 seats short of an overall majority in the Commons, and could not book his taxi to Buckingham Palace. For the first time in half a century, the Liberals, with 14 seats, held the balance of power. Heath refused to concede defeat, a stance deplored by Wilson as the action of a sportsman refusing to accept the verdict of the umpire.

Nevertheless, the Labour leader kept his counsel as Heath

tried to salvage a coalition administration from the debacle. On 1 March, as the final shape of the parliament became clear, he flew down from Liverpool and assembled the Shadow Cabinet in Transport House. Having affirmed his readiness to form a government, he adjourned to Grange Farm to await the outcome of Heath's negotiations with the Liberals. Their leader, Jeremy Thorpe, was willing to enter a coalition. His MPs were not, and after three days the talks collapsed. Armed with this bargaining chip, Wilson adamantly refused to govern with the Liberals on a joint programme. History, in the shape of Ramsay MacDonald and the great betrayal of 1931 in the National Government, was still fresh in the memory of his generation. But he would govern alone, as a minority administration, and in that capacity he was summoned to the Palace an hour after Heath resigned at 6.30 p.m. on 4 March. The media turned on the miners, and an infuriated Joe Gormley insisted that it had not been a political strike: 'it was *not* the miners but Ted Heath who brought himself down.' With a little help from the NUM, he might have conceded.

The first task of the new government was to get the miners back to work and the wheels of industry turning once again. Wilson summoned TUC leaders to Downing Street at noon on his first day in office and the CBI immediately afterwards, to discuss a settlement in the coal industry rather than the hi-falutin social contract. He appointed Michael Foot as Employment Secretary, with a brief to do a deal with the miners on the basis of the Pay Board report, which gave the NUM its pay claim for face workers in full, supplemented by further improvements approved by the new Chancellor, Denis Healey. The state of emergency was abandoned the next day, 7 March. A tumultuous period in British political history was over. It was unclear where Wilson's unlooked for success would take the nation.

Chapter 9: Two More Governments, One Last Resignation

Ten years had elapsed since the bright political morning when Wilson first entered Downing Street. He was not only older, wiser and more experienced in the ways of government, but physically diminished by a lifetime on the front line. He could not bring to his third, and then fourth, premiership the sheer drive that had informed his initial rise to power. Much of the old zest had gone, and he had returned to Number 10, if not by a deceit upon the electorate, then at least through the unsatisfactory process of an election induced by circumstances of which he could not wholeheartedly approve. It was democracy, but not at its best.

Wilson made plain from the outset that he would behave more like a guiding genius in government than a pro-active president. In football terms, he would be a 'sweeper' laying back in the field, not a 'striker' going forward. There would also be less razzmatazz, less showy use of Number 10, whether for the gliterati or guileful union bosses seeking to exploit the beer and sandwiches routine. He would delegate more to a team of experienced Cabinet ministers leaving himself to manage a party divided on the paramount issue of the day – Europe. Wilson also gave the go-ahead for all ministers to hire a political adviser, and set up the Downing Street policy unit under Bernard (now Lord) Donoughue, a very bright

LSE academic from a working class background. His semi-detachment from the trappings of power was also reflected in a decision not to live in the 'prison' of the flat above Number 10. He kept on the rented house in Lord North Street, but made full use of Chequers. Mary Wilson, never attracted to life at the top, spent more time at Grange Farm. Austen Morgan argues that the couple had 'long lived separate lives within their marriage', though there was at that time no suggestion that Wilson looked outside it for emotional sustenance.

One issue that could not be avoided was the timing of the next election. Without a Commons majority, and despite the haphazard nature of an Opposition complicated by the addition of a variety of nationalist and Ulster MPs, Labour could not avoid occasional parliamentary defeats, and indeed suffered 18 in Wilson's third administration. The situation had to be regularised, with an election giving Wilson an overall working majority. A 'June option' was considered and discarded, once Heath had been put in his place with a well-founded threat to stage a snap poll if the Tories tried to bring down the government by voting down the Queen's Speech on 18 March. They abstained.

Given his precarious parliamentary position, Wilson could not afford too radical a programme: a situation which suited his temperament. He could, and did, also plead the constraints of a continuing economic crisis flowing from the 1973 oil shock. Healey's Budget put up pensions and subsidies on food and housing, and increased the basic rate of tax by three points to 33 per cent. The Chancellor also slashed public borrowing. Unemployment was on the rise, and Labour's response to pressure inside the party was to propose industrial measures, including 'planning agreements' with private and nationalised firms. In an ideal world, these agreements would extend the government's role in the economy, in part through a National Enterprise Board. Some of the more exotic notions of intervention came, naturally, from his Industry Secretary, Tony Benn, with whom he fought a running – and ultimately successful – battle to restrain any prospect of a socialist bandwagon.

October 10th emerged as the favourite for polling day, but obstacles emerged in the path towards a peaceful victory, confirming Macmillan's rule that 'events, dear boy, events' were what Prime Ministers had to fear most. In Northern Ireland, a political strike, imposed by the threat (and use) of violence by an unknown Loyalist body calling itself the Ulster Workers' Council, brought down the power-sharing Stormont Assembly that had briefly brought together unionists and nationalists. Initially inclined to use troops and face down an even more extreme form of the industrial conflict that had propelled him into power only weeks previously, Wilson climbed down in late May and dissolved the Assembly. Direct rule from London returned to the Province.

He also had to deal with the 'Wigan Alps' scandal, which threatened for a time to drag his name in the mud along with that of his political secretary and confidante, Marcia Williams. Wilson had known during the election that Tory newspapers had been sitting on a potentially damaging story involving land speculation in Lancashire. Marcia's brother, Tony Field, a golfing friend and Wilson's one-time office manager, was the owner of pit heaps and a quarry near Wigan, which he sold with planning permission to a dodgy Wolverhampton businessman, Ronald Milhench. As a participant in her brother's business, Marcia stood to profit from the transaction. Milhench, with more enthusiasm than brains, stole a sheet of House of Commons notepaper and forged Wilson's signature to a letter purporting to encourage Field's plan to develop the land. Wilson employed Lord Goodman to prevent this piece of (quite literally) muck-raking being published in the *Daily Mail* during the election campaign. The story first appeared in mid-March, running at inordinate length for several weeks. For all that Wilson was not involved, he was deeply upset by the innuendo, and dismayed that Marcia, to whom he was exceptionally close, should have to face trial by media. He issued writs against the *Mail* and the *Daily Express*, insisting to his tormentors in the Commons that Field and his sister had been engaged in *land reclamation* not *land speculation*. Terms were important, because Labour had contemplated nationalising development land. Marcia was granted space in the loyal *Daily Mirror* to plead that she had only been trying to make provision for her retirement. As the story ran out of steam in late April, Milhench was arrested on charges of theft and forgery, and later jailed for three years.

Scandal did not end there, however. Westminster's least well-kept secret, that Marcia had two illegitimate children fathered by lobby correspondent Walter Terry, was kept out of the newspapers, but not for long. Wilson's defiant decision to ennoble Marcia as Lady Falkender in May 1974 merely added to the feeding frenzy. Wilson reacted further by setting up a Royal Commission on the Press, conveniently forgetting his rather good own joke that such inquiries consume years taking minutes. All in all, it was perhaps his worst period of relationships with the press, which is saying a great deal. His paranoia was prone to get the better of him at any time, evidenced by fears of a story about his tax returns shortly before the election was called. That he was paranoid did not mean that people were not out to get him, or at any rate, profit from stolen documents. Three years later, two men charged with burglary and receiving his private papers appeared at the Old Bailey.

Europe dogged the election timetable through the summer.

Wilson attended the EEC summits and his ministers took their place at routine meetings, though the TUC kept up its boycott of European institutions. Foreign Secretary Callaghan signalled that Labour would stay in Europe without amending the Treaty of Rome if the terms could be renegotiated. In public, Wilson remained non-committal. In private, he prepared for a referendum in which he would urge retaining membership. The anti-Market Left in the Cabinet felt betrayed, but could do nothing until he showed his hand. In July, Wilson told a joint Cabinet–NEC meeting on the forthcoming election manifesto that he wanted a firm commitment to a referendum within 12 months of returning to Number 10. He got his way. 10 October was finally confirmed as polling day in mid-September, giving only a very short, 22-day campaign. Meanwhile, he rushed out a torrent of legislative pledges on pensions, devolution for Scotland and Wales, rights at work and consumer protection. His seven-month time in office had not been idle, passing 38 Bills, including the abolition of the hated Industrial Relations Act and of tied houses for farm workers. It had been a steady, progressive government rather than a revolutionary one, more in keeping with Wilson's temperament, and, it must be said, with the mood of a nation wearied by politico-industrial strife. Considering his modest origins, Wilson chimed more with 'middle England' at this stage than his public school betters in Labour's upper echelons.

It was never going to be an easy election. Voters do not take kindly to being roused from their political slumbers too frequently. The party's insipid slogan, 'Britain *will* win with Labour' was scarcely designed to jolt them to their senses. Wilson concentrated on promises that Labour had kept. By contrast, the Tories promised lower mortgage interest rates and abolition of the rates (council taxes), and indicated a readiness to rule through coalition in the event of a hung parliament.

Wilson would have no truck with such ideas. This was his last stand. Defeat on this occasion would finish his political career. Ever the optimist, he believed he would emerge triumphant with an overall majority of around a dozen. Party officials thought he might get twice that figure. Heavy rain put a dampener on campaigning, and turnout fell by five points to below 73 per cent. Labour took 39 per cent of the popular vote, up more than three points from February and representing a swing of little more than 2 per cent from the Conservatives. Labour won 319 seats, 43 more than the Tories. However, the minor parties did even better than seven months previously, trimming Wilson's overall majority in the Commons to only three. He had squeezed in by the skin of his back teeth, as they would say in his native Huddersfield. To the question 'Who rules?' voters had answered: 'Still not quite sure.' Moreover, his fourth government would be at the mercy of death by by-election. Wilson took some comfort from the rag-bag nature of the combined Opposition. The nationalists would generally support Labour in the hope of limited home rule, while the Liberals had shown what they thought of the Tories when offered a role in a Heath government at the beginning of the year. If played right, the result was 'a firm parliamentary base'.

With a virtually unchanged Cabinet, Wilson set about turning the European initiative into reality. Labour's postponed conference in November approved, by a hair's-breadth majority, the government's direction, including a referendum. A well-pitched fraternal address from Helmut Schmidt, West Germany's Social Democrat Chancellor, heard after the vote, helped to assuage delegates' fears. He played on the economic virtues of membership, and the potential risks to jobs if Britain quit. Furious anti-marketeers such as Benn quickly latched on to Wilson's fresh tack: 'to save jobs'. This ploy naturally appealed to Labour's working class constituency, and was difficult to subvert. Schmidt spent the weekend at Chequers with Wilson, successfully urging on him a one-to-one dinner with Giscard d'Estaing at the Elysee Palace soon after. Wilson convinced the French President that Britain was in earnest, and reported genuine progress to the Commons.

There remained the awkward question of what to do with the Cabinet 'antis', chiefly Foot, Benn, Shore and Castle. Largely at their instigation, Wilson proposed the wholly novel concept of release from collective Cabinet responsibility. Ministers would be free to speak out according to personal conviction. Their freedom would be confined to Europe alone, and would not kick in until the referendum campaign began. This unique arrangement was agreed in Cabinet on 21 January 1975. Two months later, finishing touches were put to the renegotiated terms at an EEC summit in Dublin castle, on Wilson's 59th birthday. On 18 March, the Cabinet voted 16–7 on Wilson's motion to recommend the terms of continuing membership to the people.

Both sides of the argument rushed out to exploit their new-found freedom, leaving Wilson despairing of his appeal to their 'spirit of comradeship'. There is nothing like a good political fight to put asunder the brothers and sisters joined together in socialism. Wilson only secured a parliamentary majority for the EEC terms with the votes of Tories and Liberals. Thereafter, he played a low-key role. A special party conference roundly rejected the terms, but agreed not to crusade against 'its' government. The TUC, taking its cue from the Cabinet ruling, also came out against membership, but a number of unions campaigned in favour and the Congress effort was half-hearted.

The 'No' campaign had the more charismatic speakers, but not as much money as the well-heeled business lobby in favour of staying in Europe. Wilson was confident of winning, though anxious about the margin of victory. A narrow win, or a result marred by national variations that pitted the English against the Welsh or Scots, would plunge the country into lasting uncertainty. It had to be a decisive 'Yes', and in the event, it was. Opinion polls predicted a two-to-one majority, and despite being asked to go to the polls for the third time in less than 18 months, voters came out on 5 June to give Wilson a verdict of 67.5 per cent in favour. Turnout was 64.5 per cent, with 11,378,581 voting 'Yes' and 8,470,073 'No'. Every part of the country except the Shetlands and the Western Isles supported the government. It is hard to disagree with the judgement of his biographer Austen Morgan that this was Wilson's finest political hour, or with his reservation that 'few socialists were prepared to accept this'.[1] Wilson had taken on his left-wing ministers, his national executive, his party conference and his parliamentary party, and won. The negotiations were largely a side issue, if not an outright sham. Wilson had appealed to the middle-of-the-road people, of whom he saw himself as the archetypal champion. They listened to him, because their gut instinct was that he was with them.

Deliverance was short-lived, however. While Europe gripped the nation's interest, the economy was yet again heading for the buffers. In his post-referendum Cabinet reshuffle, with one eye on a restive business community, Wilson demoted Benn from Industry, where he had upset the City with plans for creeping nationalisation via the NEB, to Energy, where scope for his undoubted energies was limited. Uniquely, Wilson deliberately leaked the story of his downfall, to the Conservative *Daily Telegraph*. Benn's place was taken by Wilson loyalist Eric Varley, and the Industry Bill was diluted out of recognition before reaching the statute book. Planning agreements were quietly abandoned, along with lists of companies ripe for public ownership.

This minor step did nothing to avert a looming economic crisis. More than a million were out of work, inflation was running at 25 per cent and the pound had lost more than a quarter of its 1971 value. As the Tory wage restraint laws finally expired in July 1975, sterling came under renewed attack. The Treasury lobbied hard for a replacement statutory incomes policy but Wilson was determined to avoid legislation that would alienate the unions, his partners in the social contract. Protracted negotiations with the TUC yielded acceptance of a £6 a week flat-rate pay rise for the entire country over the next year. This levelling instrument was the idea of Jack Jones, the TGWU leader, who was flown from his union conference in Blackpool to a summit with Wilson and Healey to clinch the deal.

Those earning £8,500 a year or more would have to endure a pay freeze. However, the greatest threat came not from the salarymen but from the miners. The men who had propelled Wilson into power now looked for their reward. They were discussing a claim for £100 a week at the coalface. If they triumphed over the voluntary policy, it would be in ruins. Wilson travelled to the NUM conference in Scarborough on 7 July, and made what those who saw it regard as the greatest speech of his life.[2] The miners were not uniformly left-wing or militant, nor was their union. Some regions elected Communist leaders, others Labour moderates, and there were political tensions within individual coalfields. They were also traditionally loyal to Labour, returning the largest single group of union-sponsored MPs to Westminster. Wilson was acutely aware of these considerations, and made a direct plea to the innate fairness and patriotism of the men. *What the government has the right to ask, the duty to ask, is not a year for self but a Year for Britain.* It was emotional, sentimental, even. And it worked. The NUM posted their £100 target as an objective, not a claim. The £6 figure was accepted in a secret ballot, and with their consent the deal was secure.

Scarborough was a breakthrough, but on its own it was not enough to satisfy the financiers. Wilson pushed through a Counter Inflation Bill against strong hostility from the Tribune Group of MPs, and prepared reserve powers to control pay if the TUC deal collapsed. He set up a counter-inflation unit in Downing Street, and hired Geoffrey Goodman, respected industrial editor of the *Daily Mirror*, to run it. It was still not enough, not even for his Chancellor. In November, Healey demanded £3 billion of spending cuts. By December, he had got his way. Further draconian cuts for the next two years were outlined in a Treasury White Paper on forward spending published in February 1976. When put to a Commons vote, the White Paper was defeated by 28 votes, more than 30 Tribune MPs abstaining. On his 60th birthday, Wilson was obliged to submit his government to a vote of confidence, winning by 297 votes to 280.

> '*In 1975, his {Wilson's} one strength was that he knew he was going. He could take decisions he knew he was not going to implement.*'
>
> JOE HAINES

As Barbara Castle despaired in a note to a colleague during Cabinet, the Labour government was becoming Labour in name only. In their place, the Conservatives would have done the same, though with greater relish. But by this time, Wilson was beyond, if not caring, then certainly beyond worrying unduly. 'In 1975,' his press secretary Joe Haines said 30 years later, 'his one strength was that he knew he was going. He could take decisions he knew he was not going to implement.'[3] The only question was when he would go. In reaching his decision, Wilson was partly influenced by change at the top in the Tory Party. Amid much blood-letting, the Conservatives had replaced Heath with Margaret Thatcher in February 1975, and Wilson derived much less pleasure from his twice-weekly jousting with the new Opposition leader during Prime Minister's Questions.

Indeed, the whole political game was palling. Rewarding, punishing, reshuffling and 'treating with complete ignoral' (as George Brown would have put it) his rivals and enemies could no longer gratify his mischievous Tyke soul. And if it wasn't fun any more, what was the point of it? His single achievement of statesmanship, confirming Britain's place in Europe, was complete. Even so, argues Haines, the referendum was 'a party management function. He always wanted to stay in Europe. But more than anything else, he wanted to keep the party together.'[4] If that objective sounds less statesmanlike, the deluge that followed within five years of his departure demonstrates the value to democracy of his ambition.

Chapter 10: Spooked

Two months after his sudden resignation, Wilson called two investigative journalists, Barrie Penrose and Roger Courtiour, to his home in Lord North Street. What he had to say astounded them. MI5, he claimed, was bugging his telephone, and a 'disaffected' faction of his own security service had been secretly engaged in subversion against him, probably for many years. This was an unprecedented bombshell. Never before had a former Prime Minister made such allegations, in all likelihood because none had grounds to do so. In speeches delivered before this unorthodox initiative, Wilson had dropped heavy hints about *subversion from the Right*, which found expression in underground, well-financed organisations that did not scruple to use any weapons against British politicians and their parties. In May 1976, he singled out Jeremy Thorpe, the hapless leader of the Liberal Party facing charges of attempted murder against Norman Scott (of which he was eventually found not guilty). There was no doubt, however, that he also meant himself to be included among the victims. Chief in the list of suspects was BOSS, the South African security service, which Wilson believed had targeted him because of his refusal to sell arms to Pretoria.

But the real culprit, he knew, was his country's own security service, of which he had been titular head, on and off, for the best part of a decade. Because of its ambiguous status, being known of but not officially acknowledged, MI5 could, and did, bug and burgle its way towards objectives that bore no relation to national security but reflected the (invariably right-wing) prejudices of its officers and executives. It would be an exaggeration to say that MI5 – and MI6, the sister service responsible for intelligence gathering – was full of politicians *manqués*. Yet there were still enough to give what has accurately been called 'the secret state' a distinct political tinge. In the middle of the Cold War against Communist Russia, and given the American pre-occupation with socialism, this is not surprising. However, a blue shade has always been detectable. Both services traditionally saw their primary loyalty to the Crown and distinct from and superior to democracy. From there, it is a short step to disloyalty to an elected left-wing government, however pale pink.

Wilson attracted the attention of the 'spooks' almost from the beginning. His role at the Board of Trade in the late 1940s involved business deals with the highest levels of the Kremlin. Britain's agreement to sell Rolls-Royce aero engines in exchange for grain, cattle feed, timber and other commodities in desperately short supply, raised eyebrows among military brass hats and Ernie Bevin's Foreign Office. In the USA, this was seen as British socialists using American Marshall Aid money to

> Leader of the Liberal Party from 1967 to 1976, Jeremy Thorpe (b. 1929) is best remembered for the scandal involving the attempted murder of Norman Scott, a male model who claimed to have had a relationship with him. Although Thorpe was married, rumours about his sexuality dogged his political career. After Scott claimed publicly that the two had an affair, a bungled attempt was made on his life. Scott claimed that Thorpe had tried to have him killed. This forced Thorpe to resign and eventually face a trial.

arm the Soviets. A proposal to sell jet aircraft was abandoned after MoD intelligence chiefs and the Pentagon, acting in collusion, exercised a veto.

His card was marked, and by taking a job in 1951 with Montague Meyer, a timber merchant with considerable commercial interests in Russia, Wilson seemed almost to breathe defiance against the 'securocrats'. His consultancy work took him to Moscow several times a year, though he faithfully reported on any contacts with the Kremlin to Churchill. On one of these occasions, he was photographed in the street with an unidentified young woman. MI5 was to use this innocuous picture over and over again, to 'prove' that Wilson had either been seduced into a Soviet honeytrap (and was therefore their agent) or had failed to report a sexual advance by the KGB (which would also prove that he was a spy). Sexual peccadilloes were grist to the spooks' mill. They exposed Wilson to blackmail. Apart from the mystery woman in Moscow, MI5 was convinced that Wilson was having an affair with his political acolyte, Barbara Castle, a rising star in the Labour party. Unquestionably, Wilson liked a pretty girl, and 'Babs' was an exceptionally attractive woman, but there was nothing sexual in their relationship. On a different tack, Wilson's job at Trade had brought him into contact with other Jewish businessmen, often of east European extraction. He was a lifelong supporter of Zionism, and, unusually for a don by nature, enjoyed the company of these self-made, cut-and-thrust operators. Because they came from countries within the Soviet orbit, they, too, attracted suspicion. Their names went into MI5's burgeoning file on Wilson, code-named 'Henry Worthington', along with the women and the doubts – fostered by his successor at the BoT, Hartley Shawcross, over the jet engines.[1] Sex, soft on Commies and funny friends from behind the Iron Curtain made a heady cocktail for the spycatchers. They proceeded to get very drunk.

Hugh Gaitskell's untimely death in 1963, and Wilson's succession to the Labour leadership, provided fresh impetus for the conspiracy theorists. Smarting from their embarrassment over the defection of Kim Philby to Moscow at this time, the security services needed a boost. It came in the form of Anatoly Golitsin, a KGB defector, turned over to Britain by the CIA the month after Wilson took over. Golitsin claimed, fantastically, that Wilson was not only a Soviet agent but complicit in a successful plot to murder Gaitskell and replace him with a potential Prime Minister acceptable to the Kremlin. No evidence was advanced to support this outlandish allegation, other than Golitsin's hunch that the KGB had been planning, at least two years before, a high-level assassination somewhere in Europe to get their own man in the top place. British doctors confirmed that Gaitskell's death was from tragic but natural causes – the collapse of his immune system.

At this point, two baleful names appear: MI5 officer Peter Wright, and his American co-conspirator, James Jesus Angleton, head of counter-intelligence. It would be the understatement of the century to say that these men were obsessives. But they were also well placed to do considerable harm to Wilson. Wright, whose memoirs, *Spycatcher*, finally lifted the lid on 'the Wilson plot' two decades later, desperately wanted to believe in the spy-murder theory. So he did. And so did the equally paranoid Angleton, who circulated the conspiracy in the CIA. His actions spurred the Agency's head John McCone to contact Roger Hollis, head of MI5 for his views. Hollis, later to come under Wright's fanatical suspicion himself, cabled back that he didn't think there was anything in the Wilson case. His reassurance did not quite satisfy the Americans, who continued to mistrust Wilson for the rest of his political life. The CIA's file on him was named, curiously, OATSHEAF. It was as skimpy as MI5's was bulging.

Another cause for concern was Wilson's attitude towards CND, soon to attract strong support within the Labour Party, including the PLP. Wilson was never a ban-the-bomber, but after his 1951 resignation over defence spending versus the NHS, he had been regarded by opponents as weak on military matters. His loose membership of the Bevanites, among whom support for CND was almost an article of faith, was also held against him in this respect. In the same year, Tory War Minister John Profumo was obliged to resign after lying to the Commons about his relationship with 'model' Christine Keeler, who was also the mistress of the Soviet military attaché in London. As leader of the Opposition facing an early general election, Wilson naturally exploited the issue as best he could. Wright put round the notion that Wilson had been tipped off about Profumo by his KGB contacts. In Wright's feverish imagination, if the Russians were involved, then Wilson must be implicated.

Against this background of skulduggery, Wilson defeated the natural allies of the secret state, the Conservative Party, to win the election of 1964. Such a flagrant exercise in democracy could only inflame Wright and his friends in MI5. They probably never numbered more than half a dozen, but they had first-rate contacts in the mass media, particularly Beaverbrook's best-selling *Express* group – based in what was known as Fleet Street's black-glass 'Lubyanka', an ironic tribute to the newspapers' intellectual plurality.

One of Wilson's first acts as Prime Minister, not to be challenged for more than 40 years, was to ban MI5 tapping of MPs' phones. He also stood up for his ministers against what he thought were undeserved security fears, and he appointed George Wigg, a lugubrious ex-Army officer, to act as his eyes and ears with the security services. Wilson showed no overt hostility to the securocrats: it was always the other way round. Indeed, he ruthlessly used MI5's techniques in 1966, when faced with the seamen's strike. He was unaware that 'Five' had identified 11 MPs and party officials, two influential trade union leaders and a number of his friends as 'security risks.' With one, Will Owen, MP for Morpeth, they were correct. He was charged with taking money from the Czechs. The case collapsed, but he was ruined.

The evidence against Jack Jones of the TGWU and Hugh Scanlon of the AEU, was laughable, as were most of their other suspicions. That did not stop MI5 from ruining the ministerial careers of Niall McDermot, Financial Secretary to the Treasury who might have expected to become a Law Officer in the Cabinet, and Stephen Swingler, a Transport minister, also Cabinet material. The spooks also drove Bernard Floud MP to his death, and Floud's secretary Phoebe Pool, distraught after giving his name to MI5, to her suicide under a London tube train.

One way and another, it was a substantial haul, though not enough for Wilson's tormentors. He remained their number one target. MI5 repeatedly brought to his attention their misgivings about those around him. They never mentioned the subversion with their own ranks. Roger Hollis paid many calls to Downing Street. He did not take 'Henry Worthington' with him. The criticism of David Leigh, author of *The Wilson Plot*, that Wilson's failure to defeat – or even understand – MI5 was a significant error for which he would pay dearly, is surely unfair. Wilson was never informed about the subterranean work of Wright and his friends. Not even his bloodhound, George Wigg, got a sniff of the real plot. To cap everything he persuaded Wilson to appoint Martin Furnival Jones ('FJ'), Hollis's deputy, to succeed as Director-General of MI5, instead of his favoured external candidate, Eric St Johnston, Chief Constable of Lancashire – thereby ensuring that 'Henry Worthington' would remain a secret. If anything, Wilson was too trustful of the security services, exhibiting a Baden Powell-like faith in their probity. 'FJ' kept the Wilson file in his office safe.

Meanwhile, Wilson's strategy of withdrawal from East of Suez, pushed forward in the face of US hostility, and his cancellation of the American F111 aircraft, deepened suspicion in Washington and delighted the manic Angleton. More was to come. Joseph Kagan, a Lithuanian refugee and friend of Wilson, was discovered to be a chess companion of Richardas Vaygauskas, a fellow Lithuanian and a known KGB agent working in the Russian Embassy. Kagan, a postwar refugee, invented a waterproof material, Gannex, from which he manufactured raincoats at a factory in Huddersfield. He got to know Wilson in the 1950s, and the Labour leader made Gannex a household name by wearing one of Kagan's macs. Even the Royal Family took up this briefly-fashionable clothing, and Kagan became a regular member of the wider Wilson entourage, befriending Marcia Williams and helping with funds. He boasted of his contacts, and Wilson was warned of a possible security problem. About this time, the late 1960s, allegations of 'a Communist cell' inside Number 10, involving Marcia, Kagan and Vaygauskas began to appear. Kagan was a frequent visitor, but Wilson appeared to brush aside the suggestion that he was a risk: an indulgence that naturally fed further suspicions. They were heightened in 1969 when the defection of Czech spook Joseph Frolik brought fresh allegations. He fingered John Stonehouse, Wilson's Postmaster-General. After a personal confrontation with 'FJ', Wilson intervened to prevent a full-scale MI5 interrogation. Stonehouse survived to fake his own death and serve a jail sentence for fraud. In 2006, his guilt was finally unmasked in Czech archives. At the time, Wilson's unwillingess to co-operate fully in an MI5 investigation added further material to his four-volume intelligence file.

Oleg Lyalin, a low-level KGB officer working in the Soviet Trade Delegation in Highgate, defected in February 1971. He claimed that Vaygauskas had been introduced to Wilson by Kagan, and had even ordered the Gannex manufacturer to visit Number 10 twice in search of information about Nato and Europe. Lyalin's confession sent MI5 into overdrive, compelling Wilson to deny in person to the service that he and Kagan had ever discussed anything classified. When his MI5 interviewer cheekily asked if he had ever been put under pressure by the KGB, Wilson shot back: *I can assure you, I kept my trousers buttoned up while I was in Moscow.*[2] Having knighted Kagan in his 1970 dissolution honours list, Wilson subsequently made him a life peer. Kagan eventually went on the run to Israel to avoid fraud charges, but was extradited on a visit to Paris in 1980 and jailed for ten months. His knighthood was taken away, but he remained a peer – and a useful stick with which the conspiracy theorists could beat Wilson for years to come.

Out of power after June 1970, Wilson could not escape the machinations of the secret state. MI5 continued to keep tabs on him, and in the run-up to the February 1974 election fed to Chapman Pincher a report on Wilson's movements ahead of the miners' strike (which the CIA believed was Moscow-inspired) which expressed concerns about the return of another Wilson-led Labour government. The dirty tricks began in earnest when the Heath government fell. Pincher recorded, in

1978, that officers and retired officers of MI5 and MI6 were actually trying to bring the Labour government down. Peter Wright persuaded MI5's director, Michael Hanley, to reopen the Wilson case, partly in concert with Angleton, who was still convinced that he was a Soviet agent.

Further ammunition came from an unexpected quarter – Belfast. The minority Labour government caved in to Loyalist strikers in May 1974, whose unlawful stoppage had been allowed to bring down power-sharing in the province. The hand of MI5 was detected behind the strike. Its influence came more directly to bear through the Information Policy Unit of the Northern Ireland Office. Colin Wallace, who worked in the unit, later blew the cover of MI5's operation against Wilson, codenamed 'Clockwork Orange'.[3] Intelligence officers briefed Wallace on a smear campaign to employ against Labour, accusing the party and its leader of seeking to bring about a 'Red Shamrock Irish Workers' Republic' with the aid of Moscow. Wilson himself, said the MI5 notes, was 'under Soviet control through Vaygauskas' even though he had left the country three years previously, and was banned from returning. Wilson had promoted MPs 'believed to be communists' including Barbara Castle and Michael Foot, and his political secretary Marcia Williams had refused to be positively vetted. For good measure, the canard that Gaitskell had been murdered was disinterred. All this black propaganda was fed to any journalists who would listen in the run-up to the October 1974 election.

In the event, the dirty tricks failed, though not before putting the wind up Wilson and some of his ministers, notably Tony Benn. The spooks' campaign relied too heavily on invented material that was so over the top that not even the more naïve of Fleet Street's finest could exploit it. Failure was not for want of trying, however, and only spurred the plotters to greater ingenuity. Details of Wilson's account in the London branch of a failed Swiss bank were handed out to the media, which feasted on speculation as the origin of the £1,500 in it. The fading photograph of a moustachioed Wilson and the mystery Muscovite lady was given a fresh outing by MI5, courtesy of its sister service MI6. Sometimes, a leading public figure could be relied upon to the spooks' dirty work for them, as in 1975, when Mirror Group chairman Cecil King tried to bring together a shadow 'government of all the talents' to take over from Labour. He lectured officers at Sandhurst about the need for the armed forces to save the country. In the audience, military historian John Keegan had no doubt that he was listening to a treasonable attempt to suborn the loyalty of the Queen's officers. Elsewhere, ultra-Right wing cranks and retired generals talked airily of private armies and a coup against Wilson. Nothing came of this madcap clubland conspiracy. Nonetheless, it contributed to the general mood of unease that informed Wilson's decision-making. He was further troubled by a series of unexplained burglaries at his home and those of his associates and friends. Stephen Dorril and Robin Ramsay, authors of *Smear!*, an exhaustive account of the plot against Wilson, understand that the police came to the conclusion that MI5 were the culprits.

The trouble was that Wilson could not investigate the dirty tricks against except through the state's own political detective agency, precisely the source from which they emanated. Number 10 became paranoid with suspicion, with staffers fearing that phones were tapped and seeing security service men round every corner. Crisis point was reached in August 1975, during the parliamentary recess, when Wilson had lunch with his lawyer, Lord Goodman. London was awash with rumours about a 'Communist cell' in Number 10, he told the Prime Minister. His informant was Minnie

Churchill, wife of the Tory MP Winston, who informed him that an MI5 officer present at lunch had spoken of 'certain officers of MI5 considered the Prime Minister himself to be a security risk'.

In an effort to short-circuit MI5's control of the situation, Wilson called in Maurice Oldfield, head of MI6, and demanded to know if 'Five' was plotting against him and his government. A squirming Oldfield conceded that MI5 had an 'unreliable' section, and promised to sort it out. Nothing further was heard. Despite the traditional rivalry between the two services, descending at times into indiscreet warfare, MI6 was not in the business of exposing the Wilson plot. Had he known that Oldfield was a regular dining companion of Peter Wright, he would have been less mystified. Oldfield immediately reported the details of his confrontation with Wilson to MI5's self-appointed chief conspirator. He, in turn informed his boss Michael Hanley, who went white as a sheet on learning that 'half his staff were up to their necks in a plot to get rid of the Prime Minister'. But armed with a friendly briefing from Oldfield, sought to play down the actions of 'a small number' of his right-wing officers when hauled in by Wilson for an explanation.

The wheel had finally come full circle. Wilson's suspicions had been confirmed, and his incontrovertible knowledge that the 'secret state' had plotted against him, was plotting against him and would presumably never rest until it had destroyed him, must have weighed heavily in the balance of his decision to quit when he did. Their treachery would spook anyone, even a man as outwardly nonchalant as Harold Wilson. It is almost certainly not true that he resigned three months later solely because of the traitors to democracy in MI5. He had told his wife Mary he would go, he had littered West-minster with hints and his 60th birthday was an optimum moment. However, the fact that subversive elements in the security services over which he had titular authority had lied, cheated, burgled and spun to achieve his downfall leaves a nasty taste in the mouth. In recent times, MI5, in its new guise as the open, citizen-friendly watchdog of the nation's freedom, has sought to bury the Wilson plot by denial and obfuscation. Unfortunately for the spooks, such convenient sub-editing of history cannot wipe out the primary evidence of Colin Wallace, or the facts uncovered by investigative writers – and the testimony of Wilson himself. An internal inquiry by Sir John (later Lord) Hunt, the Cabinet Secretary established that Peter Wright had indeed been involved in plotting, along with the former deputy chief of MI6, George Kennedy Young, a leading member of the Tory Monday Club. No other British prime minister has ever been subjected to such abuse of state power. Perhaps the threat presented by Wilson's success in sustaining Labour as a governing party was indeed as great as the spooks feared – except, not in the manner they imagined.

Part Three

THE LEGACY

Chapter 11: A Moral Crusade – Or Nothing?

In the autumn of 1930, young Harold Wilson was on a scout camp at Honley, in the hills south of Huddersfield. He went to a farm to buy milk, and drank some. A few days later, he became ill and typhoid was diagnosed. He was promptly incarcerated in Meltham Isolation Hospital, where he hovered near death for six weeks. His parents nightly feared the news that he had succumbed. In the era before antibiotics, typhoid was commonly fatal. Six of the other 12 people who drank the infected milk died.

Harold, aged 14, spent four months in quarantine, before returning home weighing just over four and a half stones. As his health returned, so did his spirit, as the boy devoured Dickens, *Three Men in a Boat* and even *Whittaker's Almanac* in his hospital bed. When he returned home on 2 January 1931, grandfather Wilson said to his son: 'Herbert, that lad's been spared for something.'

If that something was anything, it was the mission he outlined at the Labour Party conference in Brighton in October 1962, when he was (though he did not know it) on the brink of becoming leader. Wilson was party chairman that year, and in his address he declared: *This Party is a moral crusade or it is nothing*. He ended with a quotation from the poet James Russell Lowell, including the lines:

He's true to God who's true to man; wherever wrong is
   done
To the humblest and the weakest, 'neath the all-
   beholding sun
That wrong is also done to us, and they are slaves most
   base
Whose love of right is for themselves and not for all
   their race.

In another context, he argued that socialism was a way of making a reality of Christian principles in everyday life. And it is surely by his own test, that there must be a moral under-pinning in politics, that he must be judged.

At first sight, he is the Prime Minister of the 20th century least likely to satisfy such a test. Derided as a Yorkshire Walter Mitty by his critics, mistrusted even by his colleagues and held in contempt as a double-dealer by his enemies, he long occupied a unique place in political demonology. Towards the end of his lifetime, opinion softened towards a kindly old man with a twinkle in his eye and an acerbic quote for the newspapers. After his death, his reputation plummeted, but first in the harsh years of Thatcherism and then the cynical decade of New Labour, revision took over from derision.

Wilson is today seen more as a man who brought his party, bruised and battered but intact, into the modern era. Had a Wilson-figure, committed and crafty enough to accommodate the strains of the opposition years of the early 1980s been at the helm, it is possible – if not probable – that the breakaway by the SDP would not have taken place, and Labour would have been spared many years in the wilderness. By the same token the people who look most to the Labour Party – in Lowell's words, 'the humblest and the weakest' – would have been spared much grief.

As it was, Wilson played little role in the tumultuous events that followed his departure. His chosen successor, Jim Callaghan, ruled until March 1979, latterly with the aid of the Lib-Lab pact that sustained his majority-free government. He chose not to go to the country in October 1978, while seeking to impose a 5 per cent pay 'norm' on the unions. The outcome was predictable: a 'Winter of Discontent' when one group of workers after another went on strike, culminating in council gravediggers whose walkout prompted the electorally-fatal headline 'Now we can't bury our dead.' In the election that followed, Thatcher came to power as Britain's first woman prime minister with a comfortable Commons majority. Wilson stood again at Huyton, for the last time, and did his bit in the national campaign but it was no longer his show. On the back benches, his voice was rarely heard. Callaghan was succeeded by Michael Foot, the dimming firebrand Wilson had brought in from the Tribunite cold. Wilson plumped for Healey in the first ballot, but coyly refused to say for whom he voted in the second.

In the summer of 1980, Wilson was diagnosed with bowel cancer and underwent a series of major operation that left him gravely weakened. Understandably, his weight fell sharply and he struggled to cope with the everyday pressures of life. His memory, hitherto prodigious, began to give way and it was clear that he was suffering from the early onset of Alzheimer's disease. Doctors ordered him to take things easily 'for a very long time'. He was no more than a helpless spectator of the catastrophic split that sundered Labour under Michael Foot in 1981, which saw Shirley Williams, once his choice as successor, defect with Roy Jenkins, David Owen and Bill Rodgers – the 'Gang of Four' – to form the breakaway SDP. Wilson was contemptuous of 'the Trots' who supported Tony Benn's leadership ambitions, though he had no time for the defectors. In any event, he retired from the Commons in 1983, the year of Labour's annihilation at the polls in the wake of the Falklands War.

His time on the back benches had not been entirely idle. In 1977, Callaghan asked Wilson to chair a committee of inquiry into the City, a task which have raised some old demons given his 1960s strictures on the 'gnomes of Zurich'. The inquiry, composed of the customary great and good but also including trade union nominees, was never going to offer radical reforms and its critics were not disappointed. Wilson himself showed how seriously he took his role by turning up with a briefcase containing nothing but his cigars. By the time the final report was published, in 1980, the Conservatives were in power and none of its recommendations, timid as they were (and rejecting outright calls for the nationalisation of financial institutions) had any political relevance. It was not debated in the Commons until the following year, when Treasury minister Nigel Lawson kindly referred to it as a 'classic textbook' that would be read for generations to come. It was then forgotten. Wilson continued to make infrequent interventions in the Commons, pointing out in a debate about the security services in March 1981 that he had been the first to instigate an independent inquiry into MI5. His intention was plainly to read this into the record, for no further action followed. His last parliamentary action was to ask a question about satellite broadcasting in 1982.

Wilson was more concerned about establishing his reputation for posterity than sustaining it on the front line. As if foreknowing that his renown would prove equivocal, Wilson did his best, while he could, to claim his place in the record with *The Governance of Britain*, published during the year he abdicated, and *A Prime Minister Among Prime Ministers* the following year. In these works, he sought to define himself against those who had gone before him. His two volumes of instant political history, *The Labour Government, 1964-1970* and *Final Term* had already appeared in 1971 and 1979 respectively, while his political manifesto, largely in the form of reprinted speeches and articles, *Purpose in Politics*, came out in the year he first became Prime Minister. Belatedly, his memoirs, *The Making of a Prime Minister*, appearing in 1986, undertook the same task in the context of his origins, political development and beliefs. While suffering the customary myopia of autobiography, this is easily his most engaging book. It was ghost-written by the journalist Brian Connell, and tells the story of a provincial boy made good, while never losing sight of what makes him go.

Wilson's motive of explaining himself before others could get the chance to do so was not entirely successful. In his controversial diaries, Crossman was often cruel to the man who had done more than anyone to advance his career. Wilson had endured more invective than praise during a long political career, but though he lived long enough to see his reputation substantially restored, he was, tragically, not capable of relishing his rehabilitation. Austen Morgan's cool and balanced biography appeared in 1992, Professor Ben Pimlott's blockbuster the next year, and the official version, by Philip Ziegler, in 1995, the year he died. Earlier, there had been Paul Foot's waspish but politically-acute paperback special, *Wilson*, and the brief hagiography by BBC journalist Leslie Smith in 1964. But the three big books of the 1990's re-established Wilson as a major figure in British political history.

A decade later, in a period when the orthodoxy of all three main parties is hostile to the 1960s, the verdict remains equivocal. It should not be. The Wilson Era may be damned as irresponsible, anarchic, immoral even, but for those who

Wilson's Premiership

'What is one to make of the Wilson style during his first two governments of 1964–6 and 1966–70? To some extent all occupants of No. 10 have to be variable geometry premiers, altering their operational patterns to suit particular circumstances, but Wilson was so to an unusual degree, which makes him especially difficult to place on the command-collegial spectrum in phase one, his self-styled 'centre-forward' period when, owing to the relative inexperience of his ministerial colleagues, he had had to try and score all the goals himself.

As a political leader who put party unity on a very high pedestal (it was, perhaps, the single consistent aspect of his thirteen years as Labour leader), Wilson had a penchant for letting the Cabinet ramble, encouraging all who wished to speak, doodling as they did so (Ted Short, his Chief Whip, called it the 'doodling Cabinet') and interjecting a little commentary when they finished before catching the eye of the next contributor. Despite his obeisance to the memory and the style of Atlee, Wilson used prolixity as a weapon, allowing the Cabinet to talk itself out.

This would infuriate the likes of Barbara Castle, no mean word-spinner herself, who recalled in her diary for 1 March 1965 that the Cabinet had spent 'three-quarters of an hour discussing the creation of new premises at Chelsea for the National Army Museum'. 'I doodled through the endless discussion,' she wrote. 'Crosland complained to me "There are twenty Ministers debating this. If only there had been as much heat generated by Vietnam." I retorted acidly "The Parkinson's Law of words operated in this Cabinet. Words expand to fill the time available for them."'

It soon became apparent, not least to the press, that there was also a group of political familiars around the Prime Minister quite separate from his Cabinet colleagues or his No. 10 or Cabinet Office advisers which has echoed through history as his 'Kitchen Cabinet'. Throughout all his years as Prime Minister the gregarious Wilson liked a group of cheerful, gossipy intimates whose company late at night he could enjoy and with whom he could mix tittle-tattle and policy. [Peter Hennessy, *The Prime Minister*, pp 288–9, 295] lived through it, it was a time of exhilarating freedom. When he was in Downing Street, Britain became a less intolerant and more agreeable place to live. The first moves towards the repeal of reactionary laws against homosexuality were made, hanging was abolished, women won the right to abortion, and safe, efficient contraception on the NHS delivered couples from the monthly fear of unwanted pregnancy. Some of these reforms were primarily the work of his liberal Home Secretary, Roy Jenkins and might even have run counter to Wilson's Nonconformist instincts. Yet he encouraged the transformation to a progressive society.

Higher education expanded dramatically, and with the aid of generous maintenance grants, the meritocratic dream of success exemplified by a Labour Prime Minister who had fought his way from the sooty terraces of Huddersfield to the very top of public life became a reality. For older people, pensions improved dramatically and Wilson's pet project, the Open University, brought into higher education many thousands of mature people who thought they had 'failed' for life. If he had only been 'spared' for that, his life would not have been wasted.

His most controversial act of public recognition – the gift of the OBE to the Beatles in 1965 – may be identified as the one piece of performance politics that sums up the man. It was a shameless act of popularity seeking, as he well knew. But it also showed his genuine regard for the four young men from Liverpool to whose music he had been introduced by 'Battling' Bessie Braddock, his fellow Labour MP in the city. It was the right thing to do, and it was one in the eye for the establishment at the same time. The Beatles achieved world-wide fame and cultural immortality. Their songs will be sung as long as people have tongues to sing.

Harold Wilson is not so assured of timeless admiration.

In the central square of Huddersfield, beside the imposing railway station and the George Hotel where Rugby League was formed in 1895, stands his statue. Right hand in his pocket, left hand clutching his lapel, buffeted by an imaginary wind, he looks purposefully ahead. The pose captures him as he would best like to remembered: a politician with his gaze on the sunny uplands of a better world, created by a visionary people's party with him as its leader.

Around its base are inscribed a tribute to the Open University, and a somewhat self-serving quotation of his: *The Leader of the Party and no less the Prime Minister has a duty to meet the people.* As they hurry through the ornate classical portico of the railway station, commuters do not stop and stare at this eight-foot high memorial to the town's greatest son. Nor is his memory commemorated

'Wilson shrewdly held Labour together, often saying "If you can't ride three horses at the same time, you shouldn't be in the circus."'

LORD DONOUGHUE

much elsewhere. A small plaque adorns the entrance to the public library. There is a Harold Wilson Suite in the George Hotel. But he goes unremarked at his birthplace and the house where he grew up, and his grave in the beachside churchyard St Mary The Virgin in the Scillies is a modest affair.

Perhaps that is how he would have liked it. Harold Wilson died on 24 May 1995, remembered briefly in the obituary columns and at a memorial service in Westminster Abbey. His will demonstrated that he had not primarily been in it for the money. Wilson left £490,092, around £550,000 in 2006 prices, or less than the cost of a semi-detached house in London.

In recent years, Harold Wilson has been consigned to political limbo, not least by New Labour career politicians who see him not as the first moderniser but the last of the *ancien regime* whose memory must be expunged from the record. Yet had it not been for his brilliant skill at holding the party together during its most disturbed years, there would have been nothing for the Blair generation to inherit. Party unity may not be the most elevated moral virtue, but without it none of the pragmatic social and political aims espoused by Labour could be realised.

Lord Donoughue, who worked closely with him, argues that even at the end of his political life, when he was tired and sick, Wilson still displayed silky skills in negotiating the treacherous currents of then Labour politics. 'The party was riven by personal jealousies and ideological splits, with the far Left trying to take control, Wilson shrewdly held Labour together, often saying "If you can't ride three horses at the same time, you shouldn't be in the circus." He had an incredibly successful political life.'[1] But perhaps the last word should go to Lord Tonypandy, as George Thomas the Speaker of the Commons in the 1970s and the man who delivered Wilson's funeral eulogy: 'He burnt himself out for Britain.'

NOTES

Introduction: Morning Departure

1. Witnessed by the author, then Labour Editor of *The Times*.
2. Peregrine Worsthorne, *Sunday Telegraph*, 23 March 1976.
3. David Leigh, *The Wilson Plot* (Heinemann, London: 1988) p 251.

Chapter 1: England Made Me

1. Harold Wilson, *Memoirs, The Making of a Prime Minister 1916-64* (Weidenfeld & Nicolson, London: 1986) p 35, hereafter Wilson, *Memoirs*.

Chapter 2: Honourable Member

1. Leslie Smith, *Harold Wilson* (Hodder & Stoughton, London: 1964) p 121.
2. Philip Ziegler, *Wilson* (Weidenfeld & Nicolson, London: 1993) p 58.
3. Ziegler, *Wilson*, p 60.
4. Wilson, *Memoirs*, p 107.
5. Wilson, *Memoirs*, p 117.

Chapter 3: Struggle for Leadership

1. Smith, *Harold Wilson*, p 42.
2. Wilson, *Memoirs*, p 111.
3. Wilson, *Memoirs*, p 182.

Chapter 4: First Government

1. Austen Morgan, *Harold Wilson* (Pluto Press, London: 1992) p 247.
2. Ziegler, *Wilson*, p 222.

Chapter 5: Second Government, Second Devaluation

1. Ziegler, *Wilson*, p 251.
2. Ziegler, *Wilson*, p 306.
3. Morgan, *Harold Wilson*, p 314.
4. Morgan, *Harold Wilson*, p 314.

Chapter 6: In Place of Harmony

1. Morgan, *Harold Wilson*, p 362, and author's recollection of newspaper headlines.
2. Ziegler, *Wilson*, p 310.

Chapter 7: Locust Years

1. Morgan, *Harold Wilson*, p 399.

Chapter 8: In Power Through Strife

1. Ziegler, *Wilson*, p 397.
2. Ben Pimlott, *Harold Wilson* (HarperCollins, London: 1992) p 608.

Chapter 9: Two More Governments, One Last Resignation

1. Morgan, *Harold Wilson*, p 469.
2. Ziegler, *Wilson*, p 447.
3. Joe Haines, BBC Radio Four interview, February 2006.
4. Joe Haines, BBC Radio Four interview, February 2006.

Chapter 10: Spooked

1. Leigh, *The Wilson Plot*, p 109.

2. Leigh, *The Wilson Plot*, p 190.
3. For a full account, see Stephen Dorril and Robin Ramsay, *Smear! Wilson and The Secret State* (Fourth Estate, London: 1991) pp 256ff.

Chapter 11: A Moral Crusade – Or Nothing?
1. Article by Donoughue, *Yorkshire Post*, 25 June 2005.

CHRONOLOGY

Year	Premiership
1964	16 October: Harold Wilson becomes Prime Minister, aged 48. Britain borrows $3,000 million to save the pound.
1965	Budget introduces 30 per cent capital gains tax. July: Emergency budget cuts spending and reimposes prescription charges. The death penalty is abolished. Britain imposes oil embargo on Rhodesia.

History	Culture
Anti-US riots in Panama lead to break diplomatic relations with USA.	OP-art emerges.
In South Africa, Nelson Mandela is sentenced to life imprisonment.	Harnick/Bock, *Fiddler on the Roof*. Saul Bellow, *Herzog*.
Turkish planes attack Cyprus. UN orders cease-fire.	Philip Larkin, *The Whitsun Weddings*.
Indonesian army lands in Malaya. Commonwealth troops move in.	Jean-Paul Sartre, *Les Mots*. Peter Shaffer, *The Royal Hunt of the Sun*.
Martin Luther King is awarded the Nobel Peace Prize.	Films: *Mary Poppins. A Hard Day's Night*.
Khrushchev is replaced by Brezhnev as first secretary of Soviet Communist Party.	TV: *Steptoe and Son. Crossroads. Top of the Pops. Match of the Day*. Radio: *Round the Horne*.
China explodes an atomic bomb.	
Lyndon B Johnson (Democrat) wins US presidential election.	

History	Culture
US aircraft bomb North Vietnam. US forces are authorised to engage in offensive operations against the Vietcong.	The Rolling Stones, *Satisfaction*. The Beach Boys, *California Girls*. Norman Mailer, *An American Dream*.
Malcolm X is shot dead in New York.	Neil Simon, *The Odd Couple*.
Clashes between India and Pakistan are ended by a cease-fire agreement. Later Pakistan crosses cease-fire lines and India bombs Lahore. Friction continues.	Frank Marcus, *The Killing of Sister George*. Films: *Doctor Zhivago. The Sound of Music. Doctor Who and the Daleks*.
France announces its boycott of all EEC meetings.	TV: *Thunderbirds. World of Sport. Horizon*.
Race riots in LA's Watts district.	
USSR admits supplying arms to North Vietnam.	
De Gaulle wins French presidential election.	

Year	Premiership
1966	31 March: Labour wins majority of 97 in general election. Budget introduces selective employment tax and corporation tax at 40 per cent. Seamen's strike. Wilson and Smith meet aboard HMS *Tiger* to plan settlement of Rhodesian dispute. Smith declares Rhodesia a republic. England win football World Cup.

History	Culture
Pope Paul VI appeals for peace in Vietnam.	Theodor Adorno, *Negative Dialectics*.
Peace agreement between India and Pakistan.	Kander/Ebb, *Cabaret*.
US resumes bombing of North Vietnam.	H W Henze, *The Bassarids*.
Unrest breaks out in Saigon.	The Beatles give their last concert in San Francisco.
USA bombs Hanoi and Haiphong. Britain dissociates itself from bombing of populated areas.	John Fowles, *The Magus*.
	Graham Greene, *The Comedians*.
	Sylvia Plath, *Ariel*.
USSR announces further aid to North Vietnam.	Joe Orton, *Loot*.
Israeli and Syrian forces clash around Sea of Galilee.	Films: *Alfie. Who's Afraid of Virginia Woolf. One Million Years B.C.*
'The Cultural Revolution': Chinese Communist Party endorses purification of Chinese communism through violent removal of intelligentsia.	TV: *Star Trek*.
Race riots in San Francisco, Chicago, Cleveland and Brooklyn.	

Year	Premiership

1967 Britain formally applies to join EEC. De Gaulle virtually vetoes Britain's entry.

Defence White Paper announces drastic reduction in commitments in Far East.

Sexual Offences Act partially decriminalises male homosexuality.

November: Devaluation of the pound: Wilson makes *pound in your pocket* speech.

George Brown resigns for the 18th and final time.

Cunard liner *Queen Elizabeth II* launched.

USA and South Vietnamese forces launch major offensive in Mekong Delta. President Johnson offers to halt US bombing if N Vietnamese halt infiltration of S. Vietnam.

Border clashes between Israel and Syria.

UAR president Nasser closes Gulf of Aqaba to Israeli shipping.

President Nasser closes Suez Canal.

Six Day War between Israel and Arab States.

Further race riots across USA.

Desmond Morris, *The Naked Ape*.

David Hockney, *A Neat Lawn*.

Andy Warhol, *Marilyn Monroe*.

G G Marquez, *One Hundred Years of Solitude*.

Tom Stoppard, *Rosencrantz and Guildenstern Are Dead*.

Lutoslawski, *Symphony No.2*.

Ragni/MacDermot, *Hair*.

The Doors, *The Doors*.

Jimi Hendrix, *Are You Experienced?*.

The Beatles, *Sgt. Pepper's Lonely Hearts Club Band*.

Sandie Shaw wins the Eurovision Song Contest for the United Kingdom.

BBC Radio 1 launched.

Films: *Far From the Madding Crowd. Accident.* Disney's *The Jungle Book*.

TV: *Omnibus. The Prisoner.*

Year	Premiership
1968	Barbara Castle's White Paper *In Place of Strife* published. Enoch Powell's 'Rivers of Blood' speech leads to his dismissal from Shadow Cabinet. Sectarian violence erupts in Armagh, Northern Ireland.

History	Culture
Over 100 Vietnamese civilians are shot by US troops at My Lai, Vietnam.	Jurgen Habermas, *Knowledge and Human Interests*.
Vietcong launches Tet offensive in South Vietnam, followed by US and ARVN offensive in Saigon area, peace talks begin.	Hubert Bennett and architects of GLC, Hayward Gallery, London.
Assassination of Martin Luther King.	Richard Hamilton, *Swinging London*.
President Johnson signs Civil Rights Bill.	Sol Lewitt, *Untitled Cube (6)*.
Student riots in Paris start in the Latin Quarter and lead to concessions by French Govt and general election.	Simon and Garfunkel, *Mrs Robinson*.
Senator Robert Kennedy is assassinated.	Theatre censorship in Britain abolished.
Greek and Turkish Cypriots negotiate.	Mexico Olympics, USA 45 Gold Medals.
Biafra refuses famine relief from Britain, which is selling arms to its enemy, Nigeria.	Murdoch beats Maxwell to the ownership of *The News of the World*.
Soviet Union invades Czechoslovakia.	
Swaziland becomes independent.	Films: *The Good, the Bad and the Ugly. Butch Cassidy and the Sundance Kid. The Graduate. If... 2001, A Space Odyssey*.
Nixon, Republican, wins election though Democrats keep control of Congress.	
Vatican bans contraception.	
Apollo 8 crew orbit the Moon.	TV: *Dads' Army*.

Year	Premiership

1969
August: British Army assumes responsibility for security in Northern Ireland.

Revival of British application for EEC membership after resignation of De Gaulle.

Anguilla coup forces British emissary to quit, British troops re-establish control.

1970
19 June: Wilson loses general election.

BP discovers oil in the North Sea.

Equal Pay act in Britain ends gender discrimination in wages.

PLO elects Yasser Arafat as chairman.

President de Gaulle resigns.

Nixon suggests withdrawal of US, Allied and North Vietnamese troops from South Vietnam.

Malays and Chinese clash in Kuala Lumpur.

Pompidou becomes French President.

Chappaquiddick, Edward Kennedy's car plunges into water, his passenger drowns.

Neil Armstrong is the first man to walk on the moon.

Millions demonstrate against Vietnam War in USA.

Willy Brandt becomes West German chancellor.

UN rejects admission of China for the 20th time.

US-Soviet talks open in Helsinki.

Isaiah Berlin, *Four Essays on Liberty*.

Kenneth Clark, *Civilisation*.

Donald Judd, *Untitled*.

Woodstock Music and Arts Fair.

John Fowles, *The French Lieutenant's Woman*.

Mario Puzo, *The Godfather*.

Rupert Murdoch buys *The Sun*.

Films: *Easy Rider*. *Oh! What a Lovely War*. *Women in Love*. *The Wild Bunch*.

TV: *Monty Python's Flying Circus*. *Civilisation*. Colour TV broadcasts begin.

Golan Heights see severe fighting between Israel and Syria.

British Guyana becomes a republic in the Commonwealth.

US ground troops withdraw from Cambodia.

PLO hijack four aircraft.

King Hussein and Yasser Arafat agree peace after Jordanian army ordered to disband PLO in Jordan.

Cambodia declares itself the Khmer Republic.

IBM invents the floppy disk.

Yamasaki, First tower of World Trade Centre completed, New York.

David Hockney, *Mr and Mrs Ossie Clark and Percy*.

Richard Bach, *Jonathan Livingston Seagull*.

Dario Fo, *Accidental Death of an Anarchist*.

The Beatles, *Let it Be*.

Led Zeppelin, *II, III*.

The Beatles split up.

Jimi Hendrix dies.

Films: *Kes*. *Love Story*. *Ryan's Daughter*.

Year	Premiership

1974 General election produces no overall majority; Labour 301,
Conservatives 297.

4 March: Wilson returns to office at head of minority government.

State of emergency in Britain ends after miners' union accepts £103
million pay deal.

Protestant general strike begins in Northern Ireland. Industrial
Relations Act in Britain is repealed and NIRC is abolished.

IRA bombs kill five and injure 65 in two public houses in
Guildford.

IRA bombs in two public houses in Birmingham kill 21 and injure
120.

10 October: general election gives Labour an overall majority of
three.

Swedish monarchy is stripped of all its remaining powers.

Willy Brandt resigns after an aide admits to spying.

Isabel Peron becomes president of Argentina on the death of her husband.

Turkey invades Cyprus.

US Judiciary Committee recommends impeachment of President Nixon. He admits complicity in the Watergate cover up and resigns.

Gerald Ford becomes President of USA.

Second cease-fire leaves 40 per cent of Cyprus under Turkish control.

Turkey demand creation of autonomous Turkish cantons in Cyprus.

Haile Selassie of Ethiopia deposed.

P F Strawson, *Freedom and Resentment*.

John Le Carré, *Tinker, Tailor, Soldier, Spy*.

Jeffrey Archer, *Not a Penny More, Not a Penny Less*.

Canadian National Tower, Toronto, is world's tallest free-standing structure.

Erica Jong, *Fear of Flying*.

Dario Fo, *Can't Pay? Won't pay!*.

Tom Stoppard, *Travesties*.

Abba, *Waterloo*, wins Eurovision Song Contest.

Films: *Murder on the Orient Express*. *The Night Porter*. *The Towering Inferno*.

TV: *The Naked Civil Servant*.

Year	Premiership
1975	Margaret Thatcher elected leader of the Conservative Party. June: Referendum votes 'Yes' for EEC membership July: Wilson's Scarborough speech to the NUM saves the government's incomes policy. Start of 'Cod War' with Iceland. 'The Guildford Four' are sentenced to life imprisonment IRA gang is besieged at Balcombe Street in London and surrenders.
1976	16 March: Wilson announces his resignation five days after his 60th birthday. 5 April: Wilson leaves office after altogether seven years and 279 days.

History	Culture
Northern Cyprus declares separate existence as the Turkish Federated State of Cyprus.	Michel Foucault, *Discipline and Punish*.
Angola is granted independence by Portugal.	H G Gadamer, *Truth and Method*.
Civil war in Lebanon.	Pierre Boulez, *Rituel in memoriam Bruno Maderna*.
In Cambodia, Khmer Rouge revolutionaries capture Phnom Penh.	Queen, *Bohemian Rhapsody*.
	Bruce Springsteen, *Born to Run*.
Last US personnel flee Saigon by helicopter from US embassy.	Saul Bellow, *Humboldt's Gift*.
	Primo Levi, *The Periodic Table*.
Saigon is surrendered to communist forces.	Athol Fugard, *Statements*.
First North Sea oil pumped ashore in Britain.	Films: *Dog Day Afternoon*. *Jaws*. *One Flew Over the Cuckoo's Nest*. *The Rocky Horror Picture Show*.
Indira Ghandi declares a state of emergency in India.	TV: *Fawlty Towers*. *The Sweeney*.

The Attack on Inflation is published.

Helsinki Conference, 30 states sign to agree to respect each others equality and individuality, avoid the use of force in disputes, and respect human rights.

General Franco dies.

Communist forces take control of Laos.

History	Culture
Argentina suspends diplomatic ties with Britain over Falkland Islands.	Brotherhood of Man win the Eurovision Song Contest for the United Kingdom.
Margaret Thatcher branded 'Iron Lady' by Soviet *Red Star* newspaper.	Alex Haley, *Roots*.
	Films: *Carrie*. *Marathon Man*. *Rocky*.
	TV: *Open All Hours*.

FURTHER READING

Harold Wilson the political historian could be as busy as the real thing. He was quick to erect a monument in words to his first government, *The Labour Government 1966-1970: A Personal Record*, published jointly by Weidenfeld and Nicholson and Michael Joseph in 1971. This volume considers in detail, as well it might in 817 pages, his 68 months in office, initially with a tiny majority in Parliament and then a decisive one. He admits mistakes, but takes pride in the *outstanding achievements* of the first Labour government since Attlee's post-war administration. His second term in office is celebrated in *Final Term, The Labour Government 1974-76*, again published jointly by Weidenfeld and Joseph in 1979 shortly after the general election that brought Margaret Thatcher to power. Wilson argues that he carried through *most of the measures foreshadowed in 1974* and blames the so-called 'Winter of Discontent' for Labour's downfall, while not excluding his successor James Callaghan for *somewhat unrealistically* nailing his colours to the masthead of wage restraint.

Wilson's first book, *New Deal For Coal*, published just before the election in 1945 and based on his wartime experience in the Ministry of Fuel and Power, is an economist's tract, but still has some claim to be the blueprint of the industry's 50-year period in public ownership. His *In Place of Dollars*, on the international monetary system, appeared in 1952 and *The War on World Poverty*, an offshoot of his co-founding of the charity War On Want, followed in 1953. In 1964, the year of his first election victory, Wilson published *The Relevance of British Socialism* and *Purpose in Politics*, both aimed at establishing an intellectual case for his brand of Labour politics and drawing heavily on speeches and journalism.

In the initial years of his retirement, Wilson busied himself with the pretentious-titled *The Governance of Britain* (Weidenfeld & Nicolson, London: 1976) and *A Prime Minister on Prime Ministers* (Weidenfeld & Nicolson, London: 1977), which sought to establish the place of his premiership in the long line of occupants of Number 10. The last book he actually wrote, *The Chariot of Israel*, which reflected his lifelong passion for the Jewish people and their state, appeared in 1981. Much later, his ghosted autobiography, *Memoirs: The Making of a Prime Minister, 1916-64* (Weidenfeld & Nicolson, London) came out in 1986. This is easily the most readable of the books that appeared under his name. For anecdotal early history, its journalist author could draw on the first biography, published in 1964 and written by Leslie Smith, a BBC current affairs producer, with Wilson's co-operation. It leans unashamedly in the subject's favour.

Later biographers were not always so generous. Paul Foot's *The Politics of Harold Wilson* (1968) is a searing indictment written from a hard-left vantage point, though with some useful insights. Other attempts followed, but it was not until the 1990s that Wilson reputation was secured, first by Ben Pimlott's magisterial *Harold Wilson* (HarperCollins, London: 1992) and then by the agnostic, exceptionally well-detailed assessment of Austen Morgan's *Harold Wilson* (Pluto Press, London: 1993). Philip Ziegler had full access to personal archives, and his authorised but well-rounded life, *Wilson* (Weidenfeld & Nicolson, London: 1993), went the final mile, and perhaps further, to establish Wilson's place in post-war political history.

He was less well served by his fellow politicians, who from the 1970s onwards took full advantage of the relatively novel freedom to publish their diaries. Richard Crossman and Barbara Castle, his allies in Labour's commanding heights and the beneficiaries of his patronage, pulled no punches in their disclosures of the Wilson era. The autobiographies of Castle, Denis Healey, Callaghan and lesser ministers of the Wilson government such as Merlyn Rees all contain valuable intelligence. This was, after all, an extended period covering several decades. Everyone, including dubious luminaries like George Wigg, had something to say about Harold. Fringe players, such as press baron Cecil King, Wilson's lawyer-confidante Arnold Goodman, and his publisher George Weidenfeld, have made free with their recollections. Wilson's 'Kitchen Cabinet' also produced a number of books. Some, like the diaries of Lord Bernard Donoughue, were respectful in an occasionally head-shaking kind of way. Others, like the volumes that flowed from his press secretary Joe Haines, contain much scandal, from murder plots to claims of adultery, and offer a seamier side to the Wilson years. That such a dimension existed is indisputable. Wilson himself started the ball rolling by spilling the beans about MI5 and 'the Wilson plot' which appeared in book form in 1978 in *The Pencourt File* by Barrie Penrose and Roger Courtior. The plot thickens in David Leigh's *The Wilson Plot* (Heinemann, London: 1988) and is vigorously stirred by Stephen Dorril and Robin Ramsay in *Smear! Wilson & The Secret State* (Fourth Estate, London: 1991). It may safely be said that no other British prime minister has attracted more speculation, investigation and exposure. And the official files have not been opened yet.

Picture Sources

Page vi
One of the many official photo portraits of Harold Wilson in his first year of premiership, 1964. (Courtesy Topham Picturepoint)

Pages 62–3
The Beatles and Harold Wilson. The Fab Four and the Prime Minister photographed together at the Dorchester Hotel, London on 19 March 1964. (Courtesy Topham Picturepoint)

Pages 140–1
Monarch and Prime Minister. Queen Elizabeth shakes hands with Harold Wilson during a reception at County Hall, Headquarters of the London County Council on 12 November 1964. (Courtesy Topham Picturepoint)

Index

S

Scanlon, Hugh 72, 82, 122
Schmidt, Helmut 111, 112
Scott, Norman 117, 118
Seddon, Ethel (mother) 14 ff., 16
Shore, Peter 55, 73, 112
Short, Ted 5, 6
Smith, Ian 57, 70
Smith, Leslie 54, 135
Smith, Tom 25
Snowden, Philip 16
St Johnston, Eirc 123
Starr, Ringo 61
Stewart Michael 55, 69
Stonehouse, John 123
Summerskill, Edith 41
Swingler, Stephen 122

T

Thatcher, Margaret 116,133
Thewlis, Elizabeth (grandmother)
    13
Thewlis, Herbert (Lord Mayor of
    Manchester)13 ff.
Thomson, George 65, 94, 139
Thorpe, Jeremy 105, 117, 118
Trend, Burke 56

V

Varley, Eric 114

Vaygauskas, Richardas 123, 125

W

Walker, Patrick Gordon 52, 54,
    70
Wallace, Colin 125, 128
Weidenfeld, George 7
Wigg, George 122
Wilkinson, Ellen 25
Williams, Marcia 2, 41, 45, 49,
    55, 108, 109, 123, 125
Williams, Shirley 133
Wilson, Giles (son) 30
Wilson, Jack (uncle) 14
Wilson, James (grandfather) 13
Wilson, James Herbert (father)
    14 ff., 20
Wilson, John (great-grandfather)
    13
Wilson, Marjorie (daughter)
    19
Wilson, Mary (wife) 18, 19, 30,
    37, 54, 64,107, 127
Wilson, Robin (son) 30
Woodcock, George 80
Wright, Peter 7, 120, 121, 127,
    128

Z

Ziegler, Philip 135